A Poem Called Karma

For my dearest friend stace
...the Bizzle Queen.
A reward for all your triumphs!

S. A.
xx

A Poem Called Karma

J.T. CROSS

To order additional copies of this book, contact:
Xlibris Corporation
0-800-644-6988
www.xlibrispublishing.co.uk
Orders@xlibrispublishing.co.uk
303046

CONTENTS

DEDICATION

This fiction is dedicated to the people of Myanmar who will always be remembered for their hospitality by those who encounter. We hope that their homeland embraces a speedy recovery from all it has suffered.

ACKNOWLEDGEMENTS

This novel would not have been possible without various people who all know who they are. I would also like to thank my travel buddies worldwide—for sharing their ideas and experiences, and of course all those people in Myanmar for their outstanding kindness and great tasting food!

Diary Entry 1

Here I am again, another flight, another border, another passport control. Feel bad for me.? I didn't think so. I don't blame you; I can never express how lucky I know I am. It's been a hell of a ride so far but I don't really know what to expect of this one. People say China is amazing and beautiful, they talk about how mystic Thailand can be, how hospitable the people of Laos are, how frightening the dizzy traffic of Vietnam is and even how the glorious neon lights in Japan all add to Asia and its culture. But here . . . nothing. What do you ever hear of Burma? Myanmar? A broken aftermath, a political war zone, a tourist death trap; personally I think it's all media fed bullshit. There is a country here, one of the biggest and most cultured in the world. I'm just not one to be told, I have to go and find out for myself. I met a guy in Thailand who had seen a Rambo film and took it from that point on that he knew everything about the place. Sure it's gonna be different, if they didn't want a difference, why the fuck did they leave home?

This is my last stop before home. I've got 15 days here and I left nine months ago. It's going to be weird going back to western life but in the meantime I'm still intrigued to know the truth about this fascinating place. I like to rough it but geez, charity begins at home. I need a shower.

Chapter I

Destination

Day 1

A mild state of confusion washed over David as he sat back in his seat—row 13 near the window of the plane. The feeling came free with the severe fatigue and discomfort that he felt caused by the major traffic and movement in Hong Kong. He had caught bed bugs from the dire room of the hostel but hadn't told anyone except his mum on the phone as he transited at Bangkok overnight.

The sleep in the airport was rough, the hard seats were the only option as the people just flowed through the place night and day. He expected it of course, everything except the bedbugs that is and he had felt a lot worse along the way at certain points, a lot better too.

Calling on his protective dragonfly he was now about to land in Myanmar, Burma. It was his 15th country this year including the odd transit countries like Chile and the USA in order to get to the other destinations he had seen. His delusion was broken and he was forced to get back to a tired reality by the beeping of the seatbelt sign lighting up when they then announced that the place was about to land. The attendant who walked by placed one hand on his shoulder gently, and asked politely if he could turn off his iPod. He now had no distraction as to what he was heading in to; the iPod was a big barrier to the world. As much as he lusted for travel he still had to create scenarios for his mind to play with what he was seeing as if it were a scene out of a movie.

With the places he had seen it was an easy task. Half of Asia, along with some of Australia and Oceania. He sat up and took a puff of his asthma pump. Holding his breath he felt the cold gas enter his lungs—he had felt it work so much more out here, being tired most of the time made his chest so heavy.

If he had infinite funds he would never had stopped, he loved travelling, it seemed that all he had feared and thought of before about being alone was now blown to dust. He now enjoyed his own company. A lot had happened for him to get to this conclusion but he was absolutely certain that someone would come along again. Finding out who was always the fun part.

The plane started to come down shaking like crazy as it always did. He gripped the arms of the seat. He still hated the landing, even after 30 flights this year. The plane taxied on the runway for a short time and lined up for arrival at the terminal building. When everyone got off they were greeted by no-one. Just cold floors and colourless walls dotted with armed guards followed by the passport control desks. He filled in the steadying his hand and got in line. It looked like this was the only flight due in, all the other people here he recognized from the plane he was on.

He spotted the toilets as the passport officer did the paperwork and hoped he wouldn't be too much longer as he was dying for a piss. Collecting his bag from the conveyor belts afterwards he turned to face the bright sun decorating the exit.

The terminal building was bland and run down as soon as you got through customs, they didn't have scanners but they hand checked bags instead. He walked up to the two female officers who gazed at him in amazement due to his height of over six feet. Slight hesitation crossed his smile before they let him through without checking. He exhaled in relief happy as a result he wouldn't have to explain the bed bugs. He still wasn't sure how bad the infestation was due to not having enough space to pack properly back in Hong Kong. He just threw everything back in unaware until Bangkok when he could feel crawling over his skin in certain places. He had the crawling feeling before when he was tired and run down. This was different though, this was *disgusting* he thought as his smile faded to a grimace. An arranged transfer was waiting for him outside with a very polite English speaking young man who asked for his name. He waited a couple of minutes as he had two more people to transfer. Two Thai women came over smiling, the language barrier was much stronger with them though. They got in the 1990s' Toyota minibus along with him.

Yangon was not a pretty city. He had read up on all of the terror and destruction it had faced from several forces of man made and natural disasters over the last ten years, but this still didn't prepare him. Ruined colonial buildings scattered the streets, weeds growing though the cracks of the derelict ones along with stained pavements where they were intact and roads that were jammed with beaten up cars dating as far back as the 80s polluting the air with relentless fumes and horn beeps.

David's analysis of the new location was interrupted along with the two Thai women when the driver started to turn the key and pump the gas. The bus had broken down, it looked like the alternator had gone. It just cut out as they stopped at the lights.

The driver was wearing a *Longyi*, traditional dress for the Burmese. It was a sarong-like garment worn by both men and women. Women had what looked like yellow face paint across their cheeks in different formations which acted as a natural perfume. It also contained a chemical which made it mimic a strong sun block, it was known as Thanakha paste. This was like another world, even after all of Asia that he had seen it just wasn't quite the same, tradition was everything, corruption was nowhere and everywhere at the same time from what he had been reading.

The driver tried starting the vehicle again and again but nothing. They had blocked traffic in the right hand lane solid. People seemed to be quite patient in the queue though. Another driver got out and started to help, but to no avail.

'May I?' asked David as if he knew what he was doing.

The driver moved over to let David into the drivers seat which turned out to be as hard and uncomfortable as the passenger seats. These vehicles were falling apart and scattered with rust. David was used to looking at brand new cars back home in England 'straight of the rack' as he would describe, but he wasn't one of these pretentious characters who got in a huff about what he was driving around it. If it moved then in his eyes it did the job, no matter how rough. He could see the driver had flooded the engine by frequently slamming the gas as he turned it over so David just did the opposite—started it after a couple of minutes letting it cool off and it fired straight off, he then held the accelerator down to get the rpm up. The two Thai women emitted a sound of surprise that the 'American' guy knew what he was doing, as did the Burmese men. It was a short lived triumph as the engine slowly died again, not even revs kept it going for long. After several more attempts it soon wouldn't even fire and a taxi with a few holes in the floor of the chassis and minimal suspension was the only option into city central.

David had once been a complex and deep thinker. Going away made him simple, more chilled out. A lot had occurred to change his state of mind, especially travelling alone. If someone were with him now it would have been very different, although he was so tired of thinking about what could have been he had now pretty much given up on it and was about to spend the last 15 days relaxing and doing something different to what he had been up to, different even compared to the last nine months he had spent running away, which he now faced was what he did.

The room was basic as expected but luxury compared to where he had been and cheap at only seven US dollars a night. He had booked in for two at the moment with a strong possibility to extend depending if he wanted to travel further north. He slung his bag into the wicker chair in the corner and raised his right eyebrow in surprise at the portable TV by the window. The generator for the electricity curfews which ravaged the country was above the window. He was then tempted to check the view and opened the straggly curtains which presented a view through misty and distorted glass to a brick wall of the next building.

'Hmph.'

He tilted his head to see through the tight gap of the alleyway it faced. There must have been less than a foot of a gap between the buildings of which pipes and rubble lined the base.

He had an en suite bathroom and a shower; impressive. He tested the water flow and it was warm too.

'Luxury,' he said to himself.

He was distracted by a knock at the door. He turned off the tap and saw to it—it was the owner. He seemed like a nice guy, very polite, apologizing for not seeing him in with the driver as he was busy with his brother or something similar. David was too tired to concentrate on details at the moment. He gave his blessing and said they could sort out all the details after he had slept a while—passport, money and so on. In his 50's, full head of hair and wearing a longyi, he was a man of tradition and said he ran the place with his wife and daughter. If David needed anything he said to contact any of them at reception. David thanked him with a smile, but mentally thanked him further for leaving as all he wanted to do was crash out. He looked at his bag as he closed the door sneering as he remembered the itchy feeling of bedbugs. It caused him to actually feel it again not sure if it was his body's senses playing with him wondering how bad it was inside there.

'Fuck it,' he said carelessly.

He left it all packed in there, would sort it out later. He headed for the shower and then the sheets for a few hours.

He awoke to the sound of the generator kicking in around 5:30pm. The lights cut out outside and then reappeared after a few seconds in fewer places than before. The emergency light was bright enough to illuminate the whole room. After one more shower he sorted out his clothes in his bag that were infected and handed them all in to the laundry service. One step outside was like opening the oven door back home, a wall of heat that hits you. He loved it though, the heat was a big favourite over the cold. England was not his idea of paradise but then everyone goes away to look for something different, everyone healthy in his opinion anyway.

The restaurant was like a barn. The staff were so polite even though they spoke very little English. A first meal in a country was never an easy choice, so much to choose from, so much that was new to try.

Day 2

The next morning he left his iPod dock on for a while whilst getting ready before taking a look around the city. He got up in time for breakfast which was included in the price of the room, just eggs and toast with coffee and orange juice. It was all that was expected though, sometimes more, and it was much nicer now that he had been eating much less over the time he had spent away. He had noticed for real now at how thin he was, he left way back in January at a decent weight for his height, now in September he was about a stone lighter, and felt half the man he used to.

The driver guy brought out the breakfast but he heard another voice in the kitchen which was almost opposite his room on the ground floor. She then appeared from around the closed edge. She stood a stunning young girl, maybe around 23 years old, long dark hair and a figure which was probably too noticeable even whilst wearing a longyi. She smiled at David as she asked the driver a question in their native language. He replied with a laugh, it appeared that they were talking about David being the only one at the table but he couldn't be sure. This language was so very hard to work out even compared to some of the others he had come across. David could only smile back obliviously as she turned back towards the cooking area. When he had finished he grabbed his daypack and changed up his US dollars for Myanmar Kyatts at the front desk. The owner's wife came to serve him—she was a petite woman with long dark hair but more pronounced face make-up. It looked quite striking to him, maybe a little intimidating, completely the wrong effect of the idea. She touched her right elbow with her left hand holding it in place when she handed over the cash, this was another tradition of respect he had not seen.

The city was demoralizing, but not exactly depressing. The people were vibrant, it had of course been through so much wear and tear due to both natural and man made disasters since the early 1990s. He was stared at just like he was in the other places he had been but not in a rude way, they more glanced and then looked away back at their business; it was a mere shock of seeing someone so different on their rugged streets. As most of his clothes were in the wash he only had a vest and his hoodie to cover his torso and shoulders. It was frowned upon here to bare shoulders, especially in temples. The last thing he wanted to do was offend. It made the walk around so damned hot, he would have been sweating just from walking around in a singlet. He didn't let it show though. As he stepped across the broken pavements and fuming crossroads he passed market stalls of all kinds selling a wide variety of food, only some of which he recognized. A myriad of smells and life flowed around him, the rush of the central locations were now all the same, he had to give it a full tour the first time to break himself into the place, still finding it overwhelming was the thrill of travelling.

A new daypack was in order. His current one had ripped and was very droopy in the way the material was stitched, the stitching had also started to come away. He had been sold it in Shanghai for about 120 Yuan, which was much better than what they originally asked for it but still not worth what he had paid considering how quickly it had fallen apart. A man approached him while he was scanning around one of the many bag shops which were not much wider than alleyways scattered off the main drag near *Sule Paya*. He introduced himself with quite good English as 'Maung Win Zaw' and he was definitely not staff at the shop. The young girls who did work there looked at him as if he was making them loose their customer already as they took a bag down from the high racks above with a broomstick for David to check.

Although he seemed very friendly, David kept the passive and polite approach. He glanced at him and smiled before turning back to the bag to inspect it further.

'Looking for a bag my friend? I can help you with that, you don't want to pay these prices,' said the man.

David checked the tag, 25000 Kyatt. The black market offered 1000 Kyatt to the US dollar, the bag itself was worth more than that, it all seemed very cheap.

'You'd say this is expensive then?' David replied.

'Ah, yes, all of these central shops will be. I can get you one for nearly half the price, or just fix your own one for much cheaper.'

He thought about it a bit and handed the bag he was inspecting back to the young girl. He felt bad already about not buying it from her reaction; she didn't speak English and therefore couldn't contend with this intrusive guy.

'Yeah I've heard that before, China can rip you off the worst in some cases.'

'Yours is from China?'

'That's right,' David said turning slightly to show the ripped seams.

'Ooh, not good, you come, I show you around. What is your name young man? And what brings you to Myanmar?'

He wished he could answer that. Lying through his teeth wasn't an enjoyment but had become somewhat of a habit over the past couple of years, not just to people away but to people at work and back home too. He preferred to think of it as a concealment of the truth with most cases. Out here people were much more direct and therefore were sometimes countered with a direct lie, just like this one.

'I've always wanted to come here, to see the temples and your amazing culture . . . and I'm David by the way.'

Maung Win Zaw took him around town for a bit. He was a strange guy, short and in his fifties, skinny and almost toothless. He coughed like he'd had a brush with tuberculosis. He found him a decent bag made in Myanmar which was much more solid than any he had previously—at 16000 Kyatt it was also borderline stealing. He then took him to a balcony which was a restaurant and bar in the Chinese quarter of town. David walked up to the edge and leaned on the rail looking down at the smoky carnage of where the Muslim quarter joined the Chinese quarter. The two houses were at peace now, they traded regularly and had remained friends for years. You would never see the divide unless informed of it. They were both as rammed with people as each other. The only difference was that one side had bars, the other had tea houses.

'What would you like sir? Any food?' asked the barman who came to their table. They seemed pleased that an Englishman had entered their joint.

'Just a beer please, and one for my friend . . .'

'Just a coffee please,' he cut in. He then switched back to Burmese ordering some cakes of some kind. 'Why do you drink that stuff?'

'Sorry, it gets the best of westerners sometimes, said David forgetting that Maung Win Zaw was Muslim.

'My brother fell to alcohol, he was a good man but nothing could save him.'

'That's a shame, how old was he?'

'Ah, a long time ago, before your time.'

He asked all the regular questions: *'How old are you?', 'Where are you from in England?', 'What are you looking for in life?'* and so on. Funny how all these questions were suddenly getting harder to answer each time he heard them.

The cakes and the beer came along with a chat about what Maung Win Zaw had really scoped him out for, he started to talk about the government and the Junta. The military regime had been enforced since the late 80s and he was already aware of most of the history since then but he listened to him anyway, to hear it from a victim face to face was what introduced the reality. David acted dumb for quite some time, he also tried changing the subject twice. He wasn't going to get involved with this conversation this early. He wanted to learn more but didn't want to be thrown in on his first day. It seemed after a while Maung Win Zaw realised this too, so he backed off.

He reached into his jacket pocket which was a bit tatty and didn't really allocate a sense of professionalism. He pulled out a small book, like a dairy, that taught David the numbers and language of Myanmar.

'If you're wanting to know how much things are here you will have to get used to the numbers. They are not like the characters used in English, the markets will fool you otherwise.'

He started writing down the symbols which at first were confusing but then suddenly made sense after a few minutes study.

'Geez, I had no idea about any of this,' he said, which was true.

'Ah, there are many things you will learn whilst here my friend. A country is only the outside, there is much more on the inside with these people here,' he said raising an arm as an invite to look around at all the people glancing over at them. They looked away as soon as David made eye contact.

'They have seen much terror over the years of your life young man.' He then started coughing and spitting into the bin under the table, from the contents it seemed to be the norm to do this.

'I can't imagine.'

'I like to check on my family myself, they live in Mandalay, that's where I'm from.'

'What are you doing in Yangon?'

'I run my shop, the work here is more, make more money.'

'Really? But I thought Mandalay was just as big as here.'

'It is, but there are less traders in what I do down here. The weather is not good though, too hot.'

'What do you do?' David asked, squinting, somehow he expected something much more sinister than what he said.

'I carve puppets and can make anything out of wood.'

'Ah, a chippie?'

'A what?'

'That's what it's called back home.'

That comment brought a broad smile to Maung Win Zaw's face, he tried to go into what David did back home but David didn't really want to get into that one. Shadow puppets were highly sought after, especially Burmese produce. They were found in many other countries, Indonesia, China but the Myanmar shadow puppets had isolated fame and caused them to soar in value. David had dropped everything and knew he would have to head back soon for a new start. It made him remember that he did still have his car to look forward to. He missed driving. Dropping things was like an alien move to these people, just never an option.

'Don't let people walk all over you here, they will find you very interesting, you are of beautiful people,' he said.

David shone a surprised but confused look at that one.

'I have found people here very friendly.'

'Yes, yes you're right, but only until they know they can catch you out . . . tell me, what are you looking for my friend?'

'Looking for?' David quizzed.

'Everyone is looking for something, everyone,' he replied as he animated his arms out wide. He called the waiter over again to help light his cigarette for him.

'Do you have to be looking for anything?'

'Of course, of course, you travel many many places across the world and you tell me you're not looking for anything?' he said whilst waving out the match. He then continued ' . . . you travel alone, no?'

'Yes . . . but you're never alone for long, right?'

Maung Win Zaw laughed, 'but a man is always alone until he finds what he is looking for.'

An odd silence fell across the table, not awkward though. David wasn't used to being cornered by conversation. He had answers for a lot, but they weren't infinite. He could tell that this guy was not all that he appeared; many people he had met along the way rang out the same way. He still didn't fully trust him though so at the same time was intrigued by his wisdom.

'Well, I guess I'll just have to let you know when I've found it,' he replied before raising his beer.

A near toothless smile formed on the old man's face again with a now lit cigar on one side.

David got the bill for both of them, he expected that at least. The barman came back with two cigarettes as change. He took them slowly not realizing that they didn't have change small enough so this is how they reciprocated. He just said thank you and looked pleased not mentioning that he was asthmatic. Maung Win Zaw suggested a cheaper hotel for him which was owned by another 'friend' of his but David would only consider it for now. He was trying to steer him away from government run hotels, he said that he wanted him to bring currency to the country and not the military. David respected this.

'Here, take this my friend, souvenir.'

He handed him four notes from his wallet, they were all Kyatt but from older times from before and during World War II. One was even called 'Rupiah' from when the Japanese held the currency. He wasn't sure that these were legal to have out here but Maung Win Zaw didn't leave him the time to ask. He hid them in the back of his journal before he took another step to keep them flat.

David headed back to the hotel along the smoky and burning bright streets taking in the array of smells again and avoiding the pavement cracks. He passed back across *Sule Paya*, it was a temple of striking colour. He was amazed at it even a second time with its decoration and detailed surroundings. The spire itself only rated as one of the smaller ones but as it remained the most central to the city it proved a good landmark. Road names were non-existent; if the streets weren't gridded navigating this place would be a nightmare. He remembered reading that a Japanese photographer was killed at the very spot of the Paya in 2007. He was 'mistaken' for a local as he was wearing a longyi and got caught up in the riots and shootings of the protests. His camera was never returned though and a bad feeling has hovered with the Japanese understandably ever since. People flocked over this spot again now, life just carried on for the people of Myanmar.

As he got back to the hotel he was dying for a piss again. The young girl was behind the desk this time—she smiled and said hello. She was about to ask him more questions but David had to cut it short by walking past quickly fumbling for his room key making it obvious he was darting for the toilet. Dropping his bag at the door as he entered he left the door open without realizing and came back out of the bathroom to find the girl at the door.

'Are you OK?' she asked.

He smiled. 'Yes, sorry, I'm fine, no public toilets here huh?'

She laughed, 'what's your name?'

'David,' he reached out his right arm to shake her hand, 'nice to meet you.'

She looked happy but stunned a little due to the handshake not being a common greeting for her. She didn't really know how to do it but placed her left hand on her right elbow whilst reaching back for his hand with her other.

David realised his schoolboy error and all he should have done was place his hands together and bow his head a little. She seemed to be intrigued though.

'How do you like Myanmar?' she asked.

'It's very nice,' lying through his teeth again. 'I've always wanted to come here.' And again.

Her English was quite good. He was surprised at how she could switch so smoothly, how many westerners did he know who could speak fluent Burmese? Her name was Khin Hla Nanda, which made sense. He had realised the word Nanda meant 'river' in English, this explained why the hotel was called The River. She loved the fact he was from England. She had met a few English people before and joked that all they ever talked about was football with her brother and father. England was like a dream to the Burmese, a land of freedom. She said her father had been a fan of the colonial times when the British were in power of Myanmar; she wouldn't have remembered then. All the regular questions followed but she seemed a bit shy to ask unlike everyone else, a sure sign she was into him but David failed to notice at first until he gave her some British coins from his wallet. He had meant to give them out throughout his whole trip but had just forgotten them until now. She looked at them all individually in her palm asking what they were worth. He had to think hard due to the different exchange rates but got a rough guess for each coin. Coins had been made redundant from new Burmese currency.

'You have plans for today?' she asked even though today was nearly over.

'Ah, not really, I'm still quite tired from jet lag' which was true. As soon as he said it though he knew there was something there. It was nearing 6pm and just starting to get dark.

They ended the conversation and he almost shut the door as she walked off, he then shook his head, *fuck it* he thought, and re-opened it.

'Hey,' he said clutching his neck with his left hand. She turned to face him again with slightly wider eyes, 'I'm going out for some dinner in a while, would you like to join me?'

She looked as if she would have jumped at the chance but then looked down and around her feet having to decline the offer. 'I am very sorry, I have to do more work here tonight.' He should have realised when he came in that she was the only one on the front desk.

'Some other time please?' she added. She smiled as she walked back to the front desk as her brother had turned up in the rusty people carrier with another guest.

Not bad, not bad he thought to himself, could have been a much worse outcome. He didn't have a plan so far for the place so he still had time to take a risk, she was such a nice girl in his head. He wasn't really looking for anyone but also had nothing to lose, still fully aware that it would be something totally different going out for dinner with a girl from Myanmar.

He thought that when in the restaurant about ten doors down that she would have been stared at violently just for being with a foreigner. He guessed it might have been illegal here like in other countries he had been to and started to get worried if he had done the wrong thing. He had gotten used to speaking openly and taking chances, the trip had forced his nature to respond when it felt right and never hold back, he didn't really have anything to hide out here, only tact remained.

The restaurant didn't appear to have a name, it was just an open building on the main road, the same road he had visited last night. The staff were so welcoming as they recognized him, a family run joint again, not very busy. Chinese food and a few beers came to his senses tonight along with the small bowl of very spicy soup which they also served the night before with the root in the bottom. It made his eyes water but made him feel better in a weird way. It was all under $6. A TV was suspended on a shelf above the opening which suited him. He didn't understand a word of what it was saying but the cheesy acting in the adverts was comical. He could just watch the world go by outside which was usually more appealing in these settings, the only problem was that people watching always made him think too much. It was so dark when it clicked round to 7pm he was glad he didn't have to go far to eat. The street lights were few and far between and the pavements were a danger to walk on in most areas. Flicking through his guide book he had bought in Hong Kong for the first time seemed like a good idea. *Shwedagon Paya*, the main temple of Myanmar was described as '*a mountain containing more gold than the bank of England*'. It made him smirk.

Diary Entry 2

Well this is . . . difficult, a real difficult one. The country of Myanmar, where do I start? In a land of amazing culture lay citizens who walk 'free' but are chained to a political wall of order. I'm not even sure if I'm allowed to write this shit so I'm gonna have to conceal it and refrain from doing so in parks and stuff. Yangon isn't that stunning, sure its buildings and architecture are wonderful little relics but most have been either levelled or left to rot from the damage of the Cyclones a few years back. It's a wonder people still flock to work here, whole blocks are just inactive. The food however is pretty good so far and the people are very polite. I can't work out some of their motives but I guess that goes hand in hand when you're barricaded in from the rest of the world. There aren't many westerners here, I think I passed one today on the street whilst watching out for the massive holes in the pavement. Things are very cheap, electric is a slight problem sometimes but it proves that you can live fine without it for a while. The temples look pretty stunning too. I'm going for the big one tomorrow at Shwedagon.

I'm going with Khin, she works at the hotel. I hope it doesn't turn out to be a pay per view tour now that I think about it, she's pretty hot anyway. I'm gonna get some sleep as it's been a long day. All I am sure of at the moment is that this one is gonna be a real experience . . . you should see the smile on my face.

CHAPTER II

Temple

Day 3

Feeling refreshed from the best nights sleep in a couple of weeks, regardless of the generator ticking over most of the night, David stepped out of the room and into the dining area for breakfast again. The brother of the family served him alone this time. He was different though, he merely smiled face to face but scowled when he looked away. David wasn't sure if he was just being paranoid about what he had said to his sister but he wouldn't be able to reverse it and just figured he had to eat now anyhow. Simple but needed. Coffee, orange juice, toast and jam with an omelette, ending with fruit. Straight after he returned to his room to get his bag.

'Ah shit' he said dropping it again realizing he had left a bag of crisps half full and open on the bedside table. It was now crawling with ants.

He plucked at the crisps holding them away, then more ants appeared under the pack and scurried off down the back of the table. The beer bottles and everything else seemed sealed and of no interest to them. Someone then appeared next to him taking the crisps from him and then spraying the table with a can of insect repellent. It was Khin. She smiled at him straight after their eyes met.

'They like salt, no worry, I fix for you,' she said.

'Thanks,' he said in surprise, 'Min-Gala-Ba,' he added, which was the main greeting in their language.

'Min-Gala-Ba! How are you today?'

'Very good thank you, I was just off to Shwedagon Paya to look around. Sorry about the ants though.'

'No, no, no problem, I can fix. Shwedagon is beautiful, looks wonderful at nigh too, many lights!' she replied.

'Really?' he said raising one eyebrow not realizing it was open at night. 'What are you up to tonight?'

'Sorry?'

'What do you do today?' he re-phrased.

'Oh, is my day off. I have no plan, just helping for fun.'

'Oh I see, well . . . you can join me if you like,' he said, feeling the painful spark of regret just after he said it.

'Oh . . .' she looked at the floor but this time in a more excited way. 'Yes please I would like to, I can show you around!' she said looking genuinely happy about it. 'You going right now?'

'Well, I could do with visiting an internet cafe first, I haven't checked in back home for a while. How about I come back here in an hour?'

Her eyes lit up. 'Yes, very good,' she said nodding, 'I wait for you here.'

'Great, I'll see you in a while then.'

'Yes, see you,' she said as he turned for the internet cafe. She looked at his door closing it for him as he had forgotten.

After the internet cafe he returned to the hotel where she waited at the front door. They grabbed a taxi which was in the same condition as the one he took when the people carrier packed in. She didn't say much when inside but kept a high mood. She spoke with the taxi driver in their language, the conversation was quite upbeat too.

'We are talking about your country,' she said turning to him.

'England is a very rich land, no?' the taxi driver cut in.

'Erm, yes, I suppose so,' he replied in reluctance.

'But you have many cars and many fine places, very much in London, yes?' Khin asked straight after.

He gave a vacant look whilst studying the question hard.

'That's right, yes, but people are not necessarily rich.' It felt like an insult saying it but felt a duty to remain defensive. He had been fooled by others with this conversation, falling into the trap of admitting you are rich is sold with the guilt of not giving away money afterwards. He wasn't so sure this was just polite conversation yet.

'Are there poor people like in Myanmar?' Khin asked again.

'Erm . . . there are poor people yes, but not like in Myanmar, things work differently,' he replied thinking of all the tax evaders and benefit cheats. At least people were honest here. Maybe they were honest only because they never had the opportunity with any of that provided by their government. This wasn't the time to be thinking about this now though.

The taxi driver started speaking with Khin again. She seemed to be clarifying something that David couldn't understand, then she turned back to him.

'He asks if the people in England are happy,' she translated for the driver.

What a question, these people really didn't skim around any crap when they spoke. He tried to back out of the inner tributaries of the question that a westerner would study so hard and look at the bigger picture. He thought of his friends and family rather than the general public he remembered walking around searching for a single smile.

'Yes . . . I think so,' he mustered.

The temple entrance was almost a cover up, only the spire could be seen from the main part when you got close to the mound. Khin started to veer off from him.

'Hey, are you OK?' he asked.

'Yes, yes, I have to go in another entrance. This entrance for visitors only,' she said.

'Oh, OK . . . shall I see you on the other side?'

'Yes, yes, I will find you,' she said walking away, smiling.

How weird, he thought. Split entrances for locals and foreigners. It was 5000 Kyatt entry. The desk was so clean, the room seemed so airtight when he stepped in and felt the cold air-conditioned wave. Even with his hoodie on that made him sweat when outside it became bitterly cold when he entered the room, he now hated air-conditioning. His eyes squinted with the white gleam and the chill as he walked up to the desk.

'Hello sir,' said the lady behind the desk, an older woman with an upright stance and no Thanakha paste at all.

She got him to sign in and place his shoes and socks into a box before entering the temple. He paid the entry fee and was walked over to a lift which he departed from a much higher point. He was met with a very modern and bland walkway. It reminded him of the airport. It was bright and stark; the windows were from floor to ceiling either side and gazed upon the whole city. It was a good photo opportunity. He carried on all the way to the end, it seemed much longer than it actually was. He walked maybe 100 metres along but it was worth the walk when the whole view in front of him opened up into the golden shimmer of the temple and its stunning surroundings.

He walked to the left around the smaller structure to get the full view of the main stupa. It was so high and stunningly beautiful. Looking up at the spire right at the top he could see the orb he had read about; it was lined with sacred jewels, rubies and diamonds. It was a shame it was a dark and overcast day. The floor was so slippery, it had been raining and what with no shoes on it was hard to keep a steady foot. The floor itself shone quite majestically, blurring everyone's vision by default from the waist down. It was an impressive effect.

'Hello,' a voice startled him as he was stuck gazing upwards. It was Khin.

People were staring as he thought they might, but she didn't seem to care much. In effect this kept him relaxed. She had also taken her shoes off. David had to turn up the end of his trouser legs to avoid them getting saturated by the thin layer of water strewn across the entire place. Many people were around worshipping, praying, just admiring the scenery; some of which were tourists. He laughed to himself quietly as he could now tell a tourist from a traveller like night from day. The little hats they wore, their cameras on their belts, their super clean clothes that stood out even more than he did, looking as rugged as the people here made him relate to them more.

'This place is wonderful, no?' she asked.

'Absolutely,' he said slowly, shaking his head in awe.

He was looking at a bell which he had recognized from the guide book. He wasn't sure of the significance but it was a very holy monument.

A very small and polite man approached them both. He had his hands placed together in front of him, he seemed to be a guide to the pagoda. He had a black backpack on which deluded the effect of his work detailing the ancient place of worship.

'Good day,' he began, 'may I be of service to you? For a small fee I can show you around this holy temple of the Buddha.'

Khin and David looked at each other. Normally he would turn down guides before they got this far in speech but it didn't seem right in this place. He was aware that the government made every scrap of money donated to this place and he wasn't sure if he should trust these ultra polite people. It was an uneasy feeling but he relented for Khin's sake.

The man introduced himself as Lak. He was a victim of cyclone Nargis back in 2007 where his home and farm were destroyed. His father and mother had been killed and his sister had been missing ever since. David couldn't help but hang on his every word. People here were very open about this sort of thing, they really didn't deserve to be hit by one of the deadliest cyclones of all time on top of being trapped by an oppressive government. The man literally had nothing left so fled to Yangon for work. Shwedagon Paya was where he found it.

Khin asked a few questions in English for the sake of David but he felt that it really wasn't necessary, two Burmese people speaking English to each other wasn't freedom of speech to him. She had asked about the 23 tonne bell they were standing by. The Maha Ganda Bell, it was beautiful in an ancient, weathered sense. Greyish bronze with rough edges decayed by years of use, it was also dropped in the Yangon River by the British back in 1825 and probably sustained some damage from the cyclone too. It was covered with scripture, like white scars all over it giving it mysticism only a monk could decode. A more modern bell was located further down the walkway which looked bigger and lined with striking red paint where it curved.

Chinthes had been staring at them the whole time as they walked around together gathering more information from Lak. Chinthes were the huge lion headed statues dotted around which protected the temple and its secrets within. They were present in some form around every surrounding part if the city-like area. Golden roofs drastically changed to red along with the detailed Baroque-esque architecture blending with smooth walls and flat plain coloured surfaces. The bland, waterlogged floor also reflected the finely and heavily painted ceilings portraying murals of grace and countless stories brought by the gods. Lak went on to explain that a cave complex was hidden under the main stupa which only the monks had access to and that held within was a chamber containing the hair of the Buddha and various relics of previous Buddhas. The age of the place was down to opinion. Science conflicted with legend but legend always held the better stories so David decided to go with that.

'When the hairs were originally taken from a casket made of gold to be enshrined in the underground complex, legend stated that wonderful things happened,' Lak said raising his hands together in font of him and meeting at each fingertip to form a casing shape.

'The people of earth and heaven felt a strong feeling of warmth that shone up with powerful light, beyond where the eye could follow, and down, beyond where the demons could trace . . . ailments were eased, diseases started to cure themselves. The earth and wind shook every last patch of ocean and dirt, causing treasures of all kinds to fall from the skies upon those who had hoped to be rewarded for their good deeds,' he animated.

They walked around to a large Banyan tree which was protruding from a purpose built platform with a Buddha image inset. The Buddha was highly reflective gold and had a spotlight mounted in front at the base for more effect at night. It was encased in a rich leaf-like decorated temple of its own. Opposite was a mural on a wall containing an amazing story of an attack which caused a flood. David didn't understand everything the guide said about it but from what he could make out he saw that the Buddha had teamed up with the angels to override the war march of the demons, and remained undamaged by everything that they could have inflicted upon him by flooding the joint. The story was much older than the mural itself.

'All this history in one place, even this place was built around 2500 years ago, huh?' David's voice frayed a little with inquisition.

'Yes, our history binds us, we are in possession of many stories of wonder,' replied Lak. 'Now, may I ask, when is your date of birth?'

'My birthday.?' David replied looking at Khin, confused at the large direction change of the conversation.

'Yes, I am nearing the end of your tour now, the last part is to allow the Buddha to bless you. In order to do this there are twelve shrines which represent the time of year you are born, the correct one must be approached,' he said now smiling.

David liked this idea, he guessed it was like a star sign thing being twelve. He told him his birthday as Khin pushed him on with the idea.

'Ah, I know, this way, we must go to the other side for your one,' Lak said, waving towards himself the way an Asian person would gesture to follow them.

They followed him to the other side of the main stupa. Khin had looped her arm around him this time, he didn't mind at the moment and didn't want to look any further into it. When they got there she let go and stepped back. Lak showed him a shrine which from the floor started as a bath shape tiled white with a small pool of water only disturbed by a cat-like creature elegantly sitting in the bottom. Stacked above this was a more golden, round, table-like structure decorated all around with tablets lined with raised dots. There was a small silver plaque with writing unreadable to David but he assumed it was the name of the shrine. This table had a bent metal rim which served as a handrail, no better than a handrail from a back alley teeming with rust but within that was an articulate statuette of a god. It looked like a Buddha but was just different enough for him to know that it wasn't. It was white faced but retained black painted lines for eyebrows and inviting dark eyes. It wore a gold breastplate appearing like armour along with what seemed like gold chain-mail down the arms. The head was crowned by a halo-like feature, again gold, but with a vertical point like the stupa itself. Golden wings draped down the back of the head behind the ears, giving an essence of power and nature. It was surrounded by donations in flowers of every colour. In front of the statue was a large round bowl holding water, three candles and a few fallen petals. Just inside the handrail was a small ledge lined with little silver cups, also full of water. The entire shrine stood as high as David.

Lak had gone and then came back in the short space of time it took to study it. He had a bunch of flowers in his hand as vibrant as the ones present. David bought them for 2000 Kyatt and placed them accordingly around the others trying not to overshadow them. Six times he then filled a silver cup with water under the guidance of Lak and six times he poured it over the head and hands of the statue. Lak and Khin watched happily seeing a young man of a foreign country respecting their tradition. After the sixth time Lak went up to the statue and spoke his own language with his eyes closed. Khin stepped forward and translated for David.

'This man I would like to grant happiness and longevity. Keep him safe and his journey not perilous. May the Buddha bring good health and much food for meals of every day.'

His expression formed a sigh from being touched by the whole thing. Under guidance from Lak and still with Khin translating he once again filled the cup six times and poured it over the head and hands. Each cup got slower and slower to his perception in time. Each one became heavier as he raised it thinking each time about his past, what he had achieved, his future, what he now was setting out to do with his direction, all the people he had met out here, even faces flashed through his memory of people turning their heads towards him whom he had just passed on the streets. The present didn't seem to matter, it seemed like fate had brought him here, to help perhaps, he didn't know. It was all still so unclear but so obvious for a split second when the water turned from spilled cups into mighty waterfalls, it was just a moment of sheer concentration. He looked up from the statue now dripping from forehead to chin and was brought back down to reality as his arm was stopped by Lak from raising another cup to pour.

'That's enough, my friend,' he said with a smile.

After handing Lak 6000 Kyatt they parted but did not leave. Khin walked over to where the Banyan tree was with the image of the flood and Buddha. She pointed to the railings just behind it.

'What's out there?' he asked.

'This is what all the problems were about in 2007.'

He could already see where this one was going—she was about to finish what Maung Win Zaw had started.

'Problems?'

'Yes, many monks gathered here and marched out of Shwedagon as protest to finish government,' she pointed to a solid, uncharismatic building shadowed behind some trees.

'This is where the military base is, they committed murder and would not release Arusa Nu Sanda.'

He knew she was referring to Arusa Nu Sanda, a revolutionist who had been imprisoned years ago under transparent circumstances or for merely 'knowing too much'. He had heard that her father had been assassinated; he was of some militant status back in the day. According to certain references he had seen before, it was an accidental incident, his body was not found. The guide book had also printed that this was not a good conversation to be having. People had looked over at them already and started walking away pretending they had no idea what they were speaking of.

'I heard she didn't want to be freed?'

She lowered her voice, 'hmm, maybe, but I'm not so sure. It's not just her though, the whole of Myanmar would like to be free. She was the first person to stand ground and demand.'

'Where do they keep her?'

'In prison on a small island just outside Yangon,' she started to say calmly but then cut straight in with 'but you must not go there.'

'It's OK, I am not here to cause waves, I was just curious.'

She relaxed and took his hand. They walked over to a small pagoda entering between the highly decorated pillars. They sat down behind a handful of people who were worshipping their beliefs in front of three golden Buddha statues, the centre of which was illuminated by a halo of electronic lights of many dazzling colours. They both sat down and shifted their feet away from the images.

'Does any of this affect you and your family?' he asked passing his thumb over the back of her hand. She looked around and then down.

'It has done, hasn't it?'

'It affects every family in Myanmar but we must not talk too much at the hotel.'

'Of course not, it must be hard to live under military law.'

'Hmm, we do not mind the military law, but the way they do things is too violent. The Myanmar people want to be looked after, not be slaves.'

'Forced labour? Does this happen everywhere?' he kept his eyes on her to attract no attention from anyone else.

'Not everywhere, mainly tourist places.'

'Places like here?'

She just looked at him and remained silent. He knew the answer before he asked the question. He sat back a little and looked around at the people bowing down in front of the Buddha images.

Religion has never showed me so much peace, he thought, *maybe I've just been fucking blind all these years.* They sat in silence for a few minutes.

'Were you here when all that shit kicked off?'

'No, but my sister was.'

'I didn't know you had a sister. Where is she?'

'She died,' she replied, emotionless.

He tilted his head up, closing his eyes.

'Oh shit, I'm so sorry.'

'It is OK, she was a student, they were in protest too. The army took her and nobody saw her since.'

'This was 2007? So she might not be dead, then?' He realised the infinite stupidity of the question as soon as he said it.

'I hope so,' she replied, just as he placed his other hand over hers.

He wasn't sure if she meant that she hoped her sister was alive or dead, either was it didn't matter. She seemed emotionless throughout the whole time; covering up seemed like a totally natural art to her. His mind darted, struggling to change the subject when suddenly she did.

'Do you see snow in England?'

'Snow? Hmm, now and again, maybe once or twice a year.'

She looked amazed, 'I have never seen snow but would like to so much.'

'Ah, it's nice to look at but way too cold for me.'

'But the weather in Yangon is too hot, no?' she said with contempt for the climate.

'Yes,' he agreed, 'but I like the heat. I like to walk around in as few clothes as possible,' he said, causing her to laugh. 'Maybe one day you will get there to see for yourself.'

She looked straight at him causing him to feel for the first time that he was too close for comfort.

'Maybe one day, yes.'

After returning to the entrance to reclaim their shoes they caught another taxi back to the hotel, where David immediately stripped off the insanely hot hoodie he had been wearing all day. Khin's brother was at the desk. He looked completely put out that they had walked in together and he started to question her in Burmese. She frowned back at him and answered very quickly, his sulking face remained with his eyes moving back to David and then down at the paperwork in front of him. David wasn't interested right now and just went back to his room. Khin swept after him and shook his left arm saying thanks for inviting her, then went back to her own room. He got straight back into the shower and turned on the air-conditioning.

'Ah shit!' he said loudly, nearly falling over in the shower as the lights went out again.

The water kept running and he carried on unfazed in the pitch darkness and kept his calm. Finding the tap to turn it off he then followed the wall where he found the door. The emergency light in the room had kicked in though, making it easier to find his clothes.

No birds flew over Yangon as he walked back out onto the broken streets around 6pm. Electricity wires bundled insecurely along the streets as if hung by threads. Cars trawled along the pot holed road and the same beggar held her thin arms up towards him for money as he passed. That's two nights he walked by unable to hide the guilty face. Her eyes told a thousand stories that no-one he knew would ever understand. He grabbed dinner from the same place trying something different again. His guide book was the reading material, that or the premier league football on TV which the indigenous people loved. David just didn't, he could barely read the score with the blurry screen anyway.

Bagan looked beautiful but full of temples, it was somewhere that was a big tourist attraction. *Enough temples,* he thought. Mandalay looked appealing with a lot going on but he was wary of it being like Yangon. *Maybe not yet.*

Hmm, Kalaw. A place near the famous Inlay Lake up in the Shan state. The food was rated highly and all home grown, distributed across Myanmar and even exported to China and Thailand. Farmers worked all day everyday to keep up with the provisions. Hill tribes and trekking were also on top of his agenda. The words of Maung Win Zaw echoed at him for some reason when he read about this place. He wasn't sure why, though, it was so small and barely on the map. He left the restaurant after the meal and three beers which tasted better with each one and another small bowl of that spicy soup with the root in the bottom. It caused sweat to run down his face. Almost straight away he booked the bus with the hotel to get to Kalaw for the day after tomorrow as that was the next available seat. Khin's brother served him at the desk with a scowl to begin with, but his mood changed and he was quite happy when he heard that he was leaving. Every sense of caution was taken when he spoke to David though, he seemed quite different from the happy-go-lucky minibus driver the day he had arrived.

Later that day his iPod was playing a song which enforced a solitary moment for him. He lay on the bed listening to the lyrics thinking about all he had done and all he had missed back home. It chanted, *'This is the place where all the wear goes thin, this is the place where the universe steps in. Too many out there are counting away their years, far too few know they're waking up to their fears'.* It was interrupted by a knock at his door. It had only been about forty minutes since he got in and he somehow knew who it was. He was however glad to have held back the smile as he opened the door topless to find Khin's father. As a restrained reaction he kept the 'how can I help you' face on.

'Hello,' he said.

'Ah, David young man, so sorry to bother you.'

'Not at all my man,' he replied whilst pausing the iPod dock.

'May we speak for a moment?' his expression happy.

'Of course, er, I'm sorry for . . .' he stammered, gesturing to his body and its lack of clothing.

The man assured it was no problem as it was his room but walked forward into it and pulled the door to behind him, making David step back and lean on the wall with one arm up casually. He wasn't sure to expect a question about the outing today.

'You like my daughter, yes?' his voice lowered.

Oh shit he thought straight away but 'she's very nice, yes,' were his words as a generic comeback.

'But you would like more of her, yes?'

David said nothing by mouth but his eyes darted from left to right in disbelief of what he might mean by that one, even the guys eyebrows raised. David could tell a liar, character trait, scenario and sometimes even the next few words from somebody. In the past he had taught people how to be dishonest, not something he was proud of but it stood as a powerful ally in situations like this.

Before he even thought of an answer the man cut back in. 'I have an offer for you my friend,' he waved him closer to his ear also checking that the door was still almost closed, 'for an extra nine dollars per night my friend she is all yours, every night, no problem,' he said as David pushed off the wall and raised his arm to brush the back of his head. He was scared not only of the comment but the fact he saw it coming. It changed his whole perspective of the place from family run hotel to some hookers joint for backpackers.

'Er, geez, I'm not sure what to say.'

'It's OK my friend, you are a good man, no problem if you not interested, eh?'

'Well, it's not that, it's just . . .'

'Just what? . . . oh, too expensive, eh? OK, OK, how about seven dollars?'

Holy shit! He didn't see that one coming, he could barely keep a straight face.

'No problem my friend, I'm sorry I embarrass you. I send her in to talk to you, you can pay later, OK?' he said as he turned to walk back out.

David was still fighting for a reply. He felt like dirt for not declining but did actually want her at the same time.

'OK,' was the best he could do as he reached the door.

Khin's father smiled and just nodded his head in understanding.

'Oh, I nearly forgot,' he said as he turned taking the bus ticket he had ordered from his back pocket, 'this is for you, to Kalaw.'

David took the ticket holding it up in one hand frozen for a moment.

'OK,' he said again not taking a breath.

Chapter III

Painted lines

Day 4

He woke silently and felt wide awake even though it was 9am, quite late. The same pinch in his chest coiled up into his throat, he coughed and took his inhaler from the bedside table taking two puffs again. He lay back down and tilted his head towards her lying next to him, still asleep, facing the other way. Still holding the second breath he looked back up at the ceiling analytically as he exhaled the white mist slowly. His heart started pounding and his head went light as it always did, it was almost enough to knock him back out to sleep. He went back into a daze but not fully unconscious until he was brought back around to find Khin, she had moved over to him and was on top of him.

'Hello' she said with a lazy smile, her yellow make-up worn off completely making her look different somehow.

'Hey' he said back as if still asleep.

She stayed in a straddle position but lowered her head and rested against his chest. He felt odd for the whole set of circumstances. Although he had technically agreed to be paying for it, it seemed it was what she wanted anyway. He didn't let his emotions get the better of him too quickly though, after all, he had just booked a bus up to Kalaw. He was a guy who did what he said he was going to do, it was mostly a saviour but sometimes a real backlash.

'What do you do . . . back in England?'

He smirked trying to avoid that one, 'I used to be a salesman, but not any more.'

'So you don't have job any more?'

'No, time for something new when I get back.'

'No girlfriend?'

'No.'

A silence followed and he could feel that she was thinking rather than pretending to be asleep. She lifted her head and inched closer to his face.

'Will you take me back with you?'

Shit . . . he froze for a moment as she stared him right in the face, it had become too serious too quickly but it was such a temptation. All the questions started to race. *How would it be possible? This is ridiculous! It would never work. What have I got to lose? Can she even get a visa?*
After the quickest deliberation of his life all he could come up with right now was, 'I'm sorry, I'd love to but can't accommodate you.'

'But I do not want to live here any more, I'll do anything,' still staring straight through him.

'What is it you hate about this place?' he asked, 'you have a loving family, a secure job, a nice place to stay.' He was genuinely quizzical.

'I want something different. I love my family and brother but it won't last forever. Everyone has to work so hard and follow the same footsteps to survive, back in England people are free. You could look after me and my English is good, no?'

This was when he relaxed in the way she was delusional about what she was asking but tensed in a way that she sounded desperate and meant every word. She even grabbed both his hands and squeezed, her eyes didn't move.

'England is not what you think it is, it has freedom, yes, but people pay a high price to live. I couldn't just 'look after you' when I get back. I'm not going to be able to support myself, my parents will bail me out, I hope.'

'But I could help, get job, make money, live together, no? I hear how it works from many travellers!' she started to sound more and more desperate.

He let go of her hands and held her against him to calm her down. It worked too; he was never going to forgive himself for this one but, 'I'll think about it for a few days, OK?' came out as he held her head up.

'I love you,' were the next quiet words out of her mouth before the kisses. *Time to get out* was the thought rapidly shooting through his head.

The day went by so slowly; they spent the entirety of it together, it was the best time they both had in a while. The stares were incriminating but David withstood the punishment and Khin just didn't seem to mind. After walking through various markets and main streets they found a cafe which had such a bad pavement outside they had to jump to get to the door. The rush of the air-conditioning was a nasty sensation after the sweating heat.

A few younger people were inside, they didn't look up once though until they sat down together.

A young female member of staff came over smiling and placed a menu in front of him. She obviously couldn't speak English and was dressed very smartly but in bright colours. Blue and red seemed to be the theme and the whole place looked co-ordinated and brand new, not quite a government run place though, it was like a fairground but without the people and with cheap pop music as background.

'What would you like to eat?' he asked Khin.

'Oh, no thank you, cannot afford, I will eat later back home.'

'Hmm, that's not an option because I will pay for you,' David countered.

'No, please, not my custom.'

'It's OK, it's mine, I would like to.'

She eventually took the deal and they each ordered a meal from their own tradition. Khin's meal was something David couldn't even pronounce but his own was the classic burger and chips. He hadn't found a place that did western food until now, it was a nice break sometimes. When it came it wasn't so inspiring though; it looked like the cheap stuff he remembered getting from festivals back home, but a lot smaller and with a tougher bun.

'Have you seen the queen?' Khin asked.

He choked with laughter on the second bite, she found that funny but couldn't work out why he laughed in the first place.

'Why do you want to leave Myanmar, Khin?'

She started on the drink that the waitress brought over and slowly replied as she lowered it from her chin. 'They are watching us all the time, there is nothing we can do.'

'What? Who?'

'The military,' her voice was now merely a whisper, 'they have no faith, they slaughter many who do not agree.'

'But you are willing to leave your family behind? Do they even know about this?'

'Yes, we talk many times but they want to stay here. I would love them to come but I need to get away for myself.'

'So why does your father rent you out?' he cut her down shaking his head slightly.

'To make more money,' she said.

'Does any of this money go to you?'

She just looked distant for that one.

'Just as I thought, and this is OK with you?'

'Up until now it has been my choice, it was not forced onto me.'

He held his head with one hand struggling with the concept. She didn't seem to want to answer each time but was relenting to everything.

'Does this happen in your country?' she asked.

'Not often, no.'

'Then there is your proof; it is not needed because England is already rich, nobody starves, nobody finds it difficult, nobody dies and you ask why I want to leave.'

He fell into that one face first he had to admit. He now had his eyes closed trying to soften his ever-sharpening tone. All he wanted to do was to help this girl, along with all the other people in the country. This was just Yangon, the worst was clearly not easily seen by tourists.

He started on his own drink, although it was some orange juice mix he really needed a seven percent beer right now.

'So, how many guys have you asked to get away with?'

'You are the first,' she said looking down at her drink, an obvious lie.

'I don't believe you.'

'OK, OK . . . four times, you are number four,' holding four fingers up.

The truth he realised was actually worse than the lies. Four rejections and many more to come was the look in her eye.

'But I'm the first one you love?' he said quietly trying not to sound condescending.

She looked back up and gave him a straight yes as if she was about to cry. He couldn't tell if he could see through this though, he wasn't sure if it was actually a stitch up by the whole family for his money or something. Committing was hard at the best of times, even when the circumstances were realistic.

After a few seconds he placed one hand over both of hers. He knew public displays of affection were frowned upon in Asia but she didn't seem to mind, it eased her quickly.

'I'm not leaving for home yet, I said I'd think about it and I mean it. I am going up to Kalaw tomorrow for a few days though, I'll come back and stay here after,' he said.

She screwed her face up as if it was an instant rejection but he kept assuring her that it wasn't a definite 'no'. She didn't have an e-mail address and the hotel one was too risky. The phone service in Kalaw had a shaky reputation but he figured to be away from her now would help him think clearly.

'You have to think about this very carefully too, you know, although we have met . . . you don't even know me,' he ended. It was a question included with a hundred more.

They spent another night together with as little stressful conversation as possible and they enjoyed each other's company. Although the whole affair was twisted there was a lot of truth in it. That's what David had come to find: how people lived on the other side, what they wanted, how they thought, and it seemed to be pretty similar to what the other side of the world was like. By this point he thought he would have had more of an idea but in fact it was even more blurry. Khin hugged him hard and followed with one more long kiss on the lips before she stepped out of his room to head back to work.

'I will miss you, but wait for you to come back.'

'I will, I promise.'

He stepped up to the desk in the morning to greet the manager. He had a large grin on his face as usual, this time interpreted as something much more sick than what met the eye. He paid up everything that was due including the laundry which he got back just in time. *Three fucking days?* he thought, *it's not as if they can't dry it out here.* It came neatly folded in a plastic bag but he literally didn't have enough time to check for bed bugs; he gave them the benefit of the doubt. He handed over the cash for the 'extras' separately. It felt so wrong.

'Thank you young man, you are coming back to us before you leave Myanmar?' he asked.

'Yes, not sure when yet though, I will be back in a few days or so. I need to fly back home from Yangon airport.'

'Ah, no problem Mr. David, we will be here and you are most welcome,' he ended.

A few minutes later the taxi pulled up outside to take him to the bus station. He slung his bag in the back and got in with relief. The taxi driver smiled in reply to his uplifting tone, 'hey, how's it been?'

Diary Entry 3

Well, I'm on the bus waiting for it to pull away, headed for Kalaw. Shwedagon was pretty impressive, although standing up was tricky and it was so overcast yesterday it was an amazing experience; pure golden places of worship, anyone can find some peace there. The monks at worship are hypnotic, I'm not technically a follower of religion but I can sure see what it means to people and what hope it holds within them. This place though is like an industrial estate depot back home, it's like the main hub of all ground transport. It's nice and sunny today. I've learnt a lot about Khin, the girl at the hotel. The people here really are from a distant land, she's an amazing human being for sharing so much with someone she has no trust in. The people here have no issues with it as what they have always been promised by their government has never come, so anything that anyone on the street does, indigenous or otherwise, holds no comparison, that's how I see it anyway. I feel bad like I've taken advantage of her though, like absolute shit in fact, but I've promised I'll come back to her before I leave. I have been granted a peaceful path by the tour guide and his

oracle though. I think I will be OK further north, from all the research I've
done it looks pretty peaceful. It's my head that's gonna need the safe travel, not
me . . . maybe that's included in the small print, here's hoping.

The bus was leaving at 2pm but he was advised to get to the station for 12pm as there could be a rush. It took about forty minutes to get there, the broken tarmac roads became rocky dust tracks as the taxi passed the personnel barrier to enter the station. It was actually more like a simplified industrial estate from back home, crawling with workers, mechanics, small office outlets and of course, buses.

They pulled up at the booth number which the ticket displayed and his driver pointed him in the right direction. The young guy at the desk spoke English but not fluently. He was like a call centre worker reading from a script, the same questions over and over, merely repeated if not understood. He was not as welcoming as most others as he took David's ticket number and passport. A few people stared and hung around outside the office smiling, intrigued that he was, again, the only white guy in the complex. He recognized a Spanish woman who was almost asleep in the corner of the larger waiting room to the right of the office. Her skin was dark enough to not be recognized as European though. Once the official gave back his details he took a seat. The heat was searing, sweat had already started to drip down both sides of his face. The midday sun wasn't easy out here. All the young guys outside were trying to sell him snacks and drinks from a line painted on the floor that they wouldn't cross. He figured it had been put there for the reason of hassle. One of them pointed to his own arm with a smile, at first he didn't realise what he meant but then it clicked that the guy liked the tribal tattoo on David's arm. He smiled back at the guy giving him the thumbs up but refused to buy any of his spicy crisps. Food was the last thing on his mind at the moment and he had enough on him already to last the fifteen hour journey. Khin had guessed he might get there around 5am. He hated bus rides, he had been so uncomfortable on them beforehand. Apart from the ones in Australia and New Zealand they were just cramped and rushed—the terrain was always difficult too. He had become accustomed to taking bets on how many people were going to throw up during the ride.

He kept his vest, t-shirt and hoodie with him knowing it would be an air-conditioned coach, it was of good quality too, one of the better looking engines he had ridden. He headed along to seat seven on the right, he was the only one on so far. The iPod came out fully charged, the biggest life saver on these journeys. As he waited for the bus to pull away a few more local people got on each giving him a smile as they walked by to their seats. The bus was only half full from what he saw, maybe less. Two seats to himself was like striking gold. Finally he felt movement and tilted his seat back as far as it would go. A few hours of daytime to stare out the window was an awesome form of entertainment.

A few more people got on and a couple got off over the following few hours. People going back home mostly, they lived in an array of towns scattered across the main drag—the famous road to Mandalay built by the British originally. It was wide, dead straight, well built and even quite smooth. The odd rock was around but it made such a nice change generally.

The sun dived quickly behind the buildings and grassy borders and the moths awoke to chase the remaining lights.

The first stop where everyone had to get off was the border crossing. Every state had to have records of where people crossed, it was one of the many ways the Junta had of keeping track of their people, and foreign business or pleasure. If you committed something they didn't like in one state it became very hard to leave—it didn't even have to be a crime in some cases. David had his passport details taken down by some soldier in a wooden booth surrounded by vigilant companions and crazy moths, funnily enough they didn't really even look at him to check his identity against it. Every bus stopped here in both directions, end everyone had to wait on the other side about twenty feet away for each bus to be driven through empty.

7pm approached and the bus pulled up at a service station, people already lined up down the aisle to get off. David followed suit and headed straight for the toilets.

The toilets were the wonderful holes in the floor as he expected, surrounded by a wooden perimeter which served as the urinals. There wasn't a sink but a tap sprouting from the far wall that people were using. He thought for a moment and then decided it was actually more hygienic to not use it. He stepped back out to the dining area looking at the huge choice of food and drink around. The station was quite impressive, it had literally been built of wood and corrugated iron but was well presented and the smell of the cooking out in the kitchens was soothing. He sat down on the entrance steps not wanting any food yet and watched them hose down the bus. It hadn't rained yet so the wheels had no chance to cool off. A few more buses pulled up as he sat. He started shaking his inhaler he took from his left leg pocket and took a large drag holding his head back to open his lungs fully. His head went slightly light again as he looked down to see two blurry figures of young boys playing a few feet away. They were shooting each other with plastic guns, rolling around having the best time. *If only it was still that easy,* he thought to himself. Khin started to creep into his head now. He had to keep her in check, he was afraid of running all this way just to forget about it for a while because he would only have to think much quicker when he returned. Getting her back to England would have to be her job, after that he guessed that it would be easy to look after someone. She wouldn't have any expectations and she honestly would think it was paradise, but then would she start to miss home? Would she start to feel the cold six months down the line? Although she was fluent in English she would still be recognized as someone who needed a lot of help, that's the way people thought back home, as other people being in the way of what they are doing. The questions from his friends and family he hadn't even thought about yet.

The two boys playing ran off when another young boy shouted something in excitement from nearer the fuel pumps to the right. He shifted his gaze back between the buses and tried focusing on the plain landscape: just fields, a few trees, telegraph poles and the road. He got up and stepped closer to the road looking both ways. *Man . . . endless.*

The bus shunted and shook as if skidding out of control, it felt much worse than it was due to him having laid down in his seat. He had drifted but not exactly fell asleep, it was an awful feeling, like a limbo of feeling rough. His heart started racing as he heard laughter and the sound of dogs squealing, the microphone-like distortion noise pierced his ear as if he was an electrical item tuning back into real time. He sat bolt upright and out of breath. It was still pitch dark outside, the guy in the opposite seat looked concerned for him and waved him calm.

'It's OK sir, we hit dog,' he said.

David didn't reply but just sat back a bit, the fatigue was a helpless feeling and he hated it. He noticed his iPod had fallen from his ears but was still playing on his lap. He illuminated his watch: 22:15, still a way to go. His watch reminded him of his old boss back home. He was a decent guy, he had given it to him just before he left. The watch was silver in colour and fitted his wrist perfectly. Durability was the biggest reason he wore it everywhere, it had fantastic illumination at night and it never seemed to stop, it was also waterproof for a few hundred metres. His boss had been in the RAF regiment when he was David's age, he had worn it on assignments. It had been to a countless amount of places in the world, he must have wanted it to see more throughout its life. He placed the earpieces of his iPod back in and leant against the window watching the dark horizon get more haunting. The road had become slightly rougher; some parts of it had been re-laid.

About twenty minutes later the bus pulled up at another station. He was ready before anyone else this time. Not many got off but he had to stretch his legs. He felt a little crushed up from the way he had relaxed, if you could call it relaxed, he looked and felt like shit. He sat on the step again, this place was empty and not nearly as decent looking as the last stop but it had a smaller, cosier atmosphere. A few people were scattered around—a couple of men drunk in the corner giggling, an old woman wiping down a few surfaces, a couple of young girl waitresses dying for something to do. They looked at David with slight confusion that he had not really acknowledged anyone or looked at any food. He just wasn't hungry, of all the strange things for an asthmatic to crave he actually wanted a cigarette.

'Hello!' said a voice from behind him. It was an unhealthy looking man. He turned to face him on the step.

'Hey, how are you?' David replied.

'I'm very good thank you, please come sit, you don't need to be on the floor, not good for you,' he said, waving him over to his table a few feet away.

He raised himself slowly and staggered over to the table with the rickety, bright green plastic chairs, took a seat and yawned.

'Not hungry this evening, eh?' he went on, 'me neither, these warm nights are beautiful in Myanmar. Where are you from?'

'United Kingdom,' he said for a change.

'Ahh, very good, very good . . . on holiday?' nodding in favour.

'Kinda.'

'Where do you go to? Mandalay?'

'No, Kalaw.'

'Ah, a man of the hills, good idea, stay out of the way, away from the junta troubles.'

'Troubles?' David asked, although he really wasn't in a mood to be lectured again about this.

'Bad news in Mandalay, someone has caused trouble, usually means protests. Not good, but Kalaw does not have problems, small town.'

'Hmm, I see.'

'You like to trek?'

'Yes, that's why I'm going.'

'Very nice too, I have only been once but is very nice, hill tribes and rice pads, no smoke, you know?' he said referring to Marijuana. He then reached into his pocket, the guy stank like shit, he offered some up and if his hygiene had been a bit better David would have actually gone for it.

'No thanks, man,' he said, nodding toward the soldier asleep at the booth by the roadside.

'Ah, yes of course, take no chances, who knows they might even arrest you,' he laughed, 'how about a beer? No law against that!'

David thought about it for a second, 'yeah OK, let's go for that . . . but I'll pay.'

The guy snapped the waitress over for two beers. David laid down the money for both of them and took a sip of Mandalay beer, warm too. It was seven percent and like acid on his tongue but it was doing the job. He only wanted to get drowsy on it.

'So what's the junta's problem then?' David asked quietly

'Not so sure any more, people are not sure what they want.'

'There must be something, people don't kill each other for no reason.'

'Very true, I think they must just be assholes, eh?' He laughed and chinked his beer against David's own making him smile. The guy only had about ten teeth, two of which were gold. He calmed down after another sip.

'Be careful who you talk to though, not everybody is against the junta. Someone could be listening in and before you know it you have someone following you, not long after you will be answering questions you have no answer to.and so on . . . understand?'

David nodded in approval with a frown and a slightly lazy eye from being so tired.

'Do many tourists have problems?'

'No, tourists are welcome, it's the people who live here they hate.'

'Sounds insane.'

'Enough to make you so if you not already are!' he laughed again. 'There have been protests, following on from two years ago in Yangon, you know where the monks started marching? Students this time in Mandalay. Nothing for you to worry about though, Myanmar is a beautiful country, the weather is much better up north too.'

'Do you know how far we are now?' David asked him, knowing he wasn't on the bus.

'Ah, not far, a few more hours, but the road is bad when it splits.'

'So what's your story? Where are you going?'

'I go to Bago to see my father, perhaps for the last time.'

'I'm sorry to hear that.'

'It's OK, it's OK, he has lived a good life. I live in Mandalay, I am a teacher.' Somehow that was hard to believe, David had him down for a drug dealer already. 'If you want something to think about doing in Kalaw apart from trekking, consider a palm reader if you find one. They are mainly by Inlay Lake but you may find one in Kalaw, they can help you if you are in need of guidance in Myanmar, trust me.'

David just looked at the guy in a scowl of confusion, from being the second person to consider him a 'lost soul' he felt he was seen by many as this somehow. He started to wonder if it was what he was wearing or the way he sat. One of the buses then beeped its horn.

'I'm sorry my friend, I must go now, many thanks for the beer. May you travel safe!' he said shaking his hand to leave.

David was too tired to think of why the guy suggested that right now, all he wanted to do was finish the beer and get back on the bus. Although it was warm it had been a long day and like the guy said he still had a few more hours to go. He looked down feeling something moving against his left ankle, it was the station cat meowing gently at him, so skinny its bones were sticking out. It wanted food but he didn't have anything but crisps anyway. He opened a bag he had bought back in Yangon. They had some highly decorated label on them but the actual pack was just clear and stapled together badly. Taking the first one he screwed his face up on one side finding them sharp and hot as hell. The flavouring was very strong but they got better. He looked down at the cat.

'If I fed you these they'd kill me.'

Back on the road was different, feeling rough as hell for the next border crossing for Shan state he wandered out of the bus in the dark blinded by the nearby high powered lights for the soldiers. He managed to take a piss by one of the barb wire fences. He just couldn't hold it in any more, it made a few people in the local queue smile anyhow. He then fumbled for his passport in his pocket on his cargo trousers and got back in the foreign visitor queue, which consisted only of himself. The local queue was a shambles this time, at least nine buses had pulled up to go in either direction and the road was swarming with people. Silhouettes shook their ID cards everywhere with the noise of a riot. There must have been about four hundred or so people around at his guess, everywhere he turned he found them and he noticed the odd shocked face as they realised he wasn't one of them. When he got to the other side he struggled to find his bus as they had all pulled through and looked the same in the dark. After a moment one of the assistants from his bus found him and grabbed his hand to pull him through the insane crowd.

After twenty minutes back on the bus he came to find that the guy at the station was highly accurate. After taking a right turn off of the backbone road to head east it became a winding road, which then became a winding dirt track wrapping around thick jungle. The altitude of the bus was elevated with the mountains and huge jungle covered chasms were inches away from the wheels as they sank into the slushy edges of the carved roads. It would look better in daylight as the golden specks of light were always dragging the eye away from the view, this time they were not temples but tribal lights. People lived out here too but there were no street lights to guide anyone. If you didn't have a light out here all you could do was sit and wait for the next one, they left the odd one on at night to navigate between settlements.

By now his back ached a lot, as did his chest, it became heavier when he was tired. His inhaler would only feel like more strain, that beer made things harder.

A couple of hours passed and he was half asleep again but the bus was now being thrown from left to right with the chasms. At 2:30am the bus suddenly stopped and the interior light flicked on blinding everyone who had their eyes half open.

'Kalaw,' one of the drivers voiced.

What?! It's two thirty AM! He thought.

He waited a second to see if he heard right. He did, one of the bus assistants flagged him over grabbing his bag for him knowing he was headed to Kalaw. It was much earlier than expected though and what with the weather being so good and the roads being quite clear. It still wasn't the timing he wanted though, he needed somewhere to lie down and although it was warm he didn't fancy a bench again.

He got off the bus and just sat on his bag after placing it on the curb. A couple of guys were nearby on scooters; one was smoking a cigarette as if on a break from a night shift or something. They saw David looking so tired and started calling out across the road. He noticed this and tried to focus as the bus pulled away to carry on to Taunggyi.

What the fuck?

'Cheylam!' they shouted, 'Cheylam!'

CHAPTER IV

Kalaw

Day 5

Cheylam was a neat girl in his opinion, especially for getting up at that time to come and accommodate him. She showed him a hotel that was cheap and included breakfast; she made a big thing of it not being government run which was good. She was a trekking guide along with her brother Shael whom he had booked straight away for the next waking day. He felt bad that the staff got up to let them all in. This town was so quiet that the bus was the only movement at night. It was an early to bed, early to rise kinda place. Right now he was in a void where only tiredness was present, he felt so much better for just dropping his gear and falling into bed fully clothed. This hotel didn't have air-con but didn't need it due to the much cooler weather. He still thought a bathroom to himself and a large bed for five US dollars was a great bargain. He crashed out straight away not waking until around 9am.

The dawn was a beautiful sight—his window faced the front of the building, the room was on the first floor and included a balcony which was shared—and the view of the hills was refreshing. The small town was like something from a fantasy film, chickens running around, clapped out cars chugging down the road with converted engines loaded with fruit and vegetables, small bikes scurrying through the streets avoiding the holes in the road. The market traders held the square in the middle of town which was about forty paces from the edge of town where he stood at the balcony sucking in air from the morning sun.

He went downstairs to the attached building where the staff lived and the dining area was. Old pictures hung on the wall of various styles of mountain scenes, mostly workers and carts with hills and sprawling greenery set behind. The room was empty, he only saw a staff member through the hole in the wall where food was passed. It didn't seem to be in use from how the tables were arranged though, about sixteen places for people to sit and eat and only one set out with a knife and fork, he guessed it was for him. A young girl walked out into the room from the kitchen, she looked surprised to see him.

'Min-Gala-Ba,' she said bowing with her whole body very slightly.

'Min-Gala-Ba,' he replied.

She turned around straight away to make the breakfast before he could even take his seat. He felt good this morning considering the rough night. The room was bright with the sun shining through what seemed to be every window but the air was so much cooler making it easier for him to breathe. He took his inhaler again whilst flicking an ant off of the table.

Something skimmed his thoughts as he heard the sizzle from an egg being thrown into a burning pan. It was Khin—he somehow missed her, even after such a short time with her and from feeling nothing more than a teenage lust. He cut himself off as the girl walked back out with a tray full of toast, eggs, orange juice, coffee and fruit. It was like a banquet and looked very welcoming.

The hotel owner was a very polite lady around 45 years old and quite tall, nearly 5"10 which was over average height for a woman. She came and spoke to him after breakfast and asked all the usual questions. Her daughter was the one in the kitchen. She explained that it was low season and that he was the only visitor in town at the moment but that he would be welcomed by everyone. Kalaw was hidden away from political fears, it was also so small geographically, shorter even than the road he lived on back home.

After their chat he walked back out of the extension building towards the hotel entrance to find a skinny guy sitting in the wicker chair just outside. He raised his eyebrows as David approached.

'Min-Gala-Ba,' he said nodding his head as he rose. 'I am Shael, you met my sister Cheylam this morning, very pleased to meet you . . .'

'Min-Gala-Ba, David, and pleased to meet you too,' he said nodding back.

'I hear you are interested in trekking? I have come to see if you would like my services, either myself or Cheylam can take you on a one, two or three day trek through the hills of Kalaw all the way up to Inlay Lake.' He then started to reach into a small shoulder bag sat beside his chair containing a map of the area.

He showed him the deal with the treks but it worked out more expensive as they were taking him alone, the fee could have been split considerably with another person. He thought two days were enough anyway; trekking had lost its edge a bit over the past few months. He had done what he had set out to do on much longer and harder hikes, this was a farewell lap before he headed home. The hills did look very rewarding he thought as he looked east. It would take him through two villages, one of which he could stay overnight with an evening meal cooked by the people there.

'This looks great, Shael,' he said reaching into his right pocket for the twenty-two dollars for the whole thing.

'Ah, my friend,' Shael said raising both hands, 'there is no need to pay now, after, after. I need to ask if you need anything?'

'Such as?' he replied, eyes rolling to one side. Offers like this in the past naturally now caused a sense of alert.

'Are you vegetarian?'

'Oh, no I'm not.'

'And would you prefer to be guided by my sister Cheylam or myself?'

David looked to the hills again and thought it would be nice to talk with Cheylam in more depth, he felt like he was indebted to her for getting up so late the previous night to collect him from the bus station.

'Cheylam would be good if that's OK.'

'Of course my friend, I shall tell her to meet you here tomorrow morning . . . is eight o'clock OK?'

David smiled, 'that's perfect my man.'

David went back up to his room to gather his pack after Shael left. He was a nice guy, and sometimes that was all it took to get you in a better mood. He still felt like a bee in a wasps' nest but more of a welcome one, and decided to head into town for a few hours. The trek was going to be a nice wind down. He did however feel dirty for wanting a beer suddenly so early in the day.

The town of Kalaw was quite upbeat for such a small area. The main temple was situated right in the centre, word had it that it was the only structure there originally and everything else had been built around it. The roads were gridded and slanted so that the one o'clock rain every day ran toward the south western corner where a small drainage system had been dug to stop the whole place becoming waterlogged. The roads were so full of gravel and holes as it was that trucks had to manoeuvre to get through. The main road that passed through from Taunggyi to Mandalay was the most preserved in this part.

Little shops selling all sorts of things were scattered throughout, the market remained more central around the temple which filtered off into smaller alleyways containing fruit and vegetables of so many colours they were dazzling against the plain brown rugged baskets that contained them. People generally smiled as he walked past holding up their items for sale.

He bought two hats, one grey with D&G 1985 written on the front and one with a denim feel looking much more worn with strands and rips. They were French style caps for sale from a young girl no older than fifteen. Three dollars each for what somebody back home in the west would pay around 25 dollars for. The surrounding stalls were full of trekking gear, boots, hats, scarves, sandals, first aid, mosquito repellent, jackets and all sorts of bangles, some were quite stylish compared to what the natives wore. People looked slightly more colourful here than what they did in Yangon. They weren't any richer but they seemed happier in general, maybe a little more secluded.

The air and the sun actually feeling refreshing rather than saturating was a big difference. He felt he could walk around with ease even though he was stared at more than usual. As he passed through the clothing section he came across what resembled a liquor store. A small inlet just off the main drag about seven feet high and twelve feet deep stacked out with all sorts of alcohol, most of which he had never heard of. Only bottles of Tiger were recognizable. He bought two large bottles to save them for after the trek. They had no refrigeration here and he had to blow the dust off the caps but it was something new to try. Mandalay beer was eight percent, with a red label and dark brown tint it looked like poison that had been drained back out of a dead animal. The other was the classic Myanmar beer which he had before. One dollar each seemed like suicide. Although he had heard of the alcoholism problems within the cities he still found it hard to believe compared to the ration of people who didn't drink.

As he left picking up a couple of bags of spicy crisps and some biscuits he was passed by a line of young monks, the one at the front clasped a bell and some further back carried large pots balanced on their heads. Only some of their eyes diverted to meet his followed by a smile, they wore loud but dark orange sheets all tied identically. Two held small umbrellas for shade from the sun but still managed to place their hands together and took a small bow to greet him. David took his iPod out after doing the same, he watched them trail slowly across a main road not even looking for traffic which stopped in wait for them to cross to a set of steep and many steps. It led to a small temple where they lived in the converted monastery attached right by it and surrounded by the woodland. He shook his in amazement of how peaceful the place was.

It seemed to brighten up very quickly as the morning ended and he found a small internet café with an old push-bike parked outside. Opening the door he discovered the place was the same size as the liquor store with four computers. They looked quite up to date and very clean as if they hadn't had much use yet. The guy reading a newspaper at the minuscule front desk to the right acknowledged him and prompted him with a smile and an open palm to take a seat at the station next to the only one occupied with a teenage girl with a pair of headphones on absolutely transfixed with her online game.

He found an arsenal of e-mails from people back home this time, they seemed to be more concerned as he hadn't been online as much. One from his mum which he replied to first, one from his friend Jo who kept him in check and up to date with the entire gang back home, one from his cousin and one surprising one from Sarah, a friend he had met in America a few years ago who had stayed in contact. *Interesting*, he thought. It turns out she had seen a photo on Facebook someone had tagged him in and decided to say hi. David couldn't see the photo due to the bad resolution on the monitor but it was quite an upbeat message using the words *'it would be great to meet up again and talk about your amazing time away . . . I really miss you, love Sarah'*. Thinking of a reply was going to overshoot on his online time so he chose to think about it over the two day trek and get back to her afterwards. It was shortly after he logged off that he started thinking about Khin again, he still felt bad for her but in the same instance was burning inside that she might have been saying all the same things and worse to another traveller guy checking into the same hotel. He suddenly realised his frown had become too pronounced thinking about all of this and relaxed back into a smile as he paid and left the café.

Some more of the day glistened by while he sat back on the balcony of his hotel with the corrugated iron roof creaking every now and again with the dragonflies hovering closely each time but never quite landing. They seemed to hover here in packs and move in circles in sync one after the other. Another shower was required along with dinner as it was nearly 6pm. The guide book was marking out a small family restaurant called Dale's a few streets down from the hotel. It seemed like a good idea so he cleaned his boots out leaving them outside the door to dry out quicker from the beams through the window. Putting on his sandals he headed down the road which was now like a dust track again after the rain had ceased.

Diary Entry 4

Kalaw . . . is awesome! Just what I need right now. The ride was a little bumpy to say the least, and dropping me off here at 2:30am was an absolute head fuck at the time. I got over the sleep deprivation earlier though and had a walk around town. It's an early rising town which is gonna help keep me in shape up here, really sleepy once it is awake though. Beautiful views over the hills, such clean air and the weather is so much easier to cope with than what saturates you in Yangon. I'm very excited to be here relaxing. I've already made a friend and will be going trekking with her tomorrow. Her name is Cheylam, a trekking guide who got up early this morning, well . . . let's say was rudely awoken due to my arrival and pointed me to this sweet little hotel, it's cheap, clean, the staff are so nice and the food is wonderful, talking of which I'd better go find some more, nearly dinnertime, I need some strength.

I also got some hats in the neat little market today, looks like I'm the only foreigner in town again though, suits me right now.

I nearly forgot to mention, as I was exploring I found a communications hut near a little place where you can rent one of their three bicycles. Their line handles long distance calls, I could call home for about half the usual rate but it's not really on my agenda right now, this place is gonna be just for me I think. I know everyone is gonna be fine back home, e-mails are enough to keep me informed but that doesn't mean I'll be glued to the internet café either.

He decided to head east along the main road to take one more walk around the block and end up at Dale's. He passed more burnt out cars, an old Skoda from the 1980's was sitting in disrepair in an old man's front garden who smiled and waved as he passed by from his large wicker chair. He also found a small sweet shop which was the size of a cupboard you would get underneath a set of stairs. The sweets were all wrapped up tight in compressed cellophane, some looked quite nice but most were highly colourful and made him feel ill thinking as to how they might taste. He greeted the shopkeeper woman who didn't seem to be very interested anyway as she was about to close up shop and walked on to the next junction finding himself bumping into a young girl with pigtails and wearing a straw hat. It struck him shortly after that it was Cheylam.

'Oh, I'm so sorry, you look so different in your hat,' he said.

She was wearing a blue chequered shirt and green cargo trousers faded with the sun, even with the pigtails and feminine looks she still gave a tomboy appearance.

'Oh, it's OK, hello again, you also look very different in yours,' she said, pointing to his new one, 'it looks very nice, you buy from the market?'

'Yes, I did, I thought it would come in handy for the trek tomorrow.'

'Yes, it will be very good, Shael has told me and I will come to your hotel at 8am tomorrow, yes?' she confirmed.

He nodded.

'You will also need sun block as your skin may burn, you are very white,' she said in a way not to cause offence, 'please bring plenty of water too, your hotel will sell you cheaper.'

'Ah, OK, I gotcha, my boots are already clean and ready to go, thank-you by the way, for getting up at some ridiculous hour to help me, Cheylam.'

'No problem, no problem.'

'Have you been anywhere nice today?' he asked, looking at her blue carrier bag of shopping.

'Ah, just the market, this is dinner, which reminds me I must go, I am cooking tonight,' she said.

'Please, don't let me stop you any more, I'll see you tomorrow,' he insisted.

'Yes, thank-you, nice to see you again,' she said as she walked off home.

David noticed she walked off north and that she waved and spoke to several people down the road, the town was so small everyone seemed to know everybody else here. He turned his head forward and back to what he came out for. To the right straight along the road he could see the sign for Dale's in the distance as it cambered downhill, so he set off in that direction.

He had trouble with the door at first and had to get the family's attention from the other end of the room to open it from the inside due to them being gathered around the television. They didn't seem to be expecting customers tonight, the place was empty. The older lady opened the door with a smile and spoke slowly in fluent English.

'Hello, very welcome sir, sorry door is sticky,' she said, forcing it open, screeching as it creased the floor, 'please come in, take a seat,' with a friendly grin.

'Thank-you—Ce-Zu-Be,' he replied, taking a seat at the right hand row of tables. The room was big and friendly, clean enough but was set out like an aircraft hanger with a row of seats against each wall either side of the room. Pictures all over the walls with a large map of Kalaw painted on one of them were present. The map showed all the trekking routes with dotted lines. All the pictures involved who he believed was Dale, he was an old man now but the pictures reflected a chronological myriad from his thirties onwards. They showed him with all the different hill tribes and a few westerners who could have been tourists or more prominent people.

Dale came out as he was looking now bringing some Chinese tea and some very colourful vegetable crackers.

'Good day, sir,' he said, bowing with a very polite tone.

He handed him a menu and welcomed him to his restaurant. David invited Dale to sit down with him as he wanted to learn more about the legend of the town and find out a few things. David had heard a few things about Dale, not just from the guide book but people had a high respect for him and soon he knew why. Dale had come from a hill tribe which was quite isolated and poor on the outskirts of Shan state. He found Kalaw as a boy when it was being created by various other tribes and decided to chip in creating a landmark town. His father's early death pushed his initiative to look after his mother and two brothers from his teenage years onwards. They all became trekking guides working from Kalaw and then Dale took the reigns and befriended a man who moved from Kalaw to work in

Mandalay, leaving his house to Dale. Dale pulled his whole family together to refurbish the house into a restaurant which they also lived in upstairs. This was where David was now sitting twenty years later. Dale now being in his early fifties left the trekking to his younger brothers but helped his wife with all the cooking and the two grandchildren who ran in and out of the dining area now and again with various toys and playful questions. Even they spoke in English. His mum eventually passed away in 1998 but he remained proud of his achievements in certainty that he had provided her and her family with an all round better life. This was a quality that all Burmese people looked up to and passed on with their accommodation of visitors regardless of how the government saw it.

David was fully attentive to his life story and showed a great deal of appreciation for his telling. Dale left him when his meal of choice came followed by the classic spicy soup and fruit serving. He paid for his meal with the tattered notes of Kyatt, as he pulled them out of his wallet a small plastic re-sealable bag came loose and some change fell out—it was full of British coins.

'Ah, you have foreign money?' asked Dale.

'Yes, coins from England, would you like one?'

'Ah, please, thank-you sir,' he replied graciously accepting a few coins with his left hand touching his right elbow. He held them up to the light to examine them one by one.

'It is very thoughtful of you to give coins, there are no coins left in Myanmar any more. People now use them as . . .' he held one to his neck trying to think of the word he wanted.

'Pendants?' David guessed.

'Yes, pendants, like charms, they bring good fortune.'

'I see, in that case . . .' he finished handing a few more to him, ' . . . for your family and children.'

By the time he had finished time was pushing on for 9pm. He took a slow walk back to the hotel to get a decent night's sleep for the trek ahead. He felt much more rewarded from Dale's story to do it now, a song came on his iPod as he paced the dark road back finding nothing but cats creeping along under the moon.

'Take a look at my dragonfly, it standing high in the clouded sky, they don't race through serene times, they only sing through the dangerous times', were the words trilled at him this time from his iPod. It made him feel content when he got back and watched over the hills from the balcony, staring into the calming light of the trees in the distance.

CHAPTER V

Dragonfly

Day 6

The first part was easy, about forty minutes into the trek was pasting David with a fresh and relaxed feeling. It was nearly 9am and the sun was out. Cheylam was very good company, she had a simple lifestyle and was quietly curious about him yet could see that he came on the trek for relaxation and didn't throw constant questions at him. Most of the beginning of the trek was uphill, straight from the front door of the hotel to the right, down the side roads climbing through the outer residential areas where the pigs and chickens roamed and straight into the dirt track. It had a reasonable amount of mud soft enough to cushion his feet but not too soft that he lost traction. His day sack was light this time and better than all the others that had suffered the heat and scrapes from nature's growth. Only a change of clothes, a first aid kit, some water, the camera, anti-diarrhoea pills, a toothbrush and paste were needed for this one. He forgot the spicy crisps and had to leave the beer in the hands of the hotel for the better. Although he was paying for the trek it also saved two nights accommodation, the hill tribes were always so friendly and looked out for foreigners. With himself being the only one they would shield him even more so than usual.

As they got further into the hills rice pads appeared, then more, and then some more to the point that they were surrounded by them and quite high. So many pads at so many heights cascaded into a valley as they trailed off onto one sticking to the sodden edge, arms out each side just a little to ensure they didn't fall to the left into a foot of muddy water and rice sprouts or to the right where the same awaited after a three foot drop. The view was breathtaking. Cheylam stopped and turned steadying herself on his arm whilst he got out the camera and took a picture. The sun was behind them and the sky was so clear he knew this photo was going to be good as the whole valley was illuminated. It was one of those moments that reminded him of how alone he had become, there was no-one to take a picture for him here, not a soul in sight. Cheylam could have taken it but it didn't feel the same even though she offered. His eyes darkened as he thought of Khin, and then wondered how low he had sunk to feel closest to someone who barely knew him, after all he didn't have anyone else's opinion.

'Very nice to look at, yes?' she said taking a long breath.

'Stunning, do you walk this way on every trek?'

'Yes, and we will stop for some rest and some lunch just on the other side of this valley,' she said, pointing to the left of it where a large hill was poking out of the horizon. There was what looked like a small hut on top where some steam was rising.

'Great, is that a hill tribe?' he asked.

'No, not yet, restaurant . . . hill tribe we will get to around 5pm where we sleep,' she replied.

'Restaurant? Up a hill?'

'Yes,' she said, submitting a small laugh, 'come, please.'

He followed her as she waved him on whilst putting the camera away and glancing one last time at the valley of beautiful loneliness.

'Eastern Promise' was the name of the song which came on his iPod whilst walking down the trenches of brush which were now appearing more like a dusty forest. It trilled at him, *'Priority rises, like the steam off the trees in the rain. Nobody hides it, and nobody is holding the flame, it categorises, several failures of man and you're still passing the blame'* It spoke of a mythical power that had been found by the wrong people who had used it in their favour rather than for the good of everyone on the planet leading to their downfall. Images of the Junta were in full mind to him with their weapons gunning down people in Yangon. The surroundings here didn't seem to coincide with any of that right now, so he skipped the track and paused it. He decided to have a chat with Cheylam who was three steps ahead of him.

'So, Cheylam, have you always lived here?' he asked.

'Yes, my brother Shael helped bring me up here, we have lived here all our lives.'

'Wow, how old are you if you don't mind me asking?'

'Thirty,' she said. He was surprised at how young she looked for her age, an easy twenty-five was in his head before she said it. 'And you?' she asked.

'Twenty-five,' he said.

'Oh, wow, you look much older!' she said.

In the west this was considered rude but in the east it was the opposite, the older you looked the more respect you gained from people. It occurred to him that he was beginning to feel how old he appeared with every step as they got closer to the restaurant hut at the top of the hill. A steep ascent began for them both, they had to stop talking for a few moments and breathe deeper to sustain momentum.

At the top another view of sheer elegance opened up, the restaurant was surrounded by flowers which had been planted selectively as a boarder for the steep drop. Cheylam asked him to wait as she went to the left to talk to an older man. He was topless, covered in muscular tone but still very slim kneeling on the ground on a large sheet picking tea leaves out of a large pile in front of him. As David passed he found that he only wore what looked like rags around his waist, he didn't even wear anything on his feet.

'Please, sit, I will be one moment, I shall see what is for lunch today,' Cheylam gestured to a picnic table that looked like it had just been carved out. He did as she asked and admired the view of farmer girls kneeling in crops below surrounded by the colours of the fields of awkward angles.

Cheylam knelt down with the man picking tea and started to laugh with him. She was talking about David in reply to the man's questions; just another traveller was the interpreted reaction from the guy. He suddenly snapped his head to the north for a rustling noise which broke through the sound of the birds and cicadas. Four soldiers appeared from a different track as to which he and Cheylam had come. They were wearing green with sleeves rolled up but had no guns, only machetes and what looked like a few other knives for hunting scattered around the harder parts of their bodies. They were all tall and slender with a red and yellow stripe, one directly above the other, on each arm. The man greeted them while Cheylam just smiled and then moved back towards David.

'Hello David, for lunch today we have Nepali food. It will be about ten minutes, would you like a drink?' she whispered.

'How much is it?' he asked.

'Food is free, already paid for, but drink, you must pay.'

'What do they have?' he asked.

'There is water, Chinese tea, Coca Cola or Tiger Beer,' she listed.

It was quite a surprising range considering where they were. He went for the coke and touched her arm just before she pulled away to fetch one. She bent down to meet his confidential look.

'Are they soldiers?' he whispered.

'Oh no . . . not soldiers, how do you say in English . . . forest people.?' she explained.

'Ah, like park rangers?' he guessed.

'Yes, nothing to worry about,' she assured him.

A few pounds seemed to lift from his shoulders after hearing that. The rangers were still laughing with the skinny man by the tea leaves, two of them had lit up a cigarette and appeared to be on their break. Cheylam went back to the hut to get the drink whilst David threw his hat down and put his feet up enjoying the view.

About fifteen minutes passed then the rangers left, the last one in line smiling at David as they entered the shrubs. Cheylam came back over with the food, he had drank half the coke and had been entertained by the amount of ants that sensed the sugar as he opened it. The food was delicious, like nothing he had ever eaten before, it was like spicy pineapple chucks in a wrap with a dark brown spice powder that you sprinkled on top. Cheylam joined him with the same meal across the table.

'Very nice place this, yes? Me and my brother used to come here all the time as children. Then the father of Mhitghal, the man over there, opened this restaurant for farmers and trekkers,' she said pointing to the man who was no longer there; he must have still been inside cooking.

'So do these people live here?'

'Yes, they live and make business, very successful and help many people cross to Inlay Lake, there is another stop station before there too,' she said.

'And do we stop there too?' he asked.

'Yes, tomorrow, but we stop and then we turn off back to Kalaw,' she replied.

The questions about the military were starting to eat away at him. He decided to approach the subject from an outer angle.

'So, what were the park rangers doing?' he asked.

'Oh, they are just checking, they cut down parts of the jungle that will need to be and make sure people are OK.'

' . . . so nothing to do with the military then?'

'No, don't worry, military rarely visit here, only Kalaw once a week. Many people here do not like the military and the government, they scare people and steal crops, some have been killed in the past,' she said.

'Crops or people?' he darted back.

'Both, but do not worry, we are safe. Tourists do not have to worry, the government likes to control, manipulate its own country,' she said, David noticing her English had expanded on this subject.

'But why? surely they would just want what everyone else wants?' he questioned.

She shrugged, 'I don't know why, people say that before I was born Myanmar was a very rich country, we have many oil producers in the south and many drug fields in the north. They take all the money from them for themselves.'

'What if the people just rebelled?' he asked, knowing it was a stupid question just as he said it.

'It has happened many times but more people are killed this way.'

'Even monks at Shwedagon.'

'Yes, even monks.'

'How did the government gain control in the first place?'

'It was overthrown by General Ne Win in 1960's, he caused many problems and corruption. The British left and gave independence and papers were signed as new laws by the military to create the Junta, it has been like it ever since.'

'Who signed the treaty, or law?' he quizzed.

'They did,' she replied.

'With indelible ink no doubt,' he said, shaking his head. He looked out across the view again with disgust at what human ignorance the landscape contained. 'And now the country is theirs, just like that.'

'Not exactly, the people still own Myanmar but only inside our minds. People here do not lust for money, it is not our way, no matter how much money we will have or not have, Myanmar will still belong to the people, not the Junta,' she said with a confident tone of a speech, giving David a wry smile of determination.

Dragonflies made themselves noticed as David tilted his head back to bathe his thoughts with Cheylam's information. They always gave him a sign that he was in a safe place and that things nearby were good. It made him think of the song he listened to in times of bad feeling, he quoted it again in his head, *'Take a look at my dragonfly, it standing high in the clouded sky, they don't race through serene times, they only sing through the dangerous times'*. He didn't know who the artist was but it was a British, female accent who sang.

'That's a great view you have Cheylam. Well, don't worry, I'm another window to the outer world who will pass on your message, I promise. Let me buy you a coke, huh?'

After leaving the restaurant the trek seemed easier. David could feel the energy from the meal and the coke pounding through his veins, it proved that he had become used to not eating so much junk food and his body was able to savour every nutrient it received. The trees had started to glisten shortly before the rain fell, not affecting the sunlight, it was like taking a warm shower. It was a euphoric feeling. He looked up through the trees at the silhouette they made from the light as the path grew narrower and went downhill. He felt like he enjoyed every step of the slow chicane watching ants scatter from giant raindrops.

'We must slow down now, the rain will make the path very muddy,' Cheylam advised.

He acknowledged her but looked at his feet ready for the big slip ahead. She wasn't kidding either, just afoot was a large descent where rocks jutted out of what looked like a ravine that seemed to shimmer with rainwater forming a colossal spout. Each step was a pinch for each calf muscle. Cheylam kept glancing back to check on him but he held his ground pretty well, holding onto the higher branches where necessary. The sound of the Cicadas came back as they got lower into the tree covered areas, his senses were heightened when the rain suddenly fell much harder and it became harder to see. The view was similar to sitting in a car with a steamed up windscreen. He could actually see steam rising from the ground, the mud became thicker like the sap from the trees and half his boot became encased as he walked. Cheylam had put her hat back onto her shoulders like a cowboy from the wild west. He figured it was easier to dry hair and skin than it was clothes so he also took his off. As he reached through some bushes, his foot was taken from under him by a strong gush of water that had built up and overturned a rock behind his heel, causing him to slip backwards and fall down the hill feet first taking out Cheylam's legs as a result. She let out a small exclamation as she went down, the force of hitting her stopped David from slipping further, but she fell on him which hurt more than the original fall. Her pack dug into his stomach but the pain was overridden for thoughts of her safety as a woman.

'Shit, are you OK?'

'Yes, yes don't worry, you fall bad?' she replied?

'Ah,' he breathed out heavily, 'I'll be OK, I might need a launderette at the next hill tribe though,' he said, failing to contain his smile.

Cheylam laughed as she got up off of him looking at their now mud laden clothes. She shook some of it off of her chequered shirt and realised the rain would do the job well enough anyway. She reached for his hand to help him up. She had obviously been used to falling over.

'You take falling very well,' said David smoothing his hair back.

'Ah, yes, don't worry, many trekkers fall and you know, the bigger they are . . .' she said suggesting his size.

'The more muddy they get?' he finished.

They both laughed and carried on after he picked up his hat which was now soaking. He put it straight back on though with the idea that it was one less thing to carry giving him a spare hand.

About thirty minutes passed and the rain had eased. The sun had dried them quicker than expected and they stopped on a rock for a drink.

'How far to go now?' he asked.

Cheylam tilted a bottle of water to her lips and pointed to the right through a set of high riding bushes where an opening was visible onto a hillside.

'This is where we will sleep tonight and stop for dinner.'

He hadn't realised the hills they had crossed had such a height to them. Although he felt they were going up and down it would appear that their altitude had risen overall. They were halfway down a hill which was about to clear with more and more distance between the bushes. The ground solidified, and then reverted to dust in their footsteps again. The hill tribe was seen through the shrubs, it looked amazing, a friendly little settlement that resembled a shanty town sitting on the side of the hill slanted towards the sun. They walked a few steps more and it reminded him of a film he had seen back home that he couldn't place as more hills of amazing crops and farmers appeared.

'Hmm, I say about twenty minutes until we get there, we have to take the long way round the hill as the short way is too dangerous after rain,' said Cheylam.

'Excellent,' said David, ecstatic with ruggedness.

They approached the village through a long slender path that wrapped around the hill at its base. From the view on the other side it looked like the whole village was slanted and ready to slip down the hill, when there you would never have noticed the gradient. It was just how he expected, there didn't seem to be many people about. He guessed they were having dinner or still out with the crops, the people he had seen from all the roadsides throughout the country seemed to work night and day to survive. They slowly navigated the tighter paths at the back of the town, it was very dusty although the grass was bright green where it was present in tufts and scattered between large patches of red soil. The earth was very rich here. Corrugated iron roofs topped decaying brick buildings with repairs of wood which looked freshly cut and nailed together.

Large green jungle leaves were lining the perimeter of the village where they stood accompanied by a feeble wire fence to separate the craps and animals. They passed a couple of large cows and a few chickens when they reached the actual house selected for them to stay the night. It was right at the back of the village but had a small balcony with a nice rear view of the flat lands.

Cheylam led him to a set of stairs where a woman and a young baby were waiting for them at the base of a staircase built into the back of the house. They greeted each other with a bow, he smiled but she could see that David was exhausted at this point. She was know as Brynnya and her baby son was only eleven months old. She spoke to Cheylam in their language.

'Brynnya does not speak English but would like to ask you if you would like dinner now?' Cheylam translated.

'That would be so good,' he replied, not even checking his watch first. It turned out to be nearly six thirty in the evening anyhow.

Cheylam led him up to their room whilst Brynnya took her child to the living room of their actual house which was directly opposite, and then to the kitchen. Cheylam explained that curry was the usual out here with rice and crackers. David wasn't going to pass up anything, he felt bad enough already that he was being fed by people with next to nothing. He took his boots off and stuffed his muddy socks in them before climbing the dark wooden steps that creaked under his weight but not Cheylam's. There seemed to be lots of space in the simple room but he figured that there was usually three or four people in here at once. The large colourful rug on the floor was the first thing he noticed, it acted as a carpet would and was pinned by a low standing table in the middle of the room. Just behind that was a bed with a pillow, it was merely a weave of blankets huddled together to form a tribal mattress on the floor. A single Buddha image with a candle yet to be lit was above the pillow. No electricity at all existed here and the windows were small and rough around the edges. A few ornaments that other travellers had left were scattered around the room but the far right corner was cut off from the rest of the room with hung sheets and a slightly nicer bed. This was for Cheylam, her space seemed to be quite cosy and more colourful. David thought she might have decorated it herself. She put her pack down and re-tied her hair.

'Dinner will be in the next thirty minutes, please make yourself at home, the tribe are very happy to have you here. If you need anything just ask me, OK?'

'No worries,' he said.

'The shower is just outside next to the toilet if you need it, but for now just relax, I will leave you to get changed and check back after dinner is served, OK?'

'Thanks Cheylam.'

She left for the stairs as he turned to sit down on his bed for a bit. He felt sore and sunburnt and a little unwell, he thought it might pass after dinner though. He took a drink of water from his bag and laid down, staring at the ceiling and listening to the birds outside. It was all he could hear as the smell of the tribe's cooking increased. He rose to check out the window; it was still light and the view of the hills in the distance was stimulating, he was far enough from Kalaw to notice the difference. He looked to the right to find that just behind the iron roof and the shower, which was a tall pipe in the ground, were the fields that seemed to be endless. He was happy in solitude for a moment and his only disappointment was that the window was facing the wrong side of the house to be able to catch the oncoming sunset. He turned back to his bed stepping on a small nail on the floorboards. He didn't have time to deal with the pain as his reaction was broken by the sound of footsteps from the stairs. A tall and skinny man in his thirties came into the room with plates and dishes filled with fruits and vegetables, chopsticks, and even a knife and fork.

Diary Entry 5

It's been a weird day, I don't feel great right now so it's probably not the best time to write. Something doesn't add up, I mean don't get me wrong, this place is amazing—I have trekked across rice pads, hills, jungles and through lush scenery that is pretty unforgettable. I feel something is wrong though, I can't tell what the problem is but it's got something to do with why I am here. This place has a nature about it that is pure and untouched. It's hard to explain, it's starting to get to me how solus I am to be here. Nobody here has anything in common, sure it's to be expected but . . . shit, I don't even know what I'm saying, the hill tribe people have just cooked me a kickass dinner and I'm complaining. Everyone is so calm and Cheylam is a great guide, she has a few stories to tell I think. All my limbs are working fine and my feet have only just started to feel the strain, tomorrow will be great. I'm sleeping in one of the better tribal buildings tonight with my iPod, a blanket, my hoodie, a candle and the Buddha figure who is watching over me. I got food in my stomach and a roof over my head, even with the luxury of an outdoor toilet and a bed that's very good for my back, what am I moaning about? I'm just a confused foreigner who doesn't know what he has.

After a fulfilling dinner by candlelight on his own Cheylam checked on him and went to bed herself. David could see she was so tired but she never let it get her down, he admired her affection to tourists. He went to bed shortly after and could hear her praying quietly behind the curtain of bed sheets for a few moments before she fell asleep. David lay down in his hoodie. He knew he needed to keep warm as the nights were much cooler in the hills. He looked up at his faded picture of the Buddha lit by the candle. He wondered if he was watching over him, he wondered if his life was being controlled, and if it was, was there ever going to be anyone with him to experience the same? He looked around the room again re-adjusting to the darkness which followed swiftly. His faced became pained the more he thought about it. He seemed to be a wanderer by nature but he considered nothing wrong with that; he was doing exactly what he wanted and loved but still felt a duty to his family back home and his own future. It seemed that he always started thinking about a career as soon as he entered his holiday and vice versa, it wasn't a mental trait he was proud of and yet he knew many people suffered from the same problem. Another perhaps bigger train of thought was that he knew he had come away searching for something. He was nearing the end of his travels and felt that he still hadn't found it. It was like a long computer game where you found that the ending wasn't great but made you look back on what you did throughout completing it. He thought of all of the decent people he had met before, back home and far away. He appreciated their time and company, spreading their many talents throughout their routes of choice, but he wasn't so good at seeing his own potential at having done the same and he always seemed to end up alone. He took a deep breath and ignored the feeling of ants and the odd flea on his skin which caused the hair on his arms to raise. He couldn't be bothered to move quickly to brush them off, instead he just leaned up to blow the candle out before pulling the provided light brown blanket over the lower half of his body and turned his head to the side. He missed Khin and he knew it wasn't healthy. He had promised that he would go back to her knowing it was a bad idea; he didn't see what he had to lose as he hadn't gained anyone else anyway. He turned his head back facing the ceiling again and blocked it all out as best he could trying not to well up as he had an idea that that tomorrow's continuation of the trek was going to be more challenging. He grabbed his iPod and pressed play hiding the light it produced to the room under his blanket. The first song rolled by slowly, a morbid but relaxing song, a band called Radiohead murmured some lines about changing luck.

Day 7

He woke to a bright morning staring at his watch that he had laid out beside him. It was blurry to begin with and then slowly focused into a sharp vision of hands pointing to an early number and a smell of a decent breakfast, and came with a dull ache in his head. Cheylam was already up and gone from her room. David felt unstable in balance as he staggered over to the balcony and looked out again. The air did surpass the aching feeling in his arms, back and hips. He took his hoodie off to flick it outside the back door freeing it of parasites.

'Good morning David!' came an upbeat cry from the doorway opposite. It was Cheylam, helping the hill tribe family with their food.

'Good morning,' he replied with a cracked smile and hair sticking up all over the place.

After adjusting his vest that he had slept in he hung his hoodie on the end banister of the stairs and sauntered toward the toilet in reverie of what he might find.

After breakfast he sat where he had the night before at the low table cross legged talking to Cheylam this time. She was very high in spirits for the day which helped him with his increasing headache. His arms were starting to become weak, he could feel the difference and remembered when he had been quite strong, he had once been able to perform thirty press-ups each morning whereas now he found he could barely hold his own weight up for twenty seconds. The toilet hut out the back was much needed which he saw as a blessing for last night's dinner not poisoning him. He did however skip the shower—the hosepipe inside connected to a tap sticking out of the ground provided freezing cold water. He splashed his face and hands slowly, that being enough on a cold morning of a warm country. Cheylam was a saviour to talk to, they talked away even as they left the tribe to continue their trek after thanking them. He gave a small donation of five US dollars as he left to the kids who waved them off by the back fence exit. Cheylam had explained that the families and tribes would be upset and questioned by the Junta if they found westerners were staying in their provinces. He didn't see the problem with it, but then nobody else did.

'Surely the government would just want to unite with westerners to share ideas and beliefs? They must realise they could benefit in so many ways,' he asked.

'This is not how they think, people of Myanmar are very open to visitors, the government used to be as well until Arusa Nu Sanda Nu Sanda was arrested. Ever since then they believe in . . . how do you say? . . . sabotage?' she replied.

'Sabotage? Like a conspiracy against them?'

'Yes, this is true.'

'Why? What does Myanmar have that the west would want to take advantage of apart from the scenery?'

'Oil,' she said as if it were a lifelong enemy to her.

Suddenly it became crystal, something Khin had said about oils fields in the south. He had read that Myanmar was dubbed the richest country in Asia due to its oil refineries. It seemed that money did change the shape of things to come. He wanted to ask how it had got so out of hand for so long in this country but couldn't bring himself to. He figured it would only upset her. He changed the subject and asked about the rest of the trek and where they were going now. She said they would pass through Myin Ma Hti first across some open fields and then through the famous cave complex. Then out through the jungle at the back and to the train station for lunch before returning to Kalaw about two hours afterwards. He checked to see how his iPod battery was holding up, priorities stood high as far as music went.

'I need to stop and put on sun-block I think, Cheylam,' he said.

'Good idea!'

The paths started to snake as they approached a dirt track that acted as a back passage for farmers transporting crops. A few streams were now in hearing distance and started to sound stronger as they got closer. Cheylam led them through a very bushy area where all the red soil of the dirt track morphed into thick shades of green which bore trees of young roots making it resemble a Canadian province rather than where they were.

'We are going to cross a river now, it is not deep at the moment so don't worry.'

'Wow . . . this is a surprise!' he said sarcastically as he stood watching it.

'Yes, Cheylam is full of surprises, plus it will wake you up, please be careful with your music playing though,' she replied with another surprising element of sarcasm.

Impressed by the comeback he smiled and stepped into it after her. It was flowing from left to right as they crossed it slowly, although it wasn't deep enough to cover the laces of their boots, the rocks were still slippery and he wasn't going to risk falling again. The stream was about thirty five feet across and was pleasant to stand in and he imagined it in full flow, only being able to cross by riding an elephant or picturing it carrying crops over.

'Come on!' Cheylam shouted from the other side, waving him over.

He was lost again and felt slightly better in the moment standing right in the middle of the stream. A song played through his head even though his iPod wasn't connected. He started singing it loudly as he dragged his now soaking feet up one after the other.

'Bring shame on me woman. This is why I cross my hands, this is why I take my soul across the . . . MIGHTY RIVER!' he sung powerfully, seeing Cheylam laughing in the distance.

About an hour passed when a singer-songwriter called Chris Cornell was the first song that came on to his iPod, as they walked through some ever thickening brush he sang, *'I wanna fly right through your oceans, sail across your dunes, set alight your fire and hope your redemption comes soon'*. He pressed pause as they took a break on a small hill with what he classed as a neat little view to another green and vibrant landscape. They drank some water as Cheylam pointed out the trees in the distance where they were heading, she said that on the other side of the trees was a small bus stop and the Myin Ma Hti caves.

'I need pee-pee, can you please stay here and watch my pack?' she asked.

He was happy to as she walked back into the brush for some privacy leaving David staring again at the horizon. He felt empty suddenly, it seemed happiness was present but not foremost as the girl from Yangon came to his thoughts again. He closed his eyes remembering everyone he had met on his travels, simply missing them. Although Cheylam was great company, he was more engulfed with solace in her country than he had been anywhere else. Regardless of how hard he found it to deal with he was now wearing a fixed sigh accepting the feeling this time rather than trying to push it away, he wasn't sure if it was any easier though.

'I need guidance from one of the monks,' he whispered to himself.

He looked back over his shoulder hearing the snap of a twig as Cheylam came out from the brush slowly. He noticed her arms were raised and gave her a confused look, she was completely blank in expression. David panicked as he saw the tip of a rifle follow her from the bushes pointed square at her back. He froze and turned slowly rising to his knees to face her along with two Burmese soldiers, both dark skinned, nearly six feet tall, skinny but muscular like the others he had seen. One was in his early twenties from what he could tell but the other one behind was much older, around forty years old. Their expression was stolid as if what they were doing was routine. He started speaking to Cheylam in their language as they stopped a few feet away from David, he tried to rise to his feet but the other soldier raised his gun and waved him back down before he could. Cheylam answered everything they asked calmly. David was left pulsing with adrenaline but kept still trying to conceal his alarm, something he happened to be very good at. The soldier holding Cheylam hostage started to get more aggressive as if he were arguing with her, nudging her arm toward her making her put her hands behind her head. She turned to David reluctantly and said that he shouldn't panic and to do the same, so he raised his arms slowly.

'What do they want?' he asked her.

'They want to know what we are doing here, I'm trying to cover for us,' she said.

The soldier was losing patience rapidly with Cheylam's replies. He barked some sort of order at his companion who then walked over to David and pointed the gun at his head. David, still with arms behind his head, heard the click of the safety catch as it came off and realised that this was not a bluff. Rather than panic he tried to assess what they were actually after, this didn't seem like lowlife theft, something more must have been at stake here. His thoughts were interrupted as the soldier grabbed his hair to taunt the now near hysterical Cheylam.

David closed his eyes tightly awaiting what seemed to be an inevitable event, not seeing an easy way out of this even if he could understand the language.

Within a second later the soldier with David slipped over and landed heavily with a thud on the bank; chaos ensued, David's mind became tunnel vision with instinct. He felt a rush of wind as somebody ran past him from behind, the only glimpse he caught was a dark pair of skinny legs with dark brown material at the waist, he definitely wasn't a soldier but didn't have time to debate it now. The younger soldier by Cheylam was distracted by his companion's slip which gave her the chance she needed to stop him. Seeing Cheylam leap at the soldier standing next to her urged David to leap on his own captor, he started punching him square in the face as hard as he could making his nose bleed. David picked up the gun and pointed it square back at the soldier more than ready to pull the trigger but he hesitated as he saw the blood run down his face and drip off his ears. Switching hands with the gun flipping it to the weighty rifle butt, he brought it down on the older soldier, and again, making sure it knocked him unconscious.

He raised his attention to the struggle in front of him. Cheylam was crawling hastily on her knees towards him on the hill whilst another man, the one who he had felt seconds before was fighting with the younger soldier; both of which had their hands on the gun. They were both of similar build but the soldier had youth on his side. Cheylam, with a look of determination on her face pulled the gun out of David's hands.

Cheylam spun around gripping the gun and fired one round into the leg of the soldier making him arch his back and lose the power struggle with the other man. His opponent could have easily shot him having gained the gun fully but instead tossed it a few feet into the brush they had entered through. He pulled out a sharp knife from his waistband before thrusting it into the soldier's neck, the sound was grotesque making David look away after the third thrust. The man was clearly trained in combat, wearing a plain brown material and harbouring a skinny muscular body like the soldiers. Although the death was gory and slow it was silent which is what the man wanted. The gunshot from Cheylam had made around twenty birds take flight from the trees above them. There was no telling how far it was heard, or if there were more soldiers nearby who would be responding already.

The man eventually rose from his opponent. He was covered in blood from his hands to his elbows. Standing fully in front of them for the first time he was wearing the same brown material wrapped around his head also creating a face-mask. David didn't need him to reveal his face as his wide eyes gave him away too much. It was Mhitgal, the man from the restaurant. He uttered instructions in his language to Cheylam whilst searching the soldier, cutting his uniform off with the knife.

'COME! RUN!' Cheylam stressed, grabbing David's hand with her free hand and then dropping the gun as they ran.

Nothing went through his head as they ran, just jungle all around him. It felt like a scene out of a movie and he wasn't entirely sure what had just happened. He followed Cheylam who was jumping over fallen branches and swinging her direction off of small tree trunks. She was on a mission to get away but kept looking over her shoulder for him. Her robotic pace was relentless but he still managed to keep up, his adrenaline was the source of stamina this time. His pack suddenly started to get very heavy, it seemed they had been running for minutes straight. His hair band had come loose and the sweat pouring from him pasted his hair to his face distorting his vision.

'I need to stop,' he gasped as he leant on a tree clutching his chest.

She allowed him this much but still seemed alert as if it were about to happen all over again. She looked around frantically and then took her own pack off to take out two bottles of water. She handed one to David and sat down.

'I think we are safe for the moment, please drink, it will calm you,' she said.

He took the bottle from her and downed half of it straight away. His breathing started to falter, he wrestled his bag off unzipping the front pouch to find his inhaler. He took it out to take two long puffs which were sorely needed. He was so hot he could barely feel the cold from the canister although the mixture inside worked in seconds as usual. He was too hot to be worried, so technically he was calm. He switched to lying down on the ground catching his breath, even though she was in a similar state Cheylam was keen to move on.

'We cannot stay for long but don't worry, we should be fine now.'

'SHOULD BE FINE?! We just killed two soldiers! Does this happen often?' he snapped back.

'Shh, shh, please, please, there may still be danger, we can avoid. Listen, we can get back to Kalaw in no time but we must not attract too much attention. Mhitgal used to be a soldier, hunter. He is well trained, he will find a way to cover up and look after us,' she explained.

'Look after us? Why should it even need to be like that?' he said.

'I know, I know it looks bad.'

'Damn straight it looks bad, we're lucky to be alive. Did he . . . did he follow us all the way from the hut?" he asked looking around violently only to see the thick brush Cheylam had led them into.

'Yes, he must have, but I didn't know he was there I swear. All we have to do now is act as if nothing happened, I will lead us back to the edge of town and everything will be back to normal.'

'Christ . . . normal . . . haven't felt that in a while,' he said, feeling like he should laugh hysterically.

The distressed couple sat in silence and took deeper breaths which became slower as time passed. The sound of the cicadas and birds in the surrounding growth took hold of their tract again.

'Come on,' said Cheylam as she put her pack on and raised her arms to aid him back to his feet, 'we should go, I will explain on the way.'

He got up, tying his hair back up with the thought that she had the right idea. There wasn't any point in standing around now.

'I get the feeling this is going to be a tough day,' he said to himself.

An edgy twenty five minute walk in silence was odd for both of them, they felt it duty to not speak and to concentrate on the steps ahead. The distress was gone, so much so it could have been questioned that it was ever actually present. The trees echoed a serene atmosphere again, like a bad dream that had passed. Cheylam stopped and turned around to question him just as they were reaching an opening.

'What hour of day is it?' she asked.

'Nearly 4pm,' he said checking his watch.

'Hmm,' screwing up her face as she looked back at the clearing.

'What's wrong?'

'We won't make it back to town before night, I think it would be best to stay at the caves.'

He paused, frowning, eventually replying:

'You're shitting me right? Sleep in the Myin Ma Hti caves?'

'No, no, not sleep in caves, I have a friend in nearby village by station, will take maybe . . . two hours to get there. We should rest there tonight and carry on to town in the morning,' she said.

'I see, well, whatever you think best. By the way I'm sorry for snapping back there.'

'It's OK, it has been a difficult day . . .' she paused again looking out to the next set of fields, 'but I think it will be OK from now on.'

'How far is it back to Kalaw?'

'About four hours, but we risk much if it is too dark. We will be safer in the village over night, no soldiers patrol, and then tomorrow I take you on short cut past the railway track and through the caves to get back.'

Two hours did indeed pass, his feet were blistered on the same outside edge of each foot when he took his boots off at the village which was similar to the last one, if not even more basic. The train station was about thirty feet away but only passed during the day three times. The villagers had built it to connect with Mandalay as a food and trading supply, the track was rusty as hell and made him wonder if it could actually support a train. It was barely visible through the long grass that had grown through it. It wasn't his concern right now though. Cheylam spoke to one of the village people and found her friend, she was a large woman with two young boys running around their plot of land. They were about eight years old, when David looked harder he thought she may have been pregnant too. He saw the concern on her face as Cheylam filled her in on the details of what had happened, they kept their voices low even from the two boys. The woman walked over to David seeing him tending to his feet. Cheylam translated for her.

'This is Shenlu, she is pleased to meet you and asks if you need medicine for your feet,' she said.

'Min-Gala-Ba. No thanks, I'll be fine, just wear and tear,' he replied.

They carried on talking while David applied plasters from his first aid kit. One of the sores had started to bleed on his right foot.

'Cheylam helped him to his feet to guide him to a room in the village hidden from the main track. The two boys rushed over to help but he put his arms up to stop the assistance, showing them that he was alright.

'Min-Gala-Ba!' they said excitedly making their mother smile.

'Their names are Shuren and Kannan, sons of Shenlu. If you don't mind, their beds will be next to yours tonight?' said Cheylam.

'That's fine, I think I just need to lie down for a while,' he said.

The boys were trying hard not to stare at him as they walked either side showing him the way to their huts. Shenlu was already in there preparing the bedding which appeared to be straw and sacks. He found it all an acceptable distraction from what had happened. Their innocence helped him appreciate the hopeful village they lived in, it reminded him of true equilibrium standing in so many countries he had seen but even more astounding being right in the centre of a country under threat of its own people. The two boys didn't speak a word of English but helped carry his boots in excitement when their mother told them they would be sharing their room with the westerner. Cheylam warned him that the comfort wouldn't be the same as the last village. A rug and a pillow were laid out for him, these were made in a factory it seemed but looked old and worn. The boys seemed to appoint themselves keeper and protector of his boots, washing them with the outside tap already from a nearby building. He sat down almost falling onto the rug. One of the boys saw him then reached for his feet again, he then shouted for his brother who then came running in with a bowl of water and a cloth. David laughed.

'No, please, it's OK, really,' he said trying to wave them away without offending them. They wouldn't have it though.

He eventually gave in and laid back with one arm over his face, thinking about nothing in particular. The boys carried on with their unprompted duties with care.

Day 8

David had fallen asleep, only realizing when he woke up in the dark. He knew exactly where he was which was surprising for first thing in the morning. It was somewhere around 4am when he raised his watch to check. The two boys were wrapped up next to him, his feet were cold but very clean and felt good for a change. He sat up to find his boots at the end of his bed, they were also much cleaner than they were before. He raised himself slowly not waking the boys and walked to the open entrance only shadowed by a hanging rug. He sat down again taking a bottle of water from his bag. Looking up at the stars again was a constant reminder of where he was, they were clearer than ever in this region with no lights around to dull them. He didn't feel normal right now, it was nothing to do with the lack of food either; it was like he had changed. He didn't care about much except the people of the village. He knew everybody else he knew in the world was relatively safe and that he himself wasn't. That was the better way around for him. Before, he never would walk out into a dark jungle-surrounded village knowing that soldiers were around looking for them. '*Too much attention is attracted when you try too hard to hide*', was what he said to himself. Given a calm attitude, he was still stressed and thought of how anyone else he knew of in this situation would be dying for a cigarette. Instead he just flicked on his iPod, it seemed to tell his story with a different set of words. He turned it right down to ensure it didn't wake anybody. He just closed his eyes, knowing it would bring Khin to him again, anything was a comfort now in comparison. Of everyone he had back home, of everyone he knew out here, only Khin stood out. He thought maybe Khin was OK in Yangon and that running off with her now didn't seem like such a bad idea.

David nearly jumped feeling the ground next to him alter; it was a tired Cheylam taking a seat. She was wrapped in a blanket.

'Can't sleep either?' she asked.

'Nah, not this time.'

A long silence stood as they stared into the distance of dark trees.

'Do you think we'll get back OK, Cheylam? I mean seriously,' he asked straight up.

She held her words for only a few seconds but finally answered, 'We have a very good chance, word from the village is that there has been another uprising in Yangon. It has already spread to Mandalay.'

'An uprising? Concerning what?'

'Not what, who. A tourist has been taken by the military for plotting to free Arusa Nu Sanda. He tried to smuggle her through Bhutan and into India.'

His jaw dropped, 'A tourist? Do you know what nationality?'

'American, he has been hiding here with a small group of people in Yangon for some time, illegally. They have stated that there are more of them hiding, so the military will search all over and all tourists are to be questioned,' she informed.

'But how it that possible, surely they can't track every tourist in the country?'

'Actually it would be easy, especially now in low season, every border has records of which state you have passed through. Yangon has been stopped, how do you say . . . isolated?'

'So what does this mean? Maybe I could just explain I am nothing to do with any of it and they'd let me leave, simple?'

'I'm afraid not, they will not take an answer from you easily, they are not to be trusted. It is likely the airports have been grounded, too.'

'Shit,' he said quietly now holding his head. It soon became clear that things had already got out of control, why else would they be so scathing with their approach, a tourist? The thought sickened him but at the same time it was what these people wanted, a freedom fighter freeing Arusa Nu Sanda Nu Sanda would be causing chaos for the government if they had succeeded, instead with failure it would cause the soldiers to tighten their grip.

'I'm guessing he didn't get through.'

'Through what?'

'The security for Arusa Nu Sanda.'

'Oh, yes, he did, he got straight in to her but she refused to come.'

'Refused?! Why?'

'It is not her way, she has had chances of freedom before but she has no-one left but her people. The only way she would go is when she knows everyone in Myanmar is free to go with her, it gives many people much hope, you understand?'

'Christ, all for one and one for all,' he said in disbelief now tilting his head back. 'So where does this leave us?'

She made a face with a fake smile which turned into a cornered look.

'I must get you back to Yangon somehow, your best chance is to hide and find a way across the border into Thailand, they will not let you fly out.'

'But you said Yangon is under isolation.'

'I can still get you in, but I will have to leave you. They will find you here. I can get through to Yangon and miss every border on the way if we are lucky.'

'Isn't that joining in with the highly illegal tribe?'

'We have been forced to avoid and kill soldiers, we are already highly illegal,' she said, handing him another sealed bottle of water. David took his eyes off her and stared back at the horizon taking a short drink.

'Holy shit.'

She rose and turned, 'I must go and get ready now, we should leave very soon, maybe 2 hours. Come over to the house when you are ready, we must eat something here before we go, it could be our last time before we get back to Kalaw.'

The two boys got up with the sun while David was re-packing, they had even washed some of his clothes for him. They both hugged him and each gave him a bottle of water, he was touched at their humanity. Pure hospitality from people who had never seen anything much further from their village, they might not have ever met anyone with a different tone of skin. Cheylam was eager to carry on and waved David on. A small part of him wanted to stay but he knew it wouldn't be a good idea, a fate worse than his would dawn on the tribe. He took a few steps before he put his hand in his pocket. Now wearing his newly washed cargo trousers he felt his wallet, something he knew he shouldn't be carrying on him visibly. He stopped and waved Kannan towards him taking his wallet out and dropping a handful of British coins and coppers into his hand. It was from the same re-sealable bag that he used to give some money to Dale and his family, it had worn slightly thinner since then already.

CHAPTER VI

Cave

One thousand and one footsteps passed in his head, his iPod was now plugged into Cheylam's ears who was in front of him yet again. He wasn't tired this time and was more attentive to his surroundings, lots of dirt tracks made up the ground they covered. They walked steadily and slowly. Cheylam was clearly affected by the music, in a good way, she had only heard of such devices. She pulled out one earpiece and turned around to him.

'The caves are not far, when we get there, you must not say anything about what has happened. OK?' she said.

'No problem,' he laughed, 'how deep do the caves go? Actually, is it even a good idea to go through them? Is there any way around?' he asked.

'There is but it's not a good idea, there are Junta outposts on both outside ridges of the caves, they will most likely not go through like us.'

'Most likely?' he said with stern question.

'Yes, there is no guarantee that the soldiers will not know what has happened already, but we will be much safer to hide and move through caves,' she replied as if not wanting to.

David thought hard about another heated reply to that but couldn't come up with one. He had to remember no matter how irate he was with the whole situation that he was in Cheylam's protection, he would be dead without her and he was no longer a tourist, he was a fraud, a fugitive, a foreigner.

'When you said not to say anything, to whom did you mean?'

Cheylam stopped and slowly admitted, 'There will be a monk at the cave entrance with a small bus stop, we will have to eat there. I have some money for us, maybe only soup is served there though, is this OK?'

'Of course, that's fine, it's OK though, I'll get it. The monk won't ask any questions, right?'

She pulled a face that suggested a lack of optimism as she walked beside him.

'He might, I don't know. Their knowledge is far greater than ours, they can see when things are not right you know. They also gain information much faster than many people.'

'I see,' he said, but he questioned himself on what a monk would have against them. If he knew that they had killed others then maybe, but was self defence even in their beliefs? They approached the caves before he even realised, they were buried between several small payas and pagodas. The green brush and grass once again turned to dirt, this time dry, very dry, it could have been mistaken for Mexico.

Cheylam led them to a small hut with a few men sitting there. It was purely wood, an open shack, not very deep but was decorated as if it were a pigsty with a small fence around one edge creating a barrier for the customers to lean on. A few plastic tables and chairs were around that led to the small inlet with a very skinny young guy sitting on a small stool surrounded by sweets, drinks, a coffee machine and even a small oven.

She asked David to sit with her this time, she seemed to recognize them all but maybe didn't know them too well. She said hello quite loud and innocently, pretending to be more tired than she was. She started speaking in her language to them and then turned to David who sat at the nearest table in the sun.

'I have asked for two soups? Is this OK?'

'Ah, that's fine . . . here,' he said and passed her some Kyatt notes. He looked around to find some colourful insect walking around, they were flocking to the odd bits of food that had been dropped on the floor. His concentration was drawn to a male voice from one of the other tables. They all looked friendly, older guys, maybe trucker types on their break he assumed.

'Hello friend! Where are you from?' asked the one sitting furthest from him.

'England,' he said as they all exclaimed.

'Ah! Manchester United!' he said. David wasn't sure if it was a question of where he lived or who he supported, or if it was even a question at all.

'No, no, south London.'

'Ah! You no support Manchester United?' asked the smallest guy sitting nearest to him on the table to his left.

He laughed, 'No, no . . . West Ham!' he made up, even though he wasn't really into football, he knew it always brought a happy reaction.

The small guy laughed and cheered and pointed as he started shaking the arm of his friend opposite who obviously was not a fan of West Ham, he smiled and muttered something before carrying on with the cigarette he had. Cheylam laughed along with them and then helped the bus stop guy bring over the soup. It was as David expected, it didn't look appetizing but he knew it was and was very much up for it. A dark yellow suggested how spicy it was going to be but was deceptive when he tried it, the famous root in the bottom was there and some herbs were floating around with a few onions, perfect timing too. The stuff tended to heat the back of his face a little and then calmed him from the unsettled situation.

'Welcome to Myanmar!' said the guy with the cigarette as he stubbed it out and got up. He then walked around the back of the stop to a small pick-up truck and drove off carrying a load of vegetation on the back with a few digging tools strapped to the sides. As he drove off, David watched him circle and re-join the dirt track road to go towards Kalaw from the way they had come. By doing this David caught sight of another small hut further towards the caves. It was barely a hut though, a pitiful sight. An old man sat with a stick, with a dark pair of glasses aiding his shade further than the tiny overhang the hut gave. It almost resembled a patrol box with only two sides. The man had long legs which were crossed and long grey hair. A board in front of him had a drawing of a hand on it with arrows marking and indicating lines. Some Burmese writing was across the top with six thousand Kyatt at the end.

'A Palm reader,' he uttered to himself. He finished his soup as to waste it wouldn't be clever and also very rude to the chef. Cheylam seemed to favour the idea of talking to the man. David was curious but not sure why he even wanted to, it was probably the worst time to hear what kind of crap he had to offer him but what the hell.

He walked over slowly trying to get a better look around the cave entrances as he stopped in front of the guy.

'He-he-he, Min-Gala-Ba,' he said nodding with a grin.

'Min-Gala-Ba,' David chanted the same.

'You have come to me for your palm reading?' he asked.

'Well, not exactly, but if fate brings us both here . . .'

He laughed some more, 'This fate you speak of, has she served you well so far?'

David paused in hesitation of this guy, these types of characters were always shady and unreadable to him. For his question though, considering everything up until now . . .

'Pretty good I guess, I'm alive and well,' he replied.

'Good, good, a man who is grateful for what he has, a traveller are you?'

'Yes.'

'And you have been many places before Myanmar I see,' he said. It seemed as if he closed his eyes but he then took off his dark glasses and stared right at him revealing his darkened eyes, one of which was scarred from an operation of some sort. He was blind.

'And see I do, very well.'

'Very true,' said David.

'Do you have the time young man?' he said raising a finger.

David checked his watch, 'Yes, it's nearly midday.'

'Where the sun rises highest, your fortune becomes more satisfying,' he said.

Suddenly David was thrown back into believing all the scam stories. He had quite a stash on him so he figured six thousand Kyatt being only around six US dollars was nothing compared to what he had paid for life preserving items in other places. He handed over the money placing it carefully in the old man's hand, he refused to take it though.

'No, please, in the bowl.' He gestured with both hands toward a small metal bowl on a small table in front of him. David pondered on how he knew it would be in the bowl without touching it, he didn't want to toy with these ideas though and did as he was asked. He realised that the man's clothes were very old and torn, an old blue shirt and baggy trousers with blankets around and a few cups he had been drinking out of marked that he may have sat out here in all weathers. His skin was leathery and dark, the sun didn't seem to bother him much. As he leant forward David noticed he had a bald patch revealing that he was a lot older than he may seem, in his early seventies maybe. His hands were scathed from past experience, a worker of the land for some years maybe, his fingernails although cracked in places were actually in a decent, shiny condition.

'Your watch, it is very fine quality yes?' he came out with.

'Err, yeah I guess so,' said David wondering how he even knew.

'It was given to you by someone very special to you? Someone you admire?'

'Admire yes, my boss from back home gave it to me.'

'It had seen many places in the world even before you wore it, yes?'

He was getting worried that he was actually right. An educated guess might have raised the same statement but his boss was an Irishman who was ex RAF regiment, and it had indeed been travelling for much longer without David than it had with him.

'I think so, yes,' is all he said.

'Please, your palm,' he said reaching out to him whilst pulling a small stool out from behind him for David to sit on. He handed him his palm and the man took his glasses off again placing his other hand on top and feeling the grooves in his hand. He concentrated hard as his brow tightened, he was silent but then after a few seconds he started uttering something in his language. About thirty seconds passed before he raised his head taking a deep breath.

'You are alone.'

'Yes,' David answered, assuming he meant right now.

'No, I mean alone, in your thoughts, in your soul, a single man.'

'Maybe, yeah,' he said wide eyed, not quite grasping what he was talking about any more.

'Your time will call you, you carry much pain from what you do not have, you have lust for life that you think you are missing out on.'

'I don't understand,' he said in slight denial.

'You do, yes you do, you are alone and are looking for something or someone, you are not yet sure,' he said raising his voice almost in anger.

David started to cringe as the guy wouldn't let go of his hand but carried on. It was as if he could see through him but still stuck in a small place in David's head was the fact he knew he may have done this a thousand times before and just developed an unnerving technique.

'You have forgotten why you have come away from your home, but you will find that what you were looking for was not so far. You have no brothers or sisters and you do not fear those who are many,' he continued, David picking up that he was now rambling at an unnatural speed, 'money is not important to you, your friends and family are, your feelings for two different women are false, another awaits you on an island. Your past is full of happiness, your year of birth is 1984, your mother and father are very proud. Your present is here in Asia. Watching over you is someone who shares the same birthday but is no longer of this world, she sees through the eyes of the Dragonfly,' he then pointed up with one hand loosely.

David's ears pricked up and he felt the cold, imaginary air hit the back of his neck raising his hairs. Dragonflies . . . someone who shared the same birthday as him was his grandmother. She passed away in the early nineties. Nobody knew this though, only his parents. *How did this stranger get this information?* was the first thought in his mind, relenting to the fact he was benign was even harder, he was about to intervene when the old man started again fading him out.

'You read much about life and follow pacifism, your ways have touched others and they will remember, however, you have a friend at home who needs you right now, she will wait for you but not forever. You are about to enter a dark period, dangerous paths lie ahead of you that could be avoided. She will be your friend when you get back, she will look after you . . .' his words came relentlessly.

'Wait, stop, enough!' said David now mildly upset, his hand held up, his heart beating so strong he thought it was going to fail. The heat above them became draining, the sweat was pouring off of him, more through anxiety and reaction from the old man.

'Why are you doing this?' he asked quickly.

'Some things happen for a reason, these are the very words you voice . . . you fight your feelings and the truth too much, it is a battle everyone is destined to lose . . . do you wish to know more?' he said putting his glasses back on his face.

David had a burning desire to know more even though he was now quite disturbed by this man. He didn't ask but David had the edge to get one up here and planted another six thousand Kyatt into the bowl.

'Please continue,' he said with a scowl.

The old man laughed so loud it turned the head of Cheylam and the bus stop café owner.

'You have stomach young man, young blood, ready for anything, you must choose your words here, use them at correct occasions, fulfil your promises that you have made to yourself . . . for the girl you think you love is not the one, there is another waiting. Your current job in sales will not follow you, your future job will be your biggest step into life at home, you will have a good job and one day you will be happy.'

The strain of his words were starting to really get to him, it caused so many images to flash from his mind, one memory led to another and then twisted his thoughts on how he could have done things differently. Sarah was the one he thought he had once liked but had then been knocked back by distance, to call it love was optimistic but it was the nearest example he could think of. Khin was another on his mind, maybe not so clear in his head but it was the *dangerous path* part that was alarming him, could this path be being walked right now?

'You will be pursued, a girl you know will cause you great harm . . .' he said.

'What . . . who.?'

'It is not clear for me, you must search yourself,' he replied.

'Is it Sarah?' he shot back not even knowing why.

'The one you love . . . she will cause you no harm.'

'That's it?' he said, hands apart waiting for something bigger. His hands were now shaking. He wanted to walk away a second ago but was now compelled to hear more.

'I only offer guidance young man, your path is yours to walk, and your path is yours to change.'

'So . . . who says change is for the better?'

The old man leaned forward and smiled, he nodded gently as if he were studying his face.

'Exactly,' he said quietly.

David smiled back wary that the man seemed to be able to pull parts of his memories from him and turn them into something directional for him.

'Are you really blind?' he asked.

'Yes, but I have seen enough in this world, and see I do . . . very well,' he said becoming less serious and more jovial again. He put his glasses back on and sat back knocking against the side of the small shelter.

'Hmm, let me guess, is the next line gonna be . . . *have you found what you were looking for?*'

'One of the many questions we can only answer ourselves.'

A few seconds of silence followed as he continued with his smile staring into space.

'I think you are needed.'

'Needed?' he asked. That exact same moment he heard Cheylam's voice call from across the flat land of the dirt track road.

'Hey David! Time to go!' she shouted with one hand cupped around her mouth, the other waving.

'OK!' he yelled to her. 'Thank you old man, Ce Zu Timbah-deh,' he said softer towards the old man whilst wiping streaks from his eyes. He went to get up but the old man had already reached for his hand and sat him back down, he held something in his hand giving it firmly to David.

'Go with your heart boy, follow the dragonfly, take this with you,' his tone more up front.

'What is it?'

'You will return here in 2014 with your loved one, bring this back to Asia and place it where your heart feels strongest,' he said before leaning back and releasing his hand again.

Cheylam hollered again from the distance. David held in his fist tight what the old man had given him, remembering that he had not given this guy any information about himself. Cheylam was the first to use his name and he hadn't been asked anything of an informative nature. He hesitated before turning towards Cheylam jogging slowly over to her.

The cave entrance was up a small slope, when they got there they found a monk sitting cross legged by a sign with a large bowl next to him, it was for donations. Cheylam pulled out two carrier bags from a roll in her pack whilst David placed a couple of notes into the bowl bowing to the monk. He received an appreciative smile back with hands placed together. The monk had jet black eyes which flickered in the light as he blinked, David was touched that he had pleased the frail man so much.

'What're the bags for?' he asked Cheylam.

'Your shoes, they are not allowed to be worn inside the cave, you must either leave them here or carry them, but as we are walking right through . . .' she said just shrugging, not needing to finish the answer.

He proceeded to take his shoes and socks off cramming them into the bag, the rustling noise caused the monk to shush him and point across the small pathway to a bush not far from them. David looked around in surprise as a soldier was just to the right of the bush with his back to them. He was slumped in a plastic chair from the bus stop, asleep from what they could make out. His cap was dropped down over his face, his gun resting on his inside leg, pointing skyward. David studied him silently for a few seconds, his boots were heavy duty and shiny as if new, his physique was thin and strong just like the others they had encountered. On his belt strapped a pistol with even a couple of small hand grenades attached behind it.

Cheylam thanked the monk for them both as they then quietly entered the cave holding their shoes in the plastic bags. The inside was dark and confined, the ceiling dripping in places, the floor very slippery and paved with tiles. To his feet it felt like they may have once been raised tiles for some grip but now they were completely flat, no sudden movements down here could be made. There were suspended lights inside which were essential to travel within. A steep set of steps unfolded in front of them, it became a tight tunnel for a while, only as wide as David's shoulders for a short time before opening up into a fork in the path. Cheylam turned around to him, spinning slowly on the saturated floor. She squatted down waving him toward her, David followed her with a squat, she whispered quietly so that the sound of the dripping ceiling could be heard as clear as her voice.

'People are asking about us, I got information from the man at the bus stop, he says soldiers are on much alert.'

'Do they know that it was us?'

'No, but they know it was a tourist.'

'What?! How?'

Cheylam glanced at his boots in the bag he held.

'Footprints,' he said quietly raising his other hand to hold his frowning forehead. The simple errors unsettled him.

'Mhitgal is a very skilled hunter, he must have hidden the bodies. The soldiers will not have found them but he must have missed some footprints as the night came. They think your make of shoes is of a tourist, not many people of Myanmar wear such boots,' she said regretfully.

David looked down at her boots.

'What about you?' he said.

She shrugged, 'They will know a trekking guide is with a tourist in the jungle.'

'So they might come for you too,' he said, guilty of tainting her just by association.

'Unlucky me!' she said laughing.

He smiled now not quite knowing what to think of her reaction. It helped him stop worrying though and it would only cripple his sound mind if he did know anyway. Sensible thought patterns took over, technically, nothing had happened to point an accusing finger straight at them, there could have been many other trekkers around that they didn't know of, even though it was low season.

'So it's easy enough then, we ditch the boots and buy some new ones from here?'

'No, that would look too obvious, we must get new boots yes but we cannot continue walking without them. The only place to sell them is Kalaw, we must be very careful when we return, but for now we are in the safest place.'

'I see, no shoes allowed huh?' he said making them both smile.

They got up and pressed on through a small alcove but reached a dead end. They couldn't help but stop and gaze at the surroundings which had been turned into a shrine. A golden statue of a god took stronghold in the centre near the back wall, it was decorated heavily within the arms and around, flowers, lights of differing colours, it was a calming spot. A scatter of statues lined the walls which made the cave very corridor like. The walls at best were only around seven feet apart without them. None of the figures could be touched, they all held meaning towards the Buddhist following. Cheylam wasn't sure of what they stood for, but the candles amongst them were still lit meaning the monks held them closely to their hearts.

'Monks may be walking around the cave today, it is very large, you must remain silent when they are praying,' said Cheylam.

'No worries,' he replied.

They turned back after retracting from the mysticism of the small inlet and attempted to go the opposite way. Slipping slightly David grabbed a scaffold bar that had been hooked up along the edge of the cave wall. The rust came off on his hand, flaky and cold, he brushed it off and continued down another set of much steeper stairs. Cheylam had to take strides to get down to each one, the handrail was secured at odd angles to hold onto. David stopped and re-tied his hair band, he didn't realise how moist the air was inside until he felt his hair become wet and heavy. As they approached the bottom of the staircase the real cave opened up before them, a massive cavern within bore a myriad of statues of all sizes, all golden, all strewn with lights, some of them intricately, some of them rather carelessly. They passed between the statues slowly, the one to the right of them towered above almost touching the roof. The air was thick enough to taste, their skin became paler under the strange lights.

'How did they get these statues in here?' he asked, knowing the entrances to the cave would be far too small.

'I don't know, maybe they build them inside,' said Cheylam shrugging again.

They looked around in amazement as they passed each one. They were scattered all over, even small statuettes lined the shelves carved into the outer walls. Several more levels of floors followed but they were taking their time, rushing wasn't a good idea knowing how little they had eaten. All David could think of as he carefully took each step was how thin and fragile he felt, if anything like what happened with the soldiers were to happen again he wasn't sure how well he could hold up, especially down here. He knew they weren't permitted by belief to enter the cave, but these were men who were also not permitted to shoot their own religious following by nature. He was prepared mentally that anything could occur, but without the fear. Cheylam stopped in front of a main statue placed within an inlet through a long winding corridor. She knelt in front and started praying in her language, feet pointed away from the image. David held back and said nothing out of respect, he found it rude just to observe. It was her time, along with everyone else in Myanmar where they could feel at ease.

He was never heavily into religion, but he could finally see the difference it made to people. Hope was well and truly kept alive here, they had made this nightmare their home and just dealt with it in any way they had to. Going home sprang to his mind where everyone would be obsessed with being successful in getting a top job, gaining more money than they can handle, boasting how much they can drink at night and how many times they could score in a month whilst moaning about charity workers trying to make them care about someone fifteen thousand miles away who they are never likely to meet. Little did they realise hell was a lot closer to heaven.

A line of monks were painted across the wall deeper inside, they were very detailed for a rock painting, bright orange robes even showing lines where the fabric would ripple as they walked. Some were carrying gifts, food, golden objects and effigies toward an actual statue within the cave, this area was dimly lit. The roof of this part of the cave was dry, the air seemed lighter but the dripping could still be heard all around. Puddles collected near the corners of the room which seemed to have been created due to its solid right angle on one side, the other half where the paintings were was concave. There was a railing in front of this piece. A group of three monks passed them silently, they backed against the wall letting them pass, they showed thanks for what they could as they were clearly in deep meditation down here. As they passed, Cheylam and David exited this room when they heard what they thought was gunshots from the outside. They froze and looked up like rabbits hearing a fox, they looked at each other and then progressed slowly, seeing the exit in the distance Cheylam stopped them to give him the lowdown.

'The exit is up ahead, one last big room to go through, many statues. It doesn't look like anyone is there but there may be soldiers waiting outside, no guarantee,' she said.

'What do we do if there is?'

'Pretend we know nothing, we are on a trek. If they start asking just say you don't know.'

'What if they don't take that for an answer?'

'We make up as we go along?' she said with no confidence.

'Great,' he said to himself suddenly feeling hungry again.

They approached the exit with caution, inching out slowly. Cheylam went first, this felt very unnatural to him but knew if they were seen they wouldn't question why the guide was in front. The stairs for the way out were much dryer than the entrance, and much wider, everything seemed to be in better condition at this end. They moved into the sunshine almost holding their breath to find silence and only trees moving in the wind, they looked around slowly . . . nothing. The jungle was cut back everyday here and a clear cut border was close by with a path carved out snaking through the long grass; it was light green, higher than both of them, swaying slowly with the little breeze there was. They both knelt down putting their boots back on.

'Well, not bad going, there's nothing to see here, which way now?' said David.

'This path, it leads to the train station. If we go now we can get something to eat there, my friend will be there, then we just follow the tracks back to Kalaw.'

Just as he turned around with a good feeling he stepped straight into the jungle path first to be hit hard on the stomach, rugby tackled. All he heard was three footsteps and then felt something slam into his centre of mass. He went down quickly but without pain, more reaction caused him to grab whoever it was; it was a small child, a girl no older than eight years old, very upset, her eyes streaming with tears as she tried to get away from him. It seemed she had not meant to run into them on purpose. Cheylam panicked and at first tried to force her off of him but she sensed the distress quickly letting her up off of David before staggering and then falling to her knees nearer the long grass that shadowed the path.

David took a deep breath as he tilted his head back lying on the ground, he shook his pack off as he got up to take out his inhaler. He took a couple of doses with his elbows raised high to open his lungs. Meanwhile Cheylam was trying to connect with the young girl now crying and wailing on the floor, arms around her knees and head down. She was wearing a nice top before she fell in the mud, it had shoulder straps, one of which was broken as if she had been in a struggle. She was from a local tribe, maybe one of the better off ones nearby the Myin-Ma-Hti caves.

'What the fuck is wrong with her?' asked David, his décor depleted.

'Junta, they were here, they attacked her village,' said Cheylam.

'Fucking great.'

Cheylam continued to calm the girl down as she questioned her softly. The girl never looked up once. Just crying as she forced her words out, she was shaking like a leaf the whole time. David had become hard to it though, his empathy was suppressed, he was concentrating on breathing and hated himself that he became helpless and cold when he needed to be the opposite. With unexpected haste, the girl got up and started running—Cheylam shouted trying to stop her and then ran after her into the long grass to the right of the path. David followed out of instinct. A furious race through the grass unfolded, the long blades cutting them both in random places along their arms. David could barely keep up with Cheylam, just seeing a blur of her back now and again. He had no idea that she had already lost sight of the little girl, one direction change would be all that she needed to do. The wall of grass just overwhelmed them very quickly slowing them both down to a tired saunter as they reached the edge. They batted away the last few blades of grass as they were side by side to find a shocking exit scene in front of them. Their eyes adjusted from the light green straight onto a war zone, another hill tribe, but this time in flames. Huts were on fire, people lay dead around them, it seemed like they were still fighting to defend themselves, cries were heard from behind what they could see. Cheylam grabbed David and pulled him back into the long grass.

'Shh, Junta are still here,' she whispered, staying close to him.

He stayed quiet as they both lay flat as they could, peering through the blades at the destruction. They stayed silent, they could see people running further back in the distance before their view was blocked by a military jeep in the foreground. The jeep stopped and three soldiers got out. They started firing their guns in the air to scare people away, this village was much poorer than they had anticipated from the girl's clothing. People ran from the huts which were only simple designs when the nearest of the three soldiers started taking pot shots at them as they ran not caring if it were women or children they fired at. They were emotionless like the two in their last encounter, like some sort of robot killing machines taught to do one thing alone. They turned around to light a cigarette causing David and Cheylam to duck back behind the grass. Another soldier came out from around the back where the brick buildings were of which even some were ablaze, he was holding a young boy by the hair; he must have been around seventeen, he was only wearing shorts which went below his knees. The boy was topless and skinny, he fought back but to little avail. Every time the soldier grabbed him he threw him back down to the ground. The young boy got up and yelled what seemed like obscenities back at him, throwing a punch and running back. Taking the blow professionally the soldier then grabbed his wrist and twisted it taking him to the floor once more as a message to state who was in charge. The other three he had brought him to were laughing and hadn't even stopped smoking before one smashed him to the ground with his rifle butt. The one who took the blow to the face fro the boy wiped the blood from his lips with the back of his hand and then turned his gun and fired a burst of bullets where he lay. Cheylam and David held their heads to the ground, so tensely, not even being able to tell the ants that were now crawling across their legs from the nerves they felt from it all. David forced his head back up, still half hidden he watched with a pained expression. The soldiers got back in their Jeep and drove off flicking their remaining cigarettes out the window towards the hut setting it ablaze. The slaughter halted when the Junta left the area and only the sound of fire and crying children filled their ears. Only the smell of smoke and sweat filled their senses and for such peace provoked people of furthest kin, only hatred reigned through their thoughts when the silence was finally broken by Cheylam . . .

'She had no parents and they killed her brother, that's why she ran.'

For the first time David realised what Khin had in her memories of her sister. The reaction of the little girl was now much stronger knowing that she most definitely was one of many before.

The smoke cleared when the few remaining people raised themselves from the ground, the few who had to pretend to be dead to stay alive. It started to rain as silky, dark grey clouds crept in from either side of the sky, it helped to put out the last of the fire but his hunger suddenly grew thick within him, twisting his stomach into what felt like knots. Cheylam walked slowly with him out from the long grass to a dry collage of reeds and stems which crackled beneath their feet. The people came to them as soon as they caught sight. She tried talking to them but nothing was consoling them, some of them were left homeless, some of them were left parentless. Nothing was going to trick them into thinking it was going to get better, most didn't even know what to say or ask. A few people of vast difference to each other in age dropped themselves near David, his knees started to tremble again like they had after running through the brush from the first two soldiers. His hands were shaking badly, he tried to hide it as they grabbed for them, his head tried to accompany their needs. *What could I do?* Was what he thought to himself.

Stuck in a trance in the main track of the broken village of Karberan it occurred to them that no matter how long they stayed to talk to them, the damage was done. Cheylam grabbed his arm in safety to pull him on, his mouth hung in disbelief, his mind lagged with confusion, he felt ashamed that his money was still in his wallet. The farmyard smell of the pigs and chickens entered the area again as the animals did, the crops and fields to the west had not been touched by the soldiers, at least they could still eat. Massive loss to them was still unfathomable after the surge of panic. To be alive had become a duty rather than a luxury, the dead were picked up and carried by two members of the families left behind and carried slowly to the fields where they started to dig their graves. Funerals were short and part of it was the digging. Everyone joined in out of respect while scarves, clothing and longyis were draped over the bodies to shelter them from the increasing sun's glare. Cheylam gave up pulling on David, she did however refuse to stand and watch them, she dropped her pack and headed over to them to help dig. David followed by default, hands were the most common tool, only few had shovels or spades. He stood over the young man who had fought back and been killed in front of him, a man with a spade started cutting into the soft crimson soil, getting softer with every minute of rain. David dropped his bag, followed the lines and removed chunks from the ground with his hands along with three others. The tears had stopped for those forced by the situation, only some were still in pieces, mainly women of the deceased, too old and weak to help. After about half an hour of labour creating the hole the body was lifted carefully by five men, one of them David. As soon as they got him in safely still wrapped in cloth bloodstained from his wounds he left to stand with Cheylam. Both were covered in mud, their clothes wrecked with red and black streaks and in regret in having to interfere, a difficult state of mind stayed upon them. The village people got on their knees and said their words to their gods around the body protecting their loss.

'What do we do now?' his tone was lower than she had ever heard.

'Nothing we can do now, we have helped a little . . . we must now let them mourn,' she said as they both watched an old woman kneeling over her sons new grave they had just made. Her blue longyi was sinking into the mud slowly as her knees pierced the shifting ground, she didn't care.

The woman looked up at them both and then fixed her gaze on David, her eyes were grey and cold, she was almost expressionless apart from the defined unhappiness. He could see that her eyes had seen this kind of tragedy before, it made him think about how many other sons she had lost to mindless violence. Feeling as if he was being stared into too deeply he turned his face away from her followed by his body and punished brow.

'I'm sorry I gotta go Cheylam,' he stated. Cheylam didn't argue, she turned right after him, gathered their packs and left straight away. The rain became heavier as they walked straight through the opposite side of the village back into the wild, the red ground appeared more often with the downpour, the rich soil was very uneven. As soon as it eased after another thirty minutes the mosquitoes started to bite, they neared the station as his iPod was about to die, another song came on which he needed to get him away from the nightmare he witnessed in recent events. It was a song about corruption. He'd heard it before but imagined it now in this new context. Cheylam was looking less chipper every step now, some weight lifted off them both as the rain leered up turning the sky back to blue and warming sun, a few seconds was all it took for their clothes to crinkle and crease with the heat again, it didn't move the dirt though.

Another upside greeted them when they caught sight of the station in the distance. It was a large shack, the light shone off the tin roof, the windows were barred this time along with kids hanging from them trying to climb on top with a woman waving a broom at them shouting them back down. The scene pleased them enough to break a smile through their rain drenched hair. The soldiers had definitely not come near here yet.

'Anything we should watch out here for Cheylam?' said David as they moved quicker down the small hill towards the smell of food.

'Yes! Food!' she shouted through a laugh.

His smile widened as he kept up with her, 'How bout a beer and a foot massage?' he threw back playfully.

'You might even be lucky enough for this!'

She slowed down as they got within view of the people there. The Shwenyaung-Thazi railroad station was thriving, a row of stacked out shops were dotted along the so called platform, it was more like a piece of land between the tracks and the shack where the grass had actually been cut.

'We should be safe, Junta will not stop trains, they use them for supplies to Yangon and Mandalay.'

Chickens and livestock were running round almost in same numbers as people. Yaks and cattle were standing by ready to be pulling carts full of fruit being loaded onto them, bright watermelons, bananas, and huge onions and potatoes on the others. Cheylam went straight to the happy shopkeeper who appeared to sell everything, fruit, vegetables, biscuits, bike parts, old radios, chewing gum, nails, hacksaws and a myriad of other next to useless items scattered over the walls and everywhere else. His till was cramped in a small space in the corner, it consisted of a calculator and a locked drawer full of cash. He fixed them both up some noodles handed to them in small intricate bowls with hand drawn pictures of farmers and fields on each side.

'I love eating here, this place has the best noodles in Kalaw. We do not have far to go now, follow the train tracks and then home, maybe one hour or less,' Cheylam assured.

'These noodles are great . . . are we going to be any better off in Kalaw?'

'We will have to see, you may have to check out of the hotel though, they will have pretended that you are not there.'

'Man, won't the soldiers check? They will find my stuff.'

'Don't worry, your stuff will be OK, they will keep it safe, people in Myanmar are very loyal, they look after each other.'

'Even foreigners it seems.'

'Yes, without tourist many people would not be living so well.'

Dust was kicked up into the air when people ran towards the tracks hearing a train approaching, it really was like an old early twentieth century steam train, but smaller than he imagined. The grass growing over the tracks bowed and burnt underneath it as it ground to a halt outside the station.

Fruit and snack sellers exchanged their goods for cash at the windows of the train, no tourists on board from what they could see, but just a scatter of arms hanging out wouldn't have been enough to be sure. People were even on the roof and hanging off the back of the train on small ledges. Some of them stepped off as it stopped and a couple of drivers wearing dirty white long sleeve shirts checked a few of the workings of the train. There were only three carriages but the last one was purely for haulage. Most people were standing on layers of hay on top helping load on more fruit and vegetables from the station tying it up tight with straggly rope. They finished the noodles pretty quick and David took it upon himself to start buying a few more snacks while he was here, the famous spicy crisps in the sealed clear packs were straight in his sight for six hundred and fifty Kyatt. Cheylam offered him a small green fruit along with it. She couldn't remember what it was called in English but assured him it was good and high in vitamins and that was all that really mattered right now. He took a bite instantly making each of the areas in front of his ears tingle from how sour it was, he could taste the vitality things held so much more now than usual. Through the noise from the people by the train he then heard a faint voice very close to him, a monk who had got off the train was introduced to him by the smiling shopkeeper. They sat down on rusty metal chairs together so he could practice his English. His face was wide, he was quite fair skinned, his head shaven and very dark eyes. Simple brown sandals and the classic light orange robes were given huge compliment by his calm and gentle nature.

He was limited with his dialogue but could answer when David spoke slowly and clearly. He used his hands to motion a lot to help.

'What is your name?' he asked.

'David, pleased to meet you,' he replied, 'and you?'

'Nanalankchara,' he said pausing getting his next question together, 'I am Bikkhu, how old are you?' he then asked.

David jumped at the chance to borrow the shopkeepers pencil stashed in his shirt pocket writing the numbers two and five in the symbols Myanmar recognized on a small piece of wood on a cluttered desk. Amazed and touched by his knowledge of this he laughed and had to pull out a phrase book from underneath his golden robes. He didn't get very clearly how old he was until Cheylam interpreted as twenty nine.

'Min-Gala-Ba! Young for your age!' he said clasping his hands and nodding his head in gesture.

Cheylam helped them with the rest of the conversation which consisted of where they had come from. His monastery was by one of the smaller payas which were further into the hills, isolated and no English due to no school nearby. He politely praised everyone in the shop and said 'very nice to meet you' with some difficulty before he left for the toilet. They revealed that he was on his way to Mandalay to see family but Cheylam and the shopkeeper were not so convinced. They spoke together after he had got back on the train more than satisfied with his traveller interaction giving David a cut on their thoughts. They were certain that he was going to join other monks in Mandalay. At times of crisis they helped promote peace but wouldn't cause alarm to anyone by admitting it. The train pulled away whilst blowing its horn and chucking out steam like a lead works. A flurry of arms from the windows were back again waving goodbye as the last snacks were traded by children chasing it down the tracks. Deciding to leave as soon as they felt better to start walking again, they bought another bottle of water each from the shop and set out, his foot was hurting now but figured that another hour wouldn't make any difference but slow them down if he tried to sort out his feet now.

'Hey Cheylam, where's the toilet in this place?'

'Ah, yes, I must go to girl's too, it is just over there,' she said pointing across the tracks to the notoriously crafted wooden hut.

He crossed the tracks taking his pack with him, realizing that there were actually seven sets of tracks making him wonder how many were actually in action. Down the other side was a small downhill path leading to the four foot square shack, he dropped his bag outside, a small hook was in the inside to lock the wooden planks together, he twisted it and turned around to see an image hung on the wall of golden sun spreading its rays across an ocean. As he was taking a piss he noticed something hanging next to it from a small nail wedged between the cracking knots in the wood. It was a piece of the robe the monk was wearing, he pulled it off the edge of the nail and felt how silky it was. Turning it over he noticed that something was written in Burmese on the back, it was a little blurred ,but certainly a message. He shoved it into his pocket as he fastened his belt again, it seemed that Nanalankchara may not have left this here by accident as it would appear to anyone else. He would have to ask Cheylam what it said but wait until they were out of the way first. Stepping outside he grabbed his pack and stepped over the train tracks scanning for Cheylam, the station seemed much quieter now the train had gone. Breathing slowly again he stopped in the centre of the tracks, he closed his eyes and raised his head toward the blue skies feeling very free again forgetting what panic stricken moments they had seen recently. He got his iPod back out ready, the battery was now flashing but he could squeeze a few more songs out of it. The train tracks and slight wind did an amazing job on both of their nerves as Cheylam stepped back out to them too.

'Ready to go?' she said.

'Definitely.'

Diary Entry 6

Today the sun is bearable, it's a nice feeling again rather than uncomfortable like back in Yangon. My hat I got from the market is excellent but has already faded with the heat. Without this soothing place I think I would be in a much worse place in my head, how do I explain? No matter how much I try to distract myself there is always the tension here, it's been a pretty terrifying ride and I feel the worst is still to come. Soldiers are now scanning the area for me, Cheylam is putting her life at risk for me. We are almost back to Kalaw, it's been difficult and many people here have lost lives, not necessarily because of me but because of western presence and stupidity. I can't help but carry some guilt, we all know what we are walking into when we get here and anyone who doesn't are idiots thinking this is just another country in Asia. I hope there aren't any problems when we get back, I picture a line of green hats waiting for me outside my hotel as I walk up. I don't know why I'm even worried here though, it will be worse in Yangon if I have to try and fly back out from there, it'll be a wonder if I even get out of Shan state . . . I have no idea how bad things are in Mandalay yet. I'm just about keeping the high jump over the bar, but each day is becoming a struggle. I move forward not looking back in a world of loneliness. I've never seen such horror. I don't know what the fuck I'm talking about any more. I really just wanna get out of here.

The track cleared completely as they followed it around the last hill that was visible for a while, about twenty minutes went by when a rusty old orange tractor passed them with three young men hanging onto it waved hello. It was now early afternoon and the remaining adrenaline was wearing off, they broke off from the track knowing they would find it again a few minutes later within an enclosed set of shrubs in the near distance crossing a marshy, sticky set of fields, boots and socks not getting any cleaner by the second. The bushes then filtered into a tunnel effect, the tracks were right down the centre. It was obvious the bushes had been planted around these tracks many years ago due to their tremendous height, they towered above both of them easily doubling David's height. Cheylam stopped a few moments in to rest but it wasn't a good time, the bushes were thick and David noticed they were full of spiders as he peered through them to the specks of sunlight that penetrated. Moths and dust were hanging from its innards. She no longer looked well as she rested her hands on her knees. This area also played havoc with David's breathing, he could feel his chest tighten feeling like the bush had sprouted growth within him labouring his breath. He unzipped the pocket on his bag for his inhaler, shook it up, held it to his mouth and forced the shaft down as if it were going to make a difference to its power.

'Is this a good place to stop?' he asked.

'Just for second, I get tired now, maybe we both sleep very well tonight in Kalaw,' she said breathless and coughing a little.

'These bushes are bad Chey, we should move out and then stop.'

'Yes, maybe you're right,' she said peeling her hands off her knees and rising back up, her sweat had increased in volume across her brow. Then she paused and froze a quizzical look with her head high and mouth slightly open.

'What is it?' said David.

'Shh,' she said silencing him with a finger to her lips, she then held out her arms and got slowly to her knees and then put an ear to the ground.

'Look out!' she said clambering back up and grabbing him, forcing him into the bushes.

'What the fu.?'

'TRAIN!' she shouted as they heard the chugging. It started hammering fiercely toward them blindly from around the bend they were on. They pushed hard into the bushes as they caught sight of the train, although it was slow it was still going at a speed dangerous enough to kill anything let alone make their hearts race. He felt the sting of the sharper edges and the dusty powder against his face that the insects had left. The locomotive headed directly toward them and then turned with the tracks just before it got too close to them. People were still hanging off of it and jumping right out at them to give high fives and cheering, it was insane. Each carriage made his head pulse as they jutted out turning the bend in an awkward fashion making it seem like it was swinging for him with a ten tonne fist as each one passed. As the last carriage passed by them they slumped back onto the tracks. Cheylam started coughing harder now, she crawled over to the bushes just opposite and coughed up, it sounded awful. David just stood up with his mouth open brushing the webs and insect dust off of his right arm and backpack. He handed Cheylam a bottle of water and spurred her on in hope that it was merely the bushes making her feel ill, somehow that hope just wouldn't stick. The more time he gave her to sort herself out the more she coughed, the dust from the train had really clouded the air and he could feel his lungs ceasing up again. He took forethought on this one and grabbed her by the arm pulling her the direction they had started in and through the dust. Holding a cloth to her face she staggered through the clearing at the other end to more fields. David joined her as she lay sprawled on the grass by the tracks. Greeted with a head rush feeling he closed his eyes trying to block out her battle with the air and took comfort on the hard ground, he could feel his back spread and click.

'Shit, it's been a hell of a long day,' were the words he forced out of his breath.

Diary entry 7

I've had a shower which actually was the best feeling of the week but now I'm so tired. We just made it back to Kalaw today around 4pm, much longer than it would normally take. The Junta are still hunting for us . . . well . . . me. The hotel still has my stuff, they have been hiding it from the inspecting troops. I owe them my life already but they are continuing to help me, never have I felt so indebted. I can't think straight right now so what I write may not make any sense to you, not that anyone will ever read this shit anyway. Cheylam is coughing hard now but is back with her brother safe, that's all I care about now, that everyone is safe. This life threatening experience has lowered my expectations of people and what is available, but heightened my senses and expectations of what is furthermore possible to come. I am still in danger here but my room is a place of rest to me either way. I am leaving tomorrow night, the hotel staff say it will be easier to move around at night. They have organized my getaway . . . this is fucking insane, I'm crashing out.

CHAPTER VII

Storm

Day 9

The forest was beautiful, he felt a small shivering feeling on the top of his head and down his neck, stimulating his next moves. He sat down with Cheylam and the three boys, Shuren, Kannan and Tenchenk. They had been picking mushrooms from the forest, they were all on the edge of the dirt track they had followed for miles. They were all happy but David was tired and his right foot was feeling like it was swollen inside his boot, the red dust had started to get to him too. The boys were very shy of him, they didn't want photos. He took the biscuits he had bought at the station earlier from his bag and handed them a couple each, Cheylam was happy to accept too. A man soon came along to join them, for a moment it appeared to be Mhitgal but as he climbed the steep bank next to them on closer inspection it was a younger man, maybe mid twenties with a broad smile, he was also happy to take a cookie. Cheylam seemed to know him and translated to David that he had been working with the three boys in hunt for herbs and small animals. David took a moment to try and taste a cookie, he wanted one that tasted like a cookie back home, not a dry, flat taste like this one. He found it disappointing but accepted that natural taste was not what he was brought up with. The hills either side of them were carved at a very steep angle, light shone through the tall trees like needles.

As he chewed slowly he saw the man become alert and jump to his feet, naturally all the adults joined him in stance. He whispered to Cheylam who then turned to David and told him soldiers were close; he figured he must have heard a march or a jeep engine or something. The boys scattered before anyone could advise them otherwise and ran into the higher grounds of the forest, the man they accompanied ran down the hill with Cheylam but away from David. He tried his best to keep up spitting out the remainder of the cookie but his physical movement seemed laboured, lethargic, his legs were solid like bars of lead yet still shaking. The downhill pace was hard on the shins. After a matter of seconds he was calling out for Cheylam as the trees thickened slowing him right down, he knew it was probably the most stupid thing to do but he was left no choice. He was forced to give up as they fell completely out of sight and tripped falling hard downhill and straight into a tree ribs first. The pain didn't really connect with his mind, he checked his ankle and caught his breath back hastily. He seemed fine so he carried straight on feeling his veins pulse. Something caught his eye which was strange, as he got back up and braced his knees for running again he looked up just above the canopy to hear a swoop from a flock of dark birds, they looked like crows but he wasn't sure what they were. He didn't have time to think but they definitely did not change his mood to pressing on and finding a hiding place. Up and running again he felt his pack from side to side before the trees opened up suddenly revealing another path that he stopped straight out in the middle of that ran horizontally across his view.

Flipping his head to the left revealed a clear path, but then to the right he was clasped eyes upon by a group of soldiers. His eyes widened as they raised their guns and shouted. Unbelievable even to his own train of thought he jumped to the left without thinking, continuing down the bank of the hill that was now becoming endless. It was a bold challenge for David, their pace was far advanced over his. He scrambled through the trees before feeling his pack being grabbed from behind, he was stopped almost instantaneously before being dragged to the floor but fought back knowing it wasn't worth giving up. Knowing he was cornered he decided to make it difficult for them, their voices echoed around him like a siren but

David remained silent grappling hard with the soldier now in front of him pulling him to the floor and tumbling down the hill together. As the straps of his pack snapped David played and lost the Russian roulette chance of where they would stop and who would be left on top, it was easily the soldier. His arms were now exhausted, he felt he had well and truly been overpowered; the soldier pulled a pistol from his belt, pointed it square between David's eyes and fired.

David awoke with a start, his right arm flailed and knocked over a bottle of water on the bedside table.

'Ah fuck!' he voiced scrambling for it.

He lay back down realizing that the bottle would have been sealed. He placed an arm across his face to comfort himself, taking deep breaths to control his heart pace he knew instantly that it had been a dream. Despite the dire turn of events within it, it didn't affect the well slept feeling he needed so badly, he also still felt fresh from the shower the night before.

He lifted his feet from the bed and sat up rubbing his head, his eyes still sensitive to light streaming through the edges of the emerald green curtains on the other side of the room. He smoothed his ruffled hair back into a reasonable tie and walked over to them holding one open and peered into the bright streets. Yaks pulling carts, kids carrying baskets of crops, an old man on a bike, it was like the beautiful little town he arrived in again. He then drew the curtains and walked into the bathroom, using the sink to wash his face he took his hair down completely and stared into the mirror for a moment reflecting on where reality was in his head. His mind was blank, instead of being upset, bewildered, frightened, vulnerable . . . nothing, he felt nothing, just the odd ache and pain through his bones with which he found strangely satisfying. He tried so hard to find an emotion but just found a robot like stare.

'Christ, what the fuck has happened to us man?' he questioned himself in the mirror shaking his head.

As the morning brightened the curtains revealed just how worn they were, he refused to open them, holding his head in the bathroom in front of the mirror he felt as if his mind were caving in. Not knowing why he was here along with what had happened became a reality, aftershocks came to him in visions and his dreams were now toying with him. He opened his mouth wide to see the new ulcers he could feel inside, they were dry and prickly as his tongue moved. Steadying one hand with the other he reached into his bag that had been hidden for days to pull out a sealed wash-bag full of shower gel, toothpaste and various other useful substances and items. He searched out his razor, a flimsy plastic handle with an attachment for blades that had rusted, he bought it in a hurry when leaving Cambodia which was some time ago now. He had one new blade left for it and seemed that it was the best time for its use. He fixed it to the end discarding the rusted one and pressed it against his face in the dimly lit bathroom, staring into the mirror as if he was staring at some stowaway who had been stranded for years. He felt sorry for himself but didn't know why, *was this the beginning of depression?* Pressing the razor into his face caused some blood to run down his cheek, he pulled it away, cleaned himself up and carried on albeit with a scowl. He managed to shave half of his face when the electricity cut out forcing him to open the curtains in the main room even though he had been advised not to. He remembered a little line he saw somebody put on internet a few weeks back that made an impression on him, it was one of his travelling friends he had met on the way. He quoted it to himself:

'Life . . . the longest multiple choice exam you will ever take . . . except there's no examiner and you might never know what grade you got at the end . . . I gotta get rid of this,' he said to himself, referring to the hair on his head. It looked long and tattered, fraying, making him look older than his years. Eight years of growth meant a lot to him but it felt dead and in the way now.

After nearly two hours of slowly getting ready, aching bones became something that he would just have to deal with, he went downstairs to take a trip out to find a barber. Before he could reach the end of the road he had the owner of the hotel running after him waving a tea towel in the air shouting after him at a volume as low as she could.

'Mister! Mister!' he turned to face her. 'Please mister, you must not leave hotel, dangerous, what do you need?'

'It's OK, I just need a haircut, you know? Barber?' he said making a scissor action with his fingers by his hair.

'Oh I see, no, this way please, this way, we can do for you, you must eat breakfast first though, no go hungry,' she said considerately.

'I thought I missed breakfast, it's like eleven twenty!' he said in a daze as they turned back towards the hotel entrance together, genuinely forgetting about eating anything. Laughing deliriously he staggered to the dining area of the hotel where a tear fell from his eye causing him to be embarrassed a little, he wasn't sure if it was joy or shock. Feeding him a larger breakfast than usual, and later than usual he sat alone making the most of each taste that served him not worrying how much it irritated the ulcers in his mouth. It was *Mohinga*, a fish soup mix which was very traditional, slightly spicy and one of his favourites. They gave him some mouthwash to alleviate the pain and about an hour later they served lunch, this time western food, an attempt at a full American breakfast without the waffles but toast instead, they called it the 'Continental'.

Shortly after lunch the daughter of the owner came out with a sheepish look and a pair of clippers in her hand.

'Hello mister, would you like cut? Electricity is working again,' she said in her slow pronounced English.

He couldn't help but crack a smile to one side, the next thing he knew he was singing loudly and carelessly but happily as they shaved his head from around seventeen inches to a grade three. The whole point was to block out the attachment he had with it for so long, he felt naked without it. He sung a song he liked that his friend back home wrote spontaneously.

'I've been fixing things. Taking a selection of my angel wings, and staring at reflections of my evil soul, nobody remind me of my evil soul . . .'

'You have beautiful voice!' she said loudly and sarcastically just to silence him.

'Why thank you my dear, some say it's my best feature, some say I don't deserve my status . . . they my dearest . . . are fools,' he said in an upper class, amusing accent whilst taking a drag from an imaginary cigar in between words.

His new short hair was refreshing; it felt much healthier and easier to deal with. He kept brushing it with his palms trying to come to terms that it wasn't going to restrict his vision any more, he didn't like it though. Sitting out on the balcony of the hotel the staff had told him that they would feed him and bring him anything he wanted provided he stayed in the hotel. He didn't really have a choice, if the wrong people were to see him walking around town someone would eventually have to tell a soldier, which would then lead to his arrest. Several beers were scattered around that he gave the young girl money for, around twice the amount they actually cost each time just to thank her for getting it. The alcohol was strong and old, dusty, as if it had been sitting on the shelves for ages, most of it was unfortunately warm too. He had drunk a bottle of Myanmar beer already and just cracked open a bottle of Dagon beer. He wasn't keen on it.

'Tastes like shit,' he said to himself almost drunk, it didn't seem to stop him from drinking it though.

A book a traveller gave him was the only saviour of boredom, called 'Tear me Down', it was about a guy who was caring for his dying brother trying to get closer to the meaning of life. For a while he was engrossed in it when his tunnel vision was broken by a dragonfly flying right past him and then circling around the balcony again. That moment he heard someone call for him and knock on the windows of the entrance. It was Shael, he had come to warn him about the escape plan, and to collect some money from him.

'Hello again my friend,' he said with a tone ready to get things done.

'Shael!' he said with glee, raising the beer with one hand to him, 'care to join me for one buddy?'

'No thank you, I do not drink any more,' he said waving it away before sitting down, 'ah I see you have shave your growings, it look very handsome,' reminding him that Shael's English was not as precise as Cheylam's.

'Ce-zu-beh, ce-zu-beh, I'm still getting used to it though. I have your money, please take this,' he said leaning over to delve into his right pocket. He took fifty United States Dollars from his wallet for him but Shael at first wouldn't accept saying it was too much.

'Twenty, please, only twenty,' he pleaded.

'Shael, let me tell you something, I may not be of sound mind right now, in fact I think I'm going fucking crazy but if there's one thing that keeps me, and everyone else in this place sane . . . it's the overwhelming relief that people can trust and help each other out. Now I feel dirty as hell giving you this because it's only money but you and Cheylam have already helped me with things worth so much more.' He rambled holding his left hand to his right elbow. Shael, even though grounded by his words was still reluctant.

After a long, friendly stare David took his palm and pressed the money into it.

'Just take it, it's my way of looking after you,' he said leaning back into his chair and cocking his finger at him.

'Min-Gala-Ba my friend, I shall not forget this.'

'It's my honour,' he replied taking another swig.

'How is Cheylam doing by the way? Any better?' he asked.

'Yes, she will be fine thank you, she must rest for a few days, she is not used to such things happening with tourists in danger.'

'Well, please let her know that I'm forever grateful to her. I owe her my life, and Mhitgal,' he replied.

'Mhitgal?!' he said with surprise.

'Yeah you know, the guy in the treetop café.'

'Ah yes, please know I have had many experience with Mhitgal, more than a few people owe their lives to him. I am happy you have told me he was there, but unhappy as I know what it must take for him to interfere,' said Shael.

'Fuck a duck my Burmese brother! His interference was shall we say, more than welcome in the heady atmosphere of terror and treachery,' he said swigging the bottle again.

From Shael's expression it seemed he had no clue what he had just said and figured the drink was taking a stronger affect on him. He got to the point before he thought that David was past the grasp of it.

'But I must inform you now of what will happen for your escape,' he cut in.

David laughed at the usage of the trivial word 'escape' but coming to terms that that was actually what it was now. Shael continued, 'I must now take you tomorrow night, it is too dangerous tonight, the patrols are to get stronger because of market day tomorrow, after then, it will be safer.'

David leaned forward with a frown suggesting his attempt at focusing on the situation, his words became slightly slurred though and his eyelids were becoming harder to co-ordinate.

'That's fine by me bud, I feel like shit today anyway, what transport do I have?' he asked.

'My friend has pick up truck that I borrow, I drive you overnight, but there are conditions. First you may need to get in the back, we disguise you as crops.'

David couldn't help but crack a smile, 'You trying to pass me off as a fruit now Shael?' he said jokingly.

'The borders will be dangerous, we must take secret routes through directions I know to get to Yangon. I must leave you in Yangon, once you are in British Embassy you will be safe, they will get you home,' he said.

'So how long will it take to get down there? Do want any petrol money?'

'It will take about . . . ten to fifteen hours if no problems, and no money for fuel, service included,' he said holding up the fifty dollars. They both laughed.

After they traded information enough to fulfil the unstable moments of concentration, Shael headed home to look after Cheylam and David was left with his fuzzy world of nonchalance. Watching the dragonflies circle closer to the ground the air became thicker, warmer, his chest became heavier. He reached in his left pocket for his inhaler, as he pulled it out he also pulled out the scrap of material he found, it had created a natural wrap around what the blind fortune teller had given him. They were mustard seeds, not regularly grown in Myanmar but used mainly in dishes. He pulled a small, transparent, re-sealable plastic bag out of his day sack which was lying next to him on the floor to contain them for the rest of his journey. He unwrapped the material, the words, stained in yellow against the dark orange were no more blurred than what they were when he had found it. They meant nothing to him now but somehow knew they would eventually.

Later that afternoon he had fell asleep in a drunken wreck on the balcony, he was only awoken by a determined mosquito gunning for his right arm. He slapped it killing it, but left a stain of blood on him. He staggered back to his room with blurry vision, after fumbling with the keys he got in to find his clothes washed, folded and laid out on the bed in a pile. It really was the simple things they did for him that touched him. Putting his iPod dock on which was fully charged again was a luxury. He got changed and put on a hoodie ready to go out against the hotels advice.

It was nearing six in the evening, he wanted an internet connection to tell people back home what had happened. As he walked up the street he realised that the hoodie, meant to disguise him a little, was of no use. However he dressed, he stuck out like a dead tree in winter with his height. A kid on a bike cycled past him smiling, 'Hello mister!' he said waving as usual. David waved back almost forgetting that it wasn't polite to give people a high five. Just as he got to the internet café it started to rain heavily, although it was well lit inside it was the perfect cover by steaming up the windows. The same guy waved him in, he was clearing up cables and sweeping the floor ready to close up but he was happy to let one more customer in. He advised that he would only be open another thirty minutes but David wouldn't even need that long, he knew exactly what he was going to say and to whom. One e-mail went to his parents, one to his best friend Richard, he worked in a high rollers lounge up in London and therefore knew he would be able to get anyone out of a few financial scrapes. His contacts would be pretty handy even in a situation like this, it was a long shot but if anything was going to be sorted out in London, Richard would be at the heart of it. His final e-mail was the reply to Sarah, he told her everything and that he wanted her back when he got home, if that was even possible. Although his deluded state warped his concentration he didn't slip up once, he double checked every line to make sure he didn't give away where he was or where he was going. Apart from some junk mail, a few offers from shopping websites and old booking confirmations he hadn't bothered to open, he noticed one from an unknown address. He clicked on it squinting his eyes, nervous that it might be an official e-mail or something. He quietly read it aloud . . .

David,

I must write to tell you, things not good in Yangon. You must be careful when you come back. Soldiers everywhere, big uprising, please when you come back contact me, will help you return home.

I wait for you.

Khin x

It was brief but pretty much clarified the situation. It was dated 8th November, anything could have worsened since then. There was no point in replying to her yet, he wasn't even sure of his plans any more. He thought for a moment that they might be able to track the IP address of the computer or a moment after logging off but just pushed the idea aside marking it as unlikely. Feeling the hunger grip his stomach he left the internet café setting out for Dale's restaurant again.

He got to the front door and knocked a few times, Dale came to the door surprised to see him.

'Oh, hello mister, please come in sit down,' he said.

He wasn't surprised to find that he was the only one in there again. People from his family were scattered around the big TV at the back of the room. They were watching Dale's videos that he had taken of his travels around Myanmar, they played out like mini documentaries trough a VCR. Now that he thought about it, it was the only time he had seen a VCR since he entered the country. Dale locked the door behind him and turned the open sign around.

'Good evening Dale! Are you even open tonight?' he asked.

'Yes, yes, please, let me get you a menu,' he said.

David noticed Dale's friend was at the back of the long room sitting in front of a chess board—Dale had been playing with him. After ordering he unzipped his pack taking out his journal.

Diary Entry 8

What the fuck have I done? It's been a blurry mess today, I've had too much to drink and too little to eat to gather sanity. I've e-mailed home explaining everything, it's been less than an hour since then but I'm regretting it already, I'm going to worry the shit outta people back home when I know there's nothing they can do about it. I also replied to Sarah, it doesn't feel like that one was real though. I let her know how I feel now and how I feel for her, usually it would bother me for hours thinking about what to say but I just typed it out once, carelessly. I don't feel like me, if I wasn't and was given a choice I wouldn't even know who to be right now. The military are like a killing machine when you're on the wrong side of it, they don't give a shit about anybody. Shael is going to try to execute my 'escape' and get me back to Yangon tomorrow night. He says it will be safer by a route he knows, it will skip all the border crossings, it's highly illegal but If I get caught I don't think I'll get lucky enough to be threatened

*with deportation somehow. Cheylam is at home recovering. I am outside my
hotel about to eat dinner at Dales when I shouldn't be. I have also cut my hair
off, it was becoming a matted tangled obstruction. It's made me feel emotionally
unprotected and cold even though it's warm. The people here are the best, they
give everything they can towards safety of visitors. Expectations of a realistic
mind only stretch so far though.*

*All the books and visions of being away from home don't add up, where do
they get all the idealistic shit from? A honeymoon on Tahiti in a three hundred
dollar a night suite with tours, transfers and free cups of coffee doesn't seem
worth it any more. What do we come away for? Are we really escaping from
what we don't want to know any more? The people here have never escaped,
but yet still embrace pride for their country, they're restricted from applying for
passports.*

*With every closing door another opens here and although they can't get out
of the prison, they wouldn't try even if they could. They strive to stand still and
change their quality of life . . . I strive to fly far away and change something
I'm not even sure of. I think my dinner is coming in a moment, smells so good.
One things for sure, there is definitely no shrink around to tell you the difference
between right and wrong. I sit here in a land that hasn't learnt stability on any
level yet. What choice do I have but to abide.*

Day 10

David got home that night after a long chat with Dale and a final game
of chess. The hotel staff had noticed he was gone but had ignored it, they
gave in to his wandering nature. The next day passed hastily, he felt better
and used the mouthwash again to soothe his now stinging mouth, it hurt
to eat breakfast. He got all of his stuff together and left it in the storeroom
of the hotel, he checked out at a time he was supposed to even though they
didn't expect it. On the upside he had slept like a baby, he felt refreshed bar
the few aches and pains in his bones and muscles. Later in the afternoon he
dropped by to say goodbye to Cheylam and load his stuff into the Toyota
pick-up. It was white and splashed with dirt. It only had two seats but

was in pretty good condition, the hotel had given him some snacks and even a bag of tea when he paid up for the room and service. Everything he had was now washed and he felt strong enough for the journey. Shael was loading up the back end with hay to conceal him near the base of the rear. The space was small but the more it was padded out the better. The hay was an added request from his cousin who wanted it delivered to a farm on the way to Yangon, after they dropped it off he had plastic covers to hide him.

'So how long do you think I will need to hide in the back?' David asked him.

'Do not worry, only about half the way, there are more border crossings down south, there will be soldiers around sometimes but if we hide you we have better chance of no worries,' he replied.

'Well, I think it's gonna be a bumpy ride whatever happens,' he said quietly to himself as he looked at the small space he would be calling home for the next few hours.

'I must now finish a few things and get ready, please come back at six o' clock to leave. I will make sure your luggage is safe and hidden with hay. We will stop at station for dinner but If you would like anything you need to take for food maybe you should go buy at the market,' he warned.

Turning out to be a great idea he did as he was advised and bought some drinks and snacks for the road. It was only three in the afternoon so he wasn't rushed, he figured he'd buy a couple of longyis to use as blankets along with a couple of beers. It could get colder later on in the open air and after all, they wasn't going to stop them for drink driving if he wasn't driving, or even present. After a stop at the market, where he discovered a new taste for rare whiskies and other very cheap alcoholics covered in dust, he went and stood in the middle of the street and looked up at the stairs by the main road that he saw the monks walk from. They had started their scheduled walk again. Paying the market stall owners for his items he then took a wander up the stairs. They passed the narrow, unlit road that Cheylam and Shael lived on and escalated further into the trees. As he climbed he felt the air lift, even the bag full of bottles felt lighter to him, it must have been a psychological reaction from the bright view in front of him as he reached the top, even the wind felt more alive where he stood now. The steps ended and a series of small wooden, hand built staircases were now in front of him to climb at all angles where the banks of grass were uneven. Seeing the temple appear slowly as he ascended he was surprised at how bright it was, white this time with hints of gold and bright colour decorating the edges, the area seemed so much more alive than the town below even though there were less people, less noise and much less conversation. Two young monks in their late teenage years approached him, they spoke clear English.

'Hello, can I help you?' one said.

Surprised by the question he didn't really know what to answer. He assumed monks could help people in some higher form that regular people didn't know of. He thought that if he reached the state of mind that they had, how would he translate help to someone who didn't understand? Realizing he was over analysing the question he just answered politely.

'Er, Min-Gala-Ba. I've just come to visit, I am leaving for Yangon very soon and never took a walk up here until now.'

They showed him around the small garden areas in between their praying times. The paya was smaller than that of the one in the town centre, they weaved around it and stepped deeper into their grounds. A small Buddha image about half the size of a fully grown human sat cross legged at the rear of the narrow hedges separating the view of everything else. The monks sat in front bowing delicately to their deity, thanking him for the life they now lead. David did the same, pointing his feet away from the image. Instead of bowing he just closed his eyes forgetting that he was actually in danger here and remembering that he was walking around breathing, eating. He was unsure of anything like a god or higher being watching over him but he was being watched over by the people here and that was more than he could ask for, a deed good enough to recognize as faith for him. He opened his eyes relaxed, his heart slowed to the point where he thought it might stop but knew it wouldn't, it wasn't his time yet, he had stories to tell when he got home, he was confident that he would actually make it now.

Before leaving he talked more with the monks and laughed at life and all the things he had experienced. He stopped out of tact not wanting them to change their pure outlook on life, temptation was void within them. It is what had kept them free of boundaries, they had helped a traveller put a smile back on his face during a time of chaos. He felt enlightened being surrounded by them, others joined and then departed leaving the two boys he had met first with him. Walking him back to the base of the staircase he said goodbye. Almost welling up inside as if he had known them for years, he looked at the floor and then back over his shoulder where Shaels Toyota awaited him. It looked like Shael was in his house still, he had ten minutes left anyway. Seeing an opportunity he pulled out the scrap of material with the writing on from his pocket and looked pained to ask the favour of translating it for him.

'Can you help me with one last thing my friends?' he said.

'Anything,' they said almost in time. He handed them the scrap.

They scanned it together, for some reason the moment felt like forever until they both smiled and looked up at him. One of them looked to the distance; his face bright with intrigue, the other gave him his answer.

'Ah my friend, you are very fortunate, this message is a blessing. It is meant only for you written by someone you have touched souls with,' he said, he then leaned closer and whispered in his ear before they turned back to their paya enclosure. David smiled and took a deep breath, by now he had heard Shael calling his from behind, he raised a hand in acknowledgement, slowly exhaling he took one last look at the scrap and then put it away again. He felt lighter than he had for ages.

The sky started to darken at an intimidating pace, the sun hid behind the trees hastily and darkness formed through the means of black rain clouds. David stepped up to Shael's car, it was ready to go, full of fuel. He double checked everything with him, the rules of the road, the bags they had, the ways they were hidden behind the hay and what to do if they were confronted. He concentrated taking every possibility into account. His efforts were shattered into a few hundred pieces when Shael told him that there would be a change of plan. Shael had been sounding uneasy and looking at his watch it made sense as to why when a white man came running towards them clumsily from the distance of the back street.

'Ah, there you are!' said Shael as the man approached taking his bags off. The young man around his late twenties took his rucksack off and stumbled onto the truck resting on the edge with both hands.

'Hey fellas! How's it hangin?! . . . Phew, what a fuckin' rush,' he said.

David looked quizzical not knowing if he was more baffled by the guys language or his general behaviour, his odour didn't do him any favours either. His shirt was long sleeve and white, torn badly in places and caked with stains, his shorts, hanging low on his waist making his boxer shorts visible, covered his knees but also looked like they had been through a few rosebushes. His boots were quite worn too but too big for him by the way he staggered. He seemed drunk.

'David, this is Tanner, you will both be travelling together tonight. I am nearly ready, just getting a can of fuel for emergency,' said Shael as he shuffled back into the house. Straight away Tanner put his hand out.

'Pleased to meet your acquaintance brother,' he said with an American accent.

'David, pleasure, so what's your story?' he asked just being polite trying not to think of what this journey might be like now.

'Ah Christ man, where do I start? How 'bout we get this show on the road then we got all night to catch up and . . .' he said before noticing the beer and snacks in David's bags, ' . . . holy shit! Now that's what I'm talkin' 'bout, hell, the back o' this baby could be the biggest party in Myanmar tonight, eh?' he said loudly causing embarrassment all round.

He wasn't drunk but David could smell that he had definitely necked a few beers during the day, he seemed to be taking it better than he was so far though. They equipped the truck to make enough space for two of them to lay down with their backs up against the cab. several waterproof sheets to cover them from rain was very necessary as it had just started to spit down.

'Come, we must go, if I go to fast just knock on the window, we stop around nine clock for dinner at service station, do you have everything you need?' said Shael hasty to get away, one leg already inside the drivers door.

'I'm ready thanks Shael,' said David.

'FUCK YEA! In the name of inhuman manipulation of the poor souls of Myanmar, lets blow this joint so we can tell the world!' said Tanner making David cringe and get in quicker.

They got in and under the rain sheets pinned to the top of the cab creating a tent effect with a couple of blankets, David made sure his iPod was there at the ready, he figured he would have to block out Tanner with something during the night. Although he annoyed him the second he met him, he remained intrigued as to why someone with his outlook on life was in a place like this. David cracked open a beer for them both and asked him outright. Shael had pulled away and was travelling slowly along the main road leading to Mandalay.

'So then, where you from Tanner? How did you wind up here under the canopy of Myanmar?'

'I like your style dude' he said as he brought his head in from the increasing rain. Sweeping his blonde shoulder length hair back he continued, 'I'm from Ohio, turned up here on a whim, been travelling for a few weeks now. Started in good old India and thought I'd stop by to see what was here on my way to Thailand where I start work.'

'Man, so was there something you wanted to see or do here?' asked David.

'Nah, check out what shit was going down, few drinks, few whores ya know?'

'Well not exactly, did you read up on any history of this place, sounds like you'd be better off going straight to Thailand for all that.'

'Hell I know that now' he said with distant eyes, he took another sip of his beer, 'this is one luxury this place has got, hey thanks for this man it's really just what I needed tonight' he said genuinely grateful holing out one hand to clasp with Davids in a brotherly manner.

'So what are you planning to work as, your job already lined up for you?' he asked.

'Pretty much, my brother runs a bar on Kho Phangan, he'll give me a guaranteed job if I don't find anything else, if he's still there that is' he pulled a cigarette from his back pocket, putting it to his mouth he cupped his hands over it to light it. He offered David one but he declined.

'Still there?' he asked.

'Well he doesn't know I'm coming.'

'He what? You're just turning up on him, that's bold.'

Tanner just coughed and smiled at him, proud of his spontaneous ways, David admired his carefree attitude but couldn't yet workout if he was here for a reason other than what he was saying.

'So what brought you to Kalaw? '

'Well I started a trek from Inlay lake, got a bit bored of the scenes and beggars over there after a couple of days, thought I'd try something I'm not used to ya know, then about half way through we got caught up in a village where we stayed overnight,' he explained.

'You mean you were with somebody else?'

'Yeah, I mean the trek guide dude' he cleared up.

The bumps in the road started to deepen as they felt Shael slow down, although it was raining harder now the temperature was still warm, David took another sip of his beer thinking of another question that would bring the lighter side of this guy to the surface. They had to raise their voices to hear each other.

'Did something happen then? Were you not meant to end up here?' he asked.

'Hell no, I didn't even know this place *was* here until yesterday, they said it'd be easier to drop me here rather than turn back cos of the shit that kicked off back there in the jungle. Back at the village I was taking a shower when my trek guy ran into some soldiers that came and questioned the village, they started pushing him around and shit so I stepped out to tell em exactly what I thought of em. After an exchange of about six disenchanting words of English, BOOM! . . . some local managed to blow up their fucking transport, I just ran back to the shower after I saw about eight locals running at me with shovels and shit'.

'Geez . . . so what did they actually want in the first place?' asked David.

'Who? . . . the locals or the soldiers?'

'Both of em.'

'Well the soldiers as far as I could work out were talking about some tourist guy who'd fucked up in Yangon with a political prisoner, wanted information from other tourists to see If they knew anything. The locals wanted to beat the shit out of them for assaulting their kids about it, I watched some of it through the cracks of the wood in the shower, looks like they weren't gonna let em go back to HQ alive you know what I'm saying?' he went on. 'By the time I stepped out it was all over, it was like a fucking revolution in front of me for all of two minutes'.

'Man, sounds like you got lucky with that one, so the trek guide brought you back to town after?'

'No, the trek guy got injured there and then, the locals got me back here. Just stayed in a hotel where Shael got in touch . . . now I'm drunk on the back of a truck with shitty suspension and an Englishman' he laughed.

Although David didn't fully trust Tanner, his suspicions were nullified from his reactions. He was quite a seedy individual, not hiding it either, but appeared honest and spoke his mind, although this was the worst place to be in to do that. David could see that it would attract the worst kind of trouble they could get, but for now it was easy, they had no choice but to contain themselves. At the moment there was no-where to go.

The darkness grew quickly, as they travelled slowly and dealt with each undulation in the road by bracing their backs for the next one. Mountainous views were now stormy night terrors, daring not to look over each side of the truck from fear of how close they came to the mountainous bends they hid beneath the blankets and covers. Even with his iPod headphones wedged firmly in his ears the driving rain, the engine and the storm were still present as if it was in his head. About two hours passed before they started talking in depth again. The rain died down and fortunately the cracks in the base of the pickup were letting the water through to the road keeping them slightly dryer.

'So what about you old bean? Age, sex, location? You don't strike me as the type who was meant to get into any of this crazy part of the world,' asked Tanner in a tone of a hooker scam.

'Ah, where do I start man? Age, 25, sex, male, and straight by the way' he added in making Tanner smile. 'location . . . the rest of the world, I got sick of being a talker like all the rest of them back home, this is my last stop before I go back home. I gotta transit through Thailand though, if I can get out of here now that is' he explained.

'Ah I'm sure you will brother, you wouldn't have made it this far if it wasn't meant to be eh?' he said patting him heavily on the shoulder.

Tanner pulled out a cigarette from his shirt pocket and offered one, to which David declined.

'Strike you as the type?' said David.

'Excuse me?' said Tanner as he lit up.

'You said I don't strike you as the type to be lost here, should I take that as a compliment? '

'Oh, yeah, I mean I just see you as a Cambridge Uni kinda guy, well educated ya know, like you're actually here working as a journalist or something undercover, not that you have to blow the lid off of it by telling me but it wouldn't surprise me anyway.' he said quite honestly but making David laugh.

'Well thanks, does the ripped shorts and sunken eyes seem like I'm trying too hard to cover it all up?'

Tanner smiled, 'Yeah! You got the idea bro.'

'No, you got me wrong pal, I'm just a . . . *was* a senior salesman who couldn't stand to rip off another undeserving customer. Wanted to see some trees as I walked around aimlessly for a while listening to the deity like presence of my iPod instead of listening to the sound of car tyres screeching to a halt at traffic lights on the way to work everyday whilst looking at miserable people who only ever looked forward to what was in front of their feet with each step they took. Sorry if I sound morbid by the way.'

Tanner looked at him stunned with a raised eyebrow and the cigarette perched in his mouth. He just held out his hand for David to shake it, as he took it he said 'Respect buddy, respect for a pure and simple idea. If my country had people who thought more like you do it might not be so wrapped up in layer upon layer of lies that people don't wanna tear through.'

David was shocked at his shared passion for words, with every sentence he grew warmer to Tanner. His alpha male appearance was becoming more transparent the more they spoke. They moved on exchanging backgrounds for a while.

'Jesus, you've been married with kids already!?' he said.

'Yeah, it sounds cute to begin with but it actually turns into a big fucking farce that I ended up walking away from. A hundred suits a day walked into a building I used to clean back home not knowing I even existed, my ex wife insisted fairly that I provided for the kids as much as I could, until I realised the company was secretly providing host for military meetings and negotiations regarding the Afghan war. Don't even get me started on any of that shit. Anyways, three nights after finding this out I come home brimming over with discontent and hungry like the wolf to find her in our bed, screwing some guy she met at the supermarket. She had some front as I left her, arguing that he had a solid job with more money to burn on her' he detailed.

'Man, I'd have left that second and not looked back, what about the kids?' asked David carefully.

'Well that's just it, I did leave but came back the next day after staying at a friends house and losing my job to check on the kids, bad on my part for not even thinking of them the whole night anyway. I turned up demanding I see the kids for that afternoon while she fucked off so I could talk to em about what was gonna happen. I had no idea myself at this stage anyhow, but on suspicious thought from my friend I managed to get a blood sample from both kids down at the clinic that day and got em checked out with blood types. They got over it after a McDonalds but guess what the Doc said three weeks later when I got the results?' he said with burned off fury.

David just shook his head and raised a lip emitting a blank mind.

'Two kids who we both named and raised until they reached three and five years old had no clue along with one of their parents that neither of em were mine anyway,' he said taking a long final drag and throwing it over the edge of the truck, he instantly lit up another one as if he were about to start chain smoking.

'No shit!' said David.

'Straight up, like I said, just one big lie after another. Not that every American boasts the same nature, don't get me wrong,' he said.

'Oh man, that's awful, and you say she knew about it from day one?' David asked.

'I'm not really sure, it doesn't really matter to me anymore ya know, she's not even with checkout Joey any more, fucking bitch.'

'Wow, that's a story! hence now you're on you're way to meet you're brother in search of party huh?'

'Oh yeah baby, the only true love I'm looking for is this, this and this!' he said enthusiastically pointing to his beer bottle, his cigarette and then his dick one after another.

'I don't know much about true love man, and I'll be honest that you live in an alien world to what I do, but out here everything becomes clearer and clarity only comes when you're embraced with it first.'

'True love exists and only exists for what you want it to and when you are around dude, don't mean that it's there. Every space in between is just down to fate . . . . aint we a pair of philosophical fucking Diablo's eh?' said Tanner laughing everything off and finishing his cigarette and beer.

His words were wise and produced a number of debates, David seemed to flow with most of them, maybe not the last about true love, but then he didn't consider himself the height of knowledge in it to cast that debate. After hours of driving they pulled over at a station, it was quite run down. The weak spotlights where a handful of other cars were parked barely displayed the obstacles. Tanner had actually fallen asleep and was awoken by the sound of the engine turning off. Shael got out and encouraged them to get some hot food here for the night. He said it was a small town called Myohla, it was not a tourist place. The station was neatly set out but in dire need of repair and at the moment held only a few people who gawped at them in amazement. Like other stations they couldn't tell if they were customers or staff. They both walked slowly as if having some sort of internal damage from the rough road and sat down like an old couple at a table with the famous small, red plastic chairs. A picnic style tablecloth with nice brightly coloured flowers decorated the table. A young waitress only recognizable from her green apron came and placed some sickly coloured crackers in front of them attracting some unpredictable flies to their direction. There didn't appear to be any soldiers here, it was so quiet they as they stared out beyond the road across into murky town back roads, beyond were fields. Mostly agriculture functioned here, the government took little notice of this place, just a notch on the map that only a tourist on a bus might glance at from the windows. They might perhaps have thought of what stories they could tell people and of how much poverty they had witnessed when they got back home.

Shael translated for them and sat opposite, nobody spoke the slightest English here. They both negotiated 'no fish' and that they just wanted something simple for dinner that would fill them until morning. Money was no object, especially at such a small price anyway, they both handed Shael twelve dollars between them. The waitress came back out to all of them with a small bowl of soup, it was chicken flavoured but not thick like they expected, just a few spring onions floating around in it. The cracked china containing it was probably their best. A couple of men in their thirties came and sat next to Shael and clearly asked him about the travellers who sat there exhaling, exhausted. He seemed to explain what they were up to and trusted them as if they had been his best friends for years. Feeling the weight ease off of their feet as time passed in the truck they were happy for, it was however quite hard on the bones. They walked around a bit in the quiet station car park getting their movement back.

They both had another beer whilst Tanner lit up another cigarette. David thought of striking up another conversation with him, just to keep them awake.

'So what are you into man? You said you're not a trekking man usually, beachcomber guy then?' said David.

'Me? Kinda. More surf for me, I'm planning to get my own board at some point, I left my old one back home, something I struggled to transport. When I get to Thailand I'm back on the coast riding the high waves, running the rip-curls just like Taylor Knox.'

'Cool, I wish I could swim well enough to be able to surf,' said David.

'You can't swim?'

'Not very well, I got my twenty five metre badge at school.'

'No Shit, you're missing out my friend.'

'Don't remind me, I can't even snorkel very well, it's too heavy on my chest.'

'Real bummer dude, even snorkelling opens up new worlds for you ya know. Floating over a coral reef watching all the sea life form in front of you is something else man, seeing everything as if it's on a HD TV and picking up every single colour you know of, even some you don't. All those colours at once in one place, that doesn't happen anywhere else above ground ya know. It's like a dream for me,' said Tanner with a glimpse of passion in his voice. 'Maybe you should try it with an expert like me; it might be easier for you.'

'Yeah, well maybe, I'll call you up when we're both outta here, until I try it I wont miss it though,' he replied.

Shael walked over to them both after he had finished talking to his new found friend, it was time to leave again. Tanner got up first, grateful for the stretch of his legs again. David followed after picking up the lighter Tanner had left on the table placing it in his back pocket. Shael informed them with new information that there were no soldiers for around the next fifty miles at least, this was a comfort to the boys. They squeezed in the larger front passenger seat with David in between them trying his best to keep his right leg away from the gearstick. The three talked possibilities and strategies on how to deal with things if they went wrong along the road. The conversation didn't last long as the small hours of the new day clicked by and they were both asleep. Tanners head rested against the window, Shael wondered how someone could sleep so peacefully feeling the shockwave of the bumpy road through the glass. David had his head tilted back, inviting whiplash in an accident but for now regenerating with his iPod headphones wedged firmly in his ears. A song helped him cloud the reality, it chanted about a road to a land of paradise, he wasn't awake for the end of it though.

Day 11

The night was easier to deal with in the cab and as dawn approached them the air became denser. The fresh country air started to thicken to remind them of the proximity to Yangon. They were greeted with half light, streaks of red and gold in the sky shone majestically over the baron fields, it looked more like a warzone from the past as they got closer to their destination.

Shael pulled over on a dusty desert highway, nothing was in sight apart from another golden temple glowing in the distance and a large building just by the road. They were just far enough away to see that it was surrounded by a low wall, the whole building was pearly white as if newly built. They stretched their legs and stepped out for a break from the road. They were now back on the main road down to Yangon. David took a long drag on his inhaler and Tanner did the same on his morning cigarette. It wasn't warm yet but they stood out with their hands in their pockets and got extra layers of clothing out of their bags in the back. Tanner was still wrapped in a blanket like a poncho draped on his shoulders, he started to sing to lighten the mood, it was about driving on the road and running into bombs. Although it was controversial they all found it funny, after all no-one was in earshot of them. Shael wanted to join in but wasn't in touch with western music much, he envied them both and felt like a father figure, he was the only one who had an idea of what danger they were in. He liked they way they kept their morale high regardless of what they had already been through. They carried on singing in time together, Tanner wrapping his arm around David and getting their cameras out. He eventually was able to join in when they saw his distance and they started to sing one he recognized. A tour bus chugged by slowly, half full of tourists, half of which were asleep but the driver and an old lady cracked a smile seeing the trio of singers performing by the side of the road, tone-deaf, ragged looking and drowned out by smoke and smiles.

CHAPTER VIII

Animal

Passing through Bago was surprisingly easy, breakfast was short but sweet. A café on the edge of the sacred city provided a comfort. The small boy who took their order was very polite, he didn't speak English but was trying his hardest to please. Tanner was also trying his best to speak his language making him giggle uncontrollably. As they were drinking and slowly sobering up they noticed that Shael was starting to lose concentration, he was stubborn and wouldn't negotiate with them on sleep. In his eyes he had a mission to fulfil and was still heading for the accomplishment, he wouldn't even let them buy him a coffee, he wasn't used to the stuff. David, who felt better in a lot of ways, noticed that the café owner and mother of the young boy started whispering to Shael. His ears pricked up like a Meer-Kat hearing a fellow Meer-Kat call saying food had arrived. They started talking as if it were a debate or like a deal were being struck, Tanner didn't notice much and was exposing the father in him with the way he had the young boy in blue jeans in stitches of laughter. Shael and the woman left them to eat and went through the kitchen toward the back of the building to talk. David appreciated the confidentiality they needed, it happened all over the country, like a secret alliance working behind the scenes. It was usually nothing suspect unless bandits were involved and they didn't operate close to big cities like Bago. David stepped outside and took in the dusty brightness that was now almost mid-morning, they were well behind schedule. Bago was bright from a distance but just as discoloured and rugged as Yangon when they got closer. Shanty towns lined the land behind the flashy government buildings and newly extended luxury business apartments, something that people like the café owner would only ever see the outside of. Tanner stepped up next to him to share the view and put on a pair of aviator sunglasses.

'What you thinking bro?' he asked.

'I'm not sure, I got a bad feeling about this now,' David replied still staring into the distance.

'Hmm, I think we'll be fine, might hit some hold ups in Yangon but there's always someone there to help someone else out right?'

'I hope so,' he said with a lack of enthusiasm.

'Lighten up bud, your shoes fit right?' he asked.

David turned to him with an obvious look of wanting to know why the hell he asked that, 'What?'

'If your shoes fit that means you're still walkin' around right? Judging from all those unmarked graves we've seen that's a fucking privilege out here man,' he said as he left, slapping him on the back.

His philosophy was straight to the point, but it was the kind they both needed. Shael returned to the truck behind them with a backpack they hadn't seen before, it was green and black with grey straps, just as big as Davids. He huffed as he lifted it over the edge into the back, David was starting to realise how much of a hard worker he must have been.

'Hey Shael, what's going on?'

'We leave in twenty minutes my friend, with a new passenger,' he replied.

Tanner cut in, 'You serious? There's no room for three of us in the back,' he stated factually.

'She take front seat, you swap around if need to,' Shael said solving the equation for them.

'She?!' They both questioned it, almost in sync. She then appeared from the stairs at the back of the café as a silhouette and started walking towards them with a smaller pack on.

'David, Tanner, please meet Katie, she will be joining us to Yangon,' he said introducing.

They all greeted the young girl, she was around twenty one with long dark hair tied tightly. She was wearing combat trousers and a tight, black, sleeveless top. She had a slim figure also topped off with a pair of dark sunglasses that wrapped around her eye line. She reminded them both of a Lara Croft type of character. She carried a small bag in each hand along with a day sack over her left shoulder to the truck as they all traded a '*hello*'. She threw them in with the décor of an army cadet. She was English, and all of this together caused Tanner to change his tune very quickly, it also caused David to shudder at what he may turn into now they were travel buddies with a female. David hung back letting Tanner make his first mistake first. He was onto her like a leech, he had seen it a hundred times before and still wasn't sure why it bothered him. This girl was nothing to him. His thoughts of Khin were becoming more distant until the actions of Tanner reminded him that he was drawing ever closer back to her. He was worried for her from the e-mail but it still didn't seem real. He pictured Yangon to be a warzone, buildings in pieces, cars dashed in the street on fire, people running for cover from fire of military tanks rolling past but deep down he would think that his over exaggerations would only console him when he arrived there to find he could walk the streets reasonably safely and into the British embassy.

They all decided to climb into the back of the truck as the café had given them some food and drink to take with them. The sun was about to pour on them again, hats went on, and this was the last stretch toward Yangon. Katie was quite practical and although she was stunning to look at, she wasn't precious with it. They swapped some stories for a while. Only about ten minutes passed and Shael stopped the truck. The traffic had been less than he thought and they were making good progress but he warned them of the next step which was the trickiest part for them so far. The Intagwa check stop was up ahead of them, it wasn't a border but it was usually manned by a small group of soldiers.

'Ok my friends, I must ask something of you, if you follow my path we will be fine but I must leave you for a little while,' said Shael.

'Leave us?' said Katie.

'It will only be for a short time, there is a checkpoint up ahead and it is unavoidable. The surrounding pathways cannot be crossed by a vehicle, too muddy,' he replied.

'That's ok, so what's the plan?' asked David.

'There is a lake, this way,' Shael informed getting straight to the point.

'It is about one kilometre this way,' he pointed west, 'when you reach it, you must follow the waterside, the banks, keep them to your left.'

They could all just about see it in the distance over the rugged terrain,

'Won't that take us way out west?' questioned Tanner as he sat on the back of the truck looking fed up.

'Yes, yes, but the lake bends back around, if you stay following then you will miss the checkpoint. You cannot be with me when I go through it, you must take your bag with you too,' said Shael.

'How far around is it? How will we know when to stop following it?' said Katie shooting out questions.

'You will see, I will wait for you around the other side of the lake. You can see the road from the edge again but will be other side of checkpoint,' he replied.

David grabbed his guide book and noticed a miniscule pair of odd shaped lakes on the map, Shael gathered them to all take a look. 'I see where you're coming from,' said David, 'this is the smaller of the two lakes right? The bigger one is up ahead say about ten kilometres but the checkpoint would be, say, somewhere around here,' he said pointing to the map. 'If we follow the line of the first lake which is kinda star shaped it should loop us back around. When we see the road again we can cut off and we would have crossed the checkpoint without knowing. I guess Shael would be waiting for us about here,' he said, pointing again.

Tanner cut in, 'that's all dandy, but that lake is surrounded by jungle right? I thought everything this side was a national park, doesn't that mean it's gonna be crawling with shit?'

'Yeah probably,' Katie replied, 'don't worry though, it only looks about maybe two kilometres in total, if we see anything it's likely to be birds.'

'You seem pretty up on the wildlife sister, would you happen to be a lover of animals?' said Tanner in a stupidly seductive voice whilst gesturing to his groin area.

'Ugh please, you're not a rare species either. There's like, a thousand guys out there like you, and to answer your question, I'm a vet back home,' she said.

'Oh, how upper class, no vets out here though huh? Out here they rate human lives above all and leave animals to die, mainly because they're more likely to kill us, that's what I'm getting at girl. ' He said, his tone becoming more impatient.

'I'm not a *girl*, *girls* can't look after themselves,' she said grabbing her stuff out of the truck and strapping it up to her, 'if you wanna whine about the jungle then fine, just go through the checkpoint on your own see how far you get,' she stabbed back.

Shael hung back saying nothing hoping the situation would calm, it did, and Tanner kept quiet. He could tell that it was not the end of the argument. David hung back in shame that the proof was right in front of them of the westerners not being able to work together, even in times of danger. They all got their bags from the truck and Shael arranged a few things ready to be searched by the checkpoint.

'I'm sorry I cannot do more for you, please take care in there, I will pick you up on the other side,' he assured.

'Hey Shael, du reckon on any animals being in there?' shouted Tanner as they backed away from the truck. Shael just shrugged and got in not wanting to enter the conversation clutching a strong possibility. Animals were everywhere in Myanmar, mostly in the jungle and marsh areas. Not many were actually harmful to humans but a few meat eaters were always to be watched out for. David could picture nothing but snakes, he had read somewhere that only one of the country's snakes was poisonous, the rest just left an uninfected wound if they even did bite you. He tried to place the idea somewhere else. They started hiking across the open area toward the lake, they had a few minutes before the jungle started to surround their vision. David was feeling better by the minute. Katie seemed to be tough as nails, she was bouncing over fallen branches and brushing trees with her fingertips as she passed. Tanner looked as if he had switched off and presented himself unapproachable. His mood had changed drastically since when he fist set eyes on Katie, her intelligence and unpredictability got to him as if she were trying to take his crown.

David started talking to Katie about her home life trying not to be too personal too quickly.

'Man, I know this is bad circumstances but I wouldn't wanna be anywhere else right now,' he said.

'I like your idea, you're a trekker huh? So what brought you to Burma?' she asked.

'Figured I'd see what was here, didn't really see what was coming though, I never do. That's the way I like I though,' he said happily.

Her smile was easily stared at, they trudged through the mud as the ground became uneven when they neared the jungle area and the edge of the lake. Tanner marched up ahead of them by about ten paces.

'So when do you go back home? Or are you even going home?' she asked.

'Yeah, I'm due home next week actually. I'm supposed to spent one night in Thailand before I go back to London, not sure how it's going to work out now though,' he said.

'Ah don't worry it'll be fine, you seem like a screwed on kinda guy, just keep your head and we'll be on the next flight out,' she said with an affirming tone.

'So when do you head home? And why Myanmar for you?'

'I live in south London with my boyfriend; he's not exactly the travelling type so I tend to take a trip out on my own now and then. I'm hoping to be back home in two weeks time, I've been here for nearly that amount of time too. I might have to cut it short though, as for Myanmar, I've always wanted to come here. I know it sounds crazy but after reading some depressing stories and watching some harsh films I go all out for it.'

'Danger junkie?' asked David.

'Yea I guess so, I would try to argue otherwise but I've already crossed Columbia, Zaire and Syria,' she said trying to cover up how proud she was of it all. David was instantly grabbed by it.

'Syria! Whoa man, that's heavy, that's near the top of my list too, can't get in at the moment now though what with the problems from the border of Israel,' he said.

'Yes I know it's a real shame, it's an amazing place though, the citadel of Damascus is worth going for alone. I love the architecture, one of the reasons I came here actually. I'm kind of a geek I know.'

'No way, you just got the same curiosity we all have. Travellers like us have just accepted that we either fit in, or we don't, so we don't worry about it and go find somewhere else to either fit in . . . or not . . . you get what I'm saying?'

'Totally, the problem with my partner is that he doesn't like heat, bugs or living life without a four start hotel waiting for him the next day. As much as I love him he's one of those that spends his life at home, trying to fit in,' she replied.

'He doesn't mind you flying off everywhere then?'

'No we've had words about it before but it's kind of expected now, I mean don't get me wrong, we go on holiday together too, but rarely out of the United Kingdom.'

'Geez, that's . . . a mechanical set-up,' said David.

'Yea, like I say it wasn't good in the beginning, big trust issues but we're over it now, four years next month,' she said.

'I envy you. I couldn't imagine being tied to someone like that and leaving them, even if it didn't matter to them.'

'Yeah I had the same feeling, now it's different, after that amount of time we know we're good for each other even though we don't admit it,' she admitted.

'So what does he do? He's gotta make some cash for those four star hotels.'

'Oh yeah!' she pronounced, 'he works with the stock market, he's definitely good for money. He's helped me out a lot too, he might be an idiot who puts odd socks on in the mornings but he can calculate percentages like nothing you've heard of before,' she said.

'Ah, a man of the stock market, I can already picture the suit and the glass of chilled wine,' he said.

'Yeah that's him, he's a great guy though, can be cold sometimes but I think he struggles to get away from work. He stresses about little things, I'm definitely the more resilient one out of us. What about you? a lucky girl waiting for you back home?'

'Not for me no, I'm not sure what's going on in that department, there's a girl in Yangon waiting for me but I'm not sure if she's genuine, and I'm not sure its just because there's no-one else showing an interest,' he said.

'Oh, harsh deal David. Are you going to find her before you go home? This could be the chance you'll never get back,' she said casting her brow higher, she took her eyes off of the grassy path to look directly at him in anticipation of his answer.

'Could be my friend, could be, I'll see how things are in Yangon,' he said.

'Is he ok?' she asked nodding toward Tanner who was racing ahead kicking out pieces of low branch that now hung from the clammy trees.

'Ah, he will be, I think he's narked off because you don't think he's gods gift. He's had a rough time with women,' said David defending his mood swing. Katie took his word for it.

'Well if he wants to carry on to them like he does to me, he's not going to get anywhere except a prostitute,' she said.

'Don't worry, he probably hates me too for even talking to you now, he'll get over it'.

Although he thought it, he didn't say that Tanner probably wouldn't have minded a prostitute, David was too occupied with the landscape now but felt troubled bringing Khin up in conversation. He didn't even have to say her name to get clouded by her memory, he was so close now, wondering if she was even still alive. None of the people around him seemed to matter when he thought about her, it wasn't the way he wanted it to be though.

After another few minutes of walking they were in full view of the lake up close, it was pounding with life—fish, birds, creepy crawlies and multi-coloured bugs that ascended the tree bark around them. The jungle grew thicker and they started to feel isolated, the road was nowhere in sight. They didn't say anything to each other for a short while due to the heat waving in their eyes, like an imaginative distortion of sound waves in a nightclub. They knew their words would make no difference, as long as they kept the lake in sight and just to their left, they would reach the next stretch of road. David had faith in Shael, he had no reason to ditch them. As a small opening appeared among some rocks, Tanner took a cigarette from his shirt pocket and sat down taking in the view. David, only a few steps behind sat on the rock opposite him just before Katie caught up. She might have started questioning why he stopped if he did it alone.

'Not so bad out here hey man?' David said as he wiped the sweat from his brow.

'No I suppose not, a joint would be fucking perfect right now though,' Tanner replied.

Katie heard the comment as she walked up and just rolled her eyes and stood waiting for them both, anxious for more walking. Her gaze followed the trees rather than the lake. David was happy either way but would have preferred to walk just to take his mind off Khin. He started flicking through his iPod.

Tanner, still with a cigarette in his mouth, had his head held high and his eyes closed sucking in every bit of smoke like some sort of perverted pyromaniac. Sweat rolled down his face and soaked his long blonde hair again.

'Does that not bother you?' asked David.

'What?' he asked snapping his eyes open.

'Wearing your hair down all the time, I recently cut mine off but I couldn't stand it in my line of sight all the time, especially when it's wet,' he said.

'Nothing much bothers me man, like I said, if you're riding a wave and you lose it then all you're gonna see is a white and blue wash of ocean. Before you know it you don't even know which way is up, hair doesn't make a difference,' he replied. As he was speaking his cigarette went out, he took the lighter to the end again but it had no fluid left in it. 'Fuck it,' he said chucking it into the lake followed by the cigarette.

'Come on Tanner, it was only going to make it harder to walk anyway,' said Katie, trying to place a positive criticism onto him.

'Who the fuck asked you?' he replied.

'You know what? I'm sick of you already, I would tell you exactly what I think of you but I'd be wasting my breath!' she said.

David could see this coming; he just didn't think it would be so soon. He stood up leaving his pack by the rock, walked over into the canopy a little and put his iPod in while they carried on. He was too tired to deal with confrontation right now.

'Please, enlighten me, I'd love to know exactly what you think of me, you never know it might make me a better person and you a more honest one!' he shouted back. Katie was forced to take her bags off as Tanner stood up and turned his back on her facing the lake again, causing her to get angrier.

'Fuck you! You have no idea of how honest the British can be and you have no idea of who I am. I haven't done anything to make you react the way you do to me except the fact that I make it clear I'm not interested in you sexually,' she said.

'Don't flatter yourself woman, this isn't about sex, I wouldn't touch you to slap you,' he retaliated.

'Thank fuck, I wouldn't want you to be going around town boasting that you slapped a woman. What is this about anyway Tanner? I've given you my end of the story and that's just your attitude in general,' she said.

'Yeah, yeah, I heard all this shit in school too.'

'Oh, you went to school? You mean you've had some education? You've obviously come such a long way to have adults saying the same thing to you now . . . so go on then what's your problem?'

'Ok, you're uptight and I don't like you, you're slowing me down and I can smoke whenever the hell I want to,' he said as they paced around each other taking verbal stabs.

David started to look around as he listened to a slow and melodic intro to a song. He breathed deeply thinking of how much easier it was going to be to take the rest of this hike, he didn't think their arguing would get them anywhere and thought about saying that to them, but he was too mesmerized by the tune. It fitted well with the scenery of the trees but knew it would end soon.

He took one ear out when he noticed movement deep in the distance, he squinted to study what it might be, it disappeared among the taller trees and every now and again he saw its dark fur flicker from behind one to the next.

He tried telling the others to '*shh*' but they had forgotten he existed and were still in full attack on each other. He turned and shouted at them.

'Hey, shut the fuck up both of you, someone might hear you. I can see something.'

By now they were almost in each others faces, Katie turned back to him, snapped two twigs off of a branch in arms reach and finished her now volatile string of sentences. 'He's right, here, take these, you wanna smoke caveman? Be my guest, you've just got to make your own fire,' she said chucking the twigs down at his feet.

'This isn't over bitch!' Tanner ended as they both walked towards David.

They stood either side of him to try and help him decipher any sounds. Although the lake was still, the sound of it and its inhabitants were drowning out anything that wasn't less than fifteen feet away.

'What do you see?' asked Tanner in a now controlled voice.

David wiped his forehead feeling the sweat from it, 'It looked like a panther,' he said.

'A Panther?' Kate wanted to confirm.

'Well, a cat like creature, kinda dark fur, I swear,' he replied

They all stood still and silent scanning what they could through the trees. They heard shrills of birds, clicks of smaller insects but nothing that would resemble a growl or whine that a feline would make. About twenty seconds passed before David broke the silence, he had been listening so hard that he couldn't even feel his heartbeat anymore.

'Ah, maybe it was nothing,' he finally said.

Tanner relaxed and acted put out, even though he was relieved slightly. He couldn't hide the stress of his conversation with Katie yet.

'Thanks bud, let me know next time you see something when I actually need to take a shit,' he said sarcastically whilst walking back for his pack. Katie got the rest of her stuff, her mood wasn't high right now either. She held a ferocious anger toward Tanner, his ignorance sickened her, she wasn't feeling the connection with David either due to the rift that had now sprung.

'Come on, let's carry on, if it was something you saw lets just hope it's not hungry,' she said, again, in a more constructive manner.

The breeze that once was felt by the bank of the water was now gone, each footstep as they carried on got heavier. The sun shone like a thousand burning hammers thought their eyes while the air was thickening and breathing became heavy. They followed the edge of the lake to each view, the next less inspiring than the last. Tanner remained behind, Katie took the lead forever looking to the distance and lifting her feet high. David felt like a wedge, a duty he hadn't sought for. He didn't have the energy to talk any sense into them and he found it unlikely that they had any more energy to waste on their petty insults. The edge of the lake they started from was now completely out of sight, they were now like blind moles following a tunnel wall, drinking bottles of water suddenly didn't feel like enough anymore. It was Katie who caved in the end.

'I need to stop, this is too much,' she said taking her pack off, the weight nearly pulled her over with it as she put it down.

Tanner and David didn't argue, David sat straight down. Tanner chucked the rest of his water bottle over his head soaking his hair and laid supine on a bald patch of land.

'What do you think this place will be like in twenty years time?' asked David.

They others looked at each other not knowing whom he was asking, Tanner just tilted his head back toward the ground and sprawled. Katie said that she hoped all the corruption was clear and that the community could work with Thailand. David agreed that it should be like she said but failed to see it; he saw a more industrialized version of the same problem. Tanner didn't want to join the conversation and made it clear that the problem was there right now, not in twenty years time. Although giving up walking was not an option, the choice to stay put was growing with each minute they sat. Tanners temper was getting shorter with the debates David was raising with Katie.

'Idiots,' Tanner murmured to himself.

'Who?' Katie rose to the insult.

'Not you, the guy whose jumped the barriers in Yangon, you know the guy who's been stirring the trouble down in Yangon. He's from my homeland too and he's probably boasting about the whole situation. You can't expect to fly home scot free pulling a dumbass stunt like that without back up, every single person I know would . . . . .'

Tanners unpredictable rantings were disturbed by Katie.

'Run! Now! Gotta go!' she shouted before acting out her own instructions.

Tanner and David were both shocked at what she was yelling about until it came close to them. Out of the longer blades of grass behind them near a tree was a face of a Clouded Leopard distorted by the strands of smooth grass, it leaped out with a slight cry at Tanner before he could know where to move to avoid it. All Tanner had time to do was raise his daypack in front of him as if protecting himself from an explosion, it worked though, saving his torso he held the Leopard off of him as it clawed and tore into his bag. It took no time to bite into the material spilling an item of clothing from its grasp through the tears. David's vision went into slow motion for the whole thing, it happened so quickly yet he envisioned the possibility of suns rising and falling again in the time that the animal pounced. Tanners face was wretched with a war like expression; he seemed to be fighting with the animal for a good escape. Just as David lurched into action running towards Tanner, Tanner shook the animal off by gusting up a huge punch of strength and launching his bag with both arms into the trees along with the animal. Instead of running toward him not knowing what he was going to do, David now knew exactly giving Tanner a quick and strong arm to haul him off the floor and run. They darted for the nearest tree they could climb. They chose a tree side by side and Katie, a few trees away, followed their lead. They scrambled as high as they could deserting their belongings until they were well out of reach. Katie's tree was stern, holding her easily. Tanners' tree was not so strong, it shook as he climbed and even though he found a perch close to the trunk it seemed like it was creaking under his weight. David kept his eyes on the creature which was snarling and prowling around in circles beneath them. It became restless and snarled louder morphing it into what sounded like a scream from a young child. It had been so quiet laying in wait for them, it was a natural, experienced predator they were dealing with making them lucky to have spotted it when they did. Although David was stable he had the most awkward position, he was holding on with all his strength to maintain safety. The muscles in his hands and biceps were at maximum volume gripping the rough, twisted coils of the tree. It was thick enough to support him but he wasn't strong enough to raise himself higher, his feet were intertwined around a larger branch beneath him, but there were no more protruding from the tree for him to use as leverage if he was able to pull himself higher. Going lower would have been a worse idea. All of them could be heard gasping for air as they found their safe positions and held them. A few seconds passed in hope that the Leopard would get tired of waiting but it remained circling, almost distracted every few seconds by noise deeper within the trees but then snapped its attention back to them increasing in anger each time.

'WHAT THE FUCK IS THIS ALL ABOUT?!' shouted Tanner in a rage as he crouched and desperately clung to the branch above him.

'Calm down,' said Katie in the distance, 'I'll try to distract him, I have a knife,' she said.

'Great, you can whittle me out a fucking crucifix,' Tanner went on.

Kate started to whistle as if it were a house trained feline in an attempt to attract it toward her. Her intention was to throw the knife, she had never done it before but was certain she could at least harm it enough to make it retreat. She pulled it out of her left boot concealed by a strap around her ankle, it was a thick blade but pointed and heavy. The hilt had the most girth and the handle was shiny and green, smooth enough for it to slip away from her hand quickly as she threw it, yet small enough for her to conceal it with her palm. She raised it with her right hand which was not the easiest angle for her to deal with but it was worth a shot. David and Tanner tried to refrain looking at it to see if it would then be interested to seek Kate's calling but it still remained under them, taunting them with its teeth. Whiskers were sprouted from its deceivingly friendly face that endorsed light, golden coloured fur which quickly contorted into silky dark fur along its body with even darker patches. If it hadn't been a dangerous animal it would have been a delight to stare at but it wasn't a pleasure they had been granted right now.

'This is insane, I'm never trusting Shael again, me and him are finished,' Tanner moaned.

'He didn't mean for this to happen huh, without him we wouldn't be anywhere right now,' replied David defending him.

'Oh as opposed to where we are now,' said Tanner.

Tanner started to lose his footing on the branch. The cat was fixed on him, it's tail thrashing every few seconds in waiting for him to fall. He clung to the branch above; it was the branch supporting his weight that was the problem.

'Kate, can you pass me the knife?' said David.

'Are you serious?' she replied. It was quite a throw if she was going to try, a few branches were in the way between them. David didn't really think it through, even if they had a clear view of each other he would use up all his strength just trying to catch it with one hand. He envisioned it slicing through his hand by accident and watching it fall, followed by himself.

'You're just going to have to try throwing it yourself Kate,' he said empty on ideas.

She didn't argue and leant back on the trunk whilst she arranged a good angle for throwing. Deep down she knew this wouldn't make a difference, it was too far away and too smaller target. Even if she did hit it with the blade it might not even tear its skin.

She took a deep breath and shuffled down the large branch she was sitting on. She held the knife steady in her right hand up by her ear. The sun was beating down hard outside the canopy turning it into a sweat box below. Her face glistened and her palm heated with each second longer she held the blade. Hearing Tanners' tree crack again she threw the knife causing it to fly dead straight toward the mammal. It struck one of its back legs making it yelp in pain for a split second but no more, it lurched away holding it up but then came straight back toward her. She shuffled back toward the trunk. She knew she was in the least danger of all of them and just sat back disappointed in herself.

This was however the best distraction so far, the cat stormed around her tree like an angry child giving David the best opportunity to retrieve the knife. A memory also struck him when he felt a burning sensation on his left buttock, it was a minimal worry but he had one of Tanners lighters and had forgotten about it. Jumping down, he landed as silently as he could but still aware that the Leopard would surely notice. He didn't even glance to check, he ran straight for the knife plucking it from the muddy ground as he ran, this time he placed it in his teeth. He kept running across the small open space to the tree opposite. He still hadn't turned to check but knew the animal was behind him gaining quickly, teeth and jaws wide in victory for its next victim.

The new tree was picked for comfort and strategy, climbing three branches up at the speed of a soldier in training he sat, legs aside a thick branch and took his top off. His top was stretched from spray of water and globules of mud it had encountered, it was finished anyway. He took the lighter and set afire the material, the branch next to his seating branch was weak enough to break off and use to hold the burning garment like a torch. When he looked down the animal had not been so keen to chase him, it sauntered over by the time he had climbed to a safe height. He held the lighter to it for a few seconds making sure the flames were visible and letting them grow enough to become intimidating, it seemed like a wasted effort though. He knew that this animal would need to be killed, it would be no use scaring it off, it would come back, possibly in greater numbers at an even less convenient time if they were to let it live.

The shirt started to ignite and soon was raging with engulfing flame.

'Be careful!' shouted Kate.

Ignoring her cry he jumped down and took the blade from his teeth, he stood warily face to face with it, and shimmied slowly to the right nearer Tanner.

'Tanner, you feeling brave?' he said.

'I hear you,' he said in difficulty as the branch under him became increasingly more unstable, 'although I don't think I have a say in this.'

The branch snapped completely from under Tanners' feet, he fell to the ground but had already accounted for it and landed on his feet. His calf and shin on his left leg grazed with blood as it caught on the sharp remains of where the branch snapped off from the trunk. He lost his breath and panted crazily. Like a knee jerk reaction he picked up the fallen snapped branch and pointed the sharp end towards the Leopard which was now trapped between what looked like two tribal men hunting dinner, one with wood, one with fire. The animal stared at both of them as it circled and for a brief glimpse it appeared to show fear. Neither of the young men were able to complete the confidence in their minds though, judging that it might have been their complacency of getting so far in such a dead end situation. The trees disappeared, Kate's voice faded, the sky grew dark, their eyes fixed on it, and nothing else seemed to exist apart from themselves and the animal, not even each other. They were a faint blur in each others distant line of sight, so was their rational thought, only reflex remained.

Tanner jumped at the Leopard as it turned toward David still holding the lit, hand made staff. He stabbed the sharp branch into its back with both hands driving into it forcefully piercing its skin. As expected blood did not go everywhere, like Tanners shin it appeared to be a flesh wound that exploded upon occurrence but was actually a mere trickle that increased over a few minutes making it look much worse. David could feel his legs shaking, every muscle was now alert. Tanner was no different, he screamed and grunted in hatred for it as he stabbed away but it wasn't giving up so easily. It seemed to jostle around in between them not giving David a clear shot with the now titled throwing knife.

The feline then started to run, it was slower to propel itself due to its injured leg and now various stab wounds in its back. Tanner slipped down to one knee from his ordeal, he was crazed with full intent to finish it off, he didn't need to though. David pulled the knife back behind his ear as Kate did and launched it as hard as he could toward it, the blade struck directly in its neck, deep and quick enough to down it instantly. Keeling straight over on its side it didn't need to call out in pain. The accuracy of the throw reminded him of a simpler time when he used to play tennis back home. The first serve was always the hardest and the most nerve wracking with the set target guidelines and although the dynamics were similar, the feeling was nothing in comparison really.

Katie climbed down slowly and rested with them, David was laying flat and retrieving his inhaler from his pack, Tanner sat with his arms rested upon his knees both of which splattered with blood from the animal and some of his own. Kate took some cleansing wipes out for Tanner to attend to his leg. After about fifteen minutes they gathered themselves and caught breath again. David felt dirty, something about the blood lust startled him, feeling no remorse for something he would have once tried to protect was now an unpredictable change in balance. If Tanner had failed to wound it as much as he did he wouldn't have hesitated to have taken his place.

He beat the burning shirt off of the stick to put it out against the ground. Tanner got up after cleaning himself up and walked over to the dead cat.

'Pretty handy with this thing bro, we did good,' he said as he pulled the knife out of its neck and handed it back to David getting more blood on them both.

'We should get going, Shael will wonder what's happened, plus I need a beer,' said Kate.

'Fuckin ey!' Tanner agreed.

Instead of changing his clothes he grabbed the cat with both hands which put into perspective of how large it actually was. He raised it up and lounged it over his shoulder and started to carry it like a prize possession, its head was hanging down his back, tongue swaying around a set of still hungry and globulous teeth. Regardless of size, it was still a baby and David didn't want to hang around to meet its family members if they were nearby.

'What are you doing with it?' he asked as he pulled a new shirt to wear out of his pack.

'Can you take a picture for me?' he said.

'What?!' they both replied.

'I want to remember this day, man was triumphant over beast. Plus, after all the trouble this thing has caused us, I'm gonna get at least one meal out of it,' he said.

'You're fucking crazy,' said David. 'You're going to carry that thing back to Yangon? who's gonna cook it for you anyway?'

Tanner stood tall and proud, one arm clinging to the tail of the animal held to his chest. 'I'm sure Shael would know how to grill something like this, man of the jungle and all,' he replied.

'Fine, fine let him bring it David, but I'm not carrying it,' said Kate putting her foot down and holding one hand up to make herself very clear.

David felt disbelief for a moment but was still fused with surviving a predator attack and brushed it off. After their muscles had stopped twitching with adrenaline they gathered their belongings, Leopard included, and started trekking again. As the trees cleared from the lake the road came back into view in the distance, the last few hundred steps were clear. They could see Shael sitting in the driver seat of the truck parked just off the road, he was reading a newspaper and smoking a cigarette. As they approached they had started to feel the hunger from their efforts. Tanner slumped the dead animal into the back of the truck still slapping blood with everything it touched. He was drenched with it himself all down his right hand side. Shael was startled and got out not believing his eyes, he crumpled his newspaper onto the dashboard and the cigarette fell out of his mouth burning his leg a little, they smiled trying not to laugh as he tried to cover up his surprise.

'Where have you been? What is this?' he exclaimed.

'Little snack for us all Shael, hunters' glory!' said tanner loudly, he had quickly got over his dull and vicious mood.

'We ran into some trouble in the trees, this animal started to attack us, lucky we had a knife on us,' Kate explained.

Shael looked at each one of them in amazement not able to believe them. He looked closer at the majestic creature now smothered in wounds in the back of his truck.

'Oh dear, this is not good fortune my friend,' he said shaking his head.

'Not good? you're telling me, I got one shirt less because of that thing,' said David.

Shael didn't care much, he was straight to the point with his instructions that Tanner could not bring it with him to Yangon. He pointed out that it was a Clouded Leopard and was a protected species, only around ten thousand of them existed worldwide. Bringing it to Yangon would only cause disgrace and the wrong kind of attention.

Mid afternoon followed, the three stowaways were back in the truck listening to music, but not tired for a change. They started to feel quite good for some reason, the morning events had made them pulse with fear and relief. They felt less bumps in the road on the way down further into Yangon, the traffic became less when it should have intensified like the air had. They were about to enter a place that they had all been before but with totally new expectations. Tanner tapped the side of the truck as they approached the outer edge of the city. Shwedagon Paya was seen in the distance. The roads became quiet, nothing moved, the far east was now similar to the wild west after a shootout had occurred. They all paid close attention and peeked over the edges of the truck feeling that Shael had taken a few turns to avoid the main roads in fear of being seen, he had also slowed down to try and disguise the sound of the engine. Kate held a heart shaped pendant in her hand, lapping over into the other hand with every two seconds passing. She kept vigilant along with David whilst Tanner turned back and just whispered to himself in a strange voice whilst shifting his eyes around.

'Shut up you moron,' Kate said softly with a smile.

'Well, this is it people, if anything is gonna happen, it's gonna happen now, good luck to you both if I don't see you again huh?' said David.

'Jesus, make it sound like we had a chance why don't you?' said Kate.

Tanner raised one eyebrow, 'If something's gonna happen dude, it's gonna happen because of us. I say we split straight for the embassy.'

'Not me, I got something to take care of first,' said David.

'What?' said Kate, 'oh, you're seriously gonna go find this girl?'.

'Yeah.'

'She's not gonna be there man, looks like the city has taken a walk,' said Tanner.

'He's right David, you need to make sure you're safe first, you can't go risking your life for a girl you hardly know,' said Kate in agreement.

'No she'll be there, if she isn't then I'll come straight to the embassy and meet you there,' he insisted.

Although they didn't think his idea was sane in any way they abided and were in no position to argue his choices. They knew deep down that no-one would be there and he would end up chasing them. David felt strongly against them, even if she wasn't waiting he would find a way to catch up with her. Kate became indecisive for the first time, she wasn't afraid of going to the British embassy by herself but going with someone would definitely help. Tanner had no choice, the American embassy was nearer to them now, which would be the second stop, the first being the hotel David wanted. He leaned over the edge of the truck holding the hotel business card up for Shael to read, he took it from him and held a thumbs up out the window.

Something must have happened, something bad, they thought. The streets were soulless and empty compared to the last time they were here. They echoed with sounds of cracking walls and scurrying feet, people were seen for seconds at a time and no more whilst closing windows, ducking behind doorways, walking around corners out of sight as if frightened by the sound of the truck, soon no vehicles were present. Rubble was heaped in corners, litter had gathered in drains and eyes were watching them from the distance, they could feel it.

David readied his stamina and got everything together on the back of the truck for a quick exit, the hotel wasn't far away now.

'Not far now, not far,' said Shael as he lowered his window.

Silence rang in their ears, then as Shael turned the last corner the River hotel came into view. They pulled up directly outside for him, he scanned it quickly, it was hard to tell it was even open from the outside. It was so dark inside, he looked up to find an out of focus set of windows, around six floors. The sun glared heavily stopping him from seeing any real activity but he was willing to take the risk. He turned back to Shael who was itching to get away.

'Thanks for everything Shael, it's been a pleasure, I really appreciate it,' he said.

'Please, take care my friend, safe journey back home,' he returned.

Kate and Tanner said a brief goodbye and helped shove his pack off the back of the truck.

'Good luck, I'll meet you at the embassy later on either way huh?' said Kate, pressing him like a big sister would.

'Right behind you Kate, take care, tell em I'm here for me,' he said not knowing if it would make any difference.

She nodded in certainty and Shael pulled away slowly. The British embassy was about twelve blocks away; the American was only about nine so they started crawling the roads to match tuk-tuk speed. Every crossroads they came to forced them to look both ways to find a bleak vision of emptiness, slight wind blew the weeds that were growing from the cracks in the mortar, traffic lights were only half active, young children usually playing on corners were gone and hiding in the high rises. The danger potential felt closer and was becoming painfully clearer when they passed a junk shop on a corner with six television sets of varying sizes in the window of which all screens were blank. Kate and Tanner crouched, still in the back, eyes perched over the sides hoping for movement soon. She clutched the small heart shaped pendant in her hand she had been playing with for some time, kissing it with her eyes closed tight.

'Something wrong here, very wrong,' Shael said, slowly shaking his head and lighting a cigarette.

Chapter IX

Call Me Corruption

The truck crawled forward and came to a crossroads nearly five hundred metres away from David. Shael touched the heavy brakes to stop the car. They peered through the rear window of the cab to see a line of soldiers in the distance causing a barricade. Each of the soldiers held a rifle over their shoulder amongst the dusty streets which were strewn with litter and the odd riot shield from what they could see. Shael turned the engine off and got out into the back with them.

'What's happening?' said Kate.

'Not sure, big problems here. American embassy is near them, too dangerous to go now,' Shael replied.

Tanner just threw his hands up in a silent disappointment. Kate suggested for him to come with her to the British embassy as taking a detour would be just as risky, none of them were sure how far the barricade stretched.

Military movements used tactics to close in on a target. If something had happened they would surely be on the opposite side or closing in from a similar angle, there was no telling of how many of them were scattered about. They agreed they could only try. The risk was even with the odds of success of actually getting to a safe stronghold.

Driving around slowly only attracted more attention, gunshots pulsed in the air, not at them directly but it was a clear warning for them and others around. The thick air had made them sticky and tired; they were running out of patience, ideas and were scared to blink. Shael suddenly stopped and shifted the gearstick into reverse.

'What's up?' Kate asked through the glass behind him.

'This is over, too dangerous, I can see soldiers around every corner, the embassies may not be open for you,' he said.

'If we don't get somewhere, I'm gonna start walking through them,' said Tanner, losing concentration.

'That's insane, you're not going to get through them without being seen, you'll be detained or worse, we're not even supposed to be in Yangon state,' Kate reminded him.

He knew she was right but he was beyond caring, he thought that even if he was detained he might have been able to get a shower and some food. The further possible consequences were what stopped him from arguing, he held his head in confusion like he did after the leopard incident. It seemed humans were an equally dangerous animal.

'What about David? maybe we should go back and get him, check if he found the girl, you know, we could grab him and head over the border,' he said, Kate sensing the slight hesitation in his tone.

'This is a good idea, I cannot get you all the way though, they will only let me so far but you could cross the border, may be a small fee,' said Shael.

Tanner started getting his wallet out on the misunderstanding that Shael wanted more money, he was urged to put it away when he realised that the toll booth at the border was what he meant. Shael felt he had to do a duty now, getting these travellers young enough to be his sons and daughter to safety was a task fit for a well respected hunter like he was, he decided to turn around. Finding David was the next problem, they had hoped he hadn't moved on already.

David tugged at the handle of the sliding door one last time, it didn't budge. His head spun with what to do, nothing to climb, no small window to get through, the side of the building had a gap but it was too slim to get anything down, except the broken piles of bricks and rusty tin cans that were there already. He rubbed his head with a questioning smirk and looked in several directions down the streets as if an answer were laying in wait.

Hearing the distant gunshots he could only think of Khin, nothing else mattered. He did throw out a thought for Kate and Tanner and wondered if Shael had managed to get them to the embassy but what was left for David to do now wasn't an obvious choice. Seconds now seemed like hours as the sun continued it's shining, he paced around feeling gradually more sick in his stomach knowing he might have fucked this up entirely. He questioned his decisions he had made now rather than what he was going to do next, *had he traded rational thought for reckless chance?, Or perhaps personal safety for an unhinged relationship with this girl that didn't really exist?* He finished his rant in his head and tried to calm down by sitting on the dusty curb, the sun was becoming like Japanese water torture. Nurtured by the emotion he was desperately trying to control he almost forgot where his was for a brief moment, the heat was making the veins in his head pulse as sweat began to appear again. Embarrassment was to blame this time along with self exposure.

After a minute of holding his head and brushing his hair with his palms he heard a whistle. He snapped his head up and scanned the street, nothing, the gunshots had faded so it was clear as day. He pondered to think he had finally gone mad and was hearing things, but no, it happened again. He scanned the nearby buildings rapidly and then as he looked up he saw something falling towards him from above, a shingling sound rattled closer as if in slow motion, it was a set of keys thrown down from the top floor balcony. They hit the floor before he could catch them but looking up he couldn't see anyone. He forced himself up off the curb and grabbed them. He counted six keys attached to a metal bar and a Manchester United key ring, somebody knew he was here.

Snatching at the keys he went to the lock below the handle of the sliding door and tried them one by one. The first two didn't work but the third did, hearing the lock click on the other side he wrenched the handle back and the door opened. He slung his larger pack in the lobby and closed the door behind him locking it again. Running through the main corridor past the breakfast table the place seemed dark and deserted but as he ran for the stairs he was confronted with Khin. His heart thudded as she quickly ran down to him, she hugged him briefly. She seemed to be taken with his new hairstyle and stroked his head lightly.

She whispered in his ear 'I'm so glad you came back, I knew you would.'

Before he could answer she grabbed his wrist and pulled him up to the top level. The door was held open for them as they ascended and closed quickly behind them as they entered the room. Standing in the room with a scowl was her brother and another young man who was topless, they both had rifles in their hands, no doubt loaded along with a pistol under each of their belts. The room was not the clean rentable room that he would have expected this time, the bed had been shoved over to the far wall and another mattress was laid on the floor next to it. The phone was unhooked from the wall and a small stove was near the windows with a few pots and pans, their edges burnt with rings of cooking sauce and flavoursome extras. A small bathroom with a sink with running water was present next door so it seemed they had been living up here on this floor.

Khin seemed to start explaining who David was in her own language to the other man in the room. He seemed rugged, moody and ready for action. David was most wary of her brother and learned that his name was Senal. He was surprised that he actually held his hand out to shake first, David complied and held his left elbow the same as he did. He also handed him the keys, guessing they belonged to him because of the key ring.

'What happened here?' he asked Khin and Senal.

'Small uprisings started when a man broke through fences to an area he was not allowed to go. Many people have to stay inside or get out of Yangon, now everyone is in danger because of further violence in other places,' answered Khin.

She pretty much summed it all up in that sentence, the uprisings had escalated to an enormous level here and ended in violence. Once the violence reached a certain level the government used force from there on until everything turned back under their control, seizing all visitors was only to track where they were at the time. It didn't seem so significant when they explained to him further, and it still didn't justify the way they conducted it. There was a TV in the corner of the room on top of a small bedside cabinet that the other guy turned on, he turned the volume down low. It showed a news report but nothing of what was happening, no riots, no gunshots, it just seemed to go on about the sewage system and farming equipment trade in Mandalay. Senal told him of how it was all kept under wraps as if nothing was wrong. Only outside countries could tell something was wrong from reports that leaked across the border, this caused problems for anyone who attempted to cross one. Canning people in was the first port of call.

Khin translated the end of the news report that provided a small warning that people should stay in their homes and comply with any instructions given by the military. The whole scene was sick, he asked of the whereabouts of Khin's mother and father, she went quiet and hung her head trying to find the words. Senal stepped forward and said outright that they were killed in an earlier conflict. David had already worked it out though.

Dismissing the idea of any certainty from the broadcasts he introduced himself to the moody, topless man. The man lit a cigarette and sat on the edge of the window which looked out over the balcony and held out his hand as willingly as Senal did. It seemed they were more willing to pull together as a team for the good of everybody regardless of danger, in their eyes they all had a common enemy now, that enemy happened to be more powerful right now. The man said his name was something like *'Than-Shen-Kau-Tsik'*. David repeated it back to him slowly with the handshake to try and make it stick, he had to resort to calling him 'Dan' in the end. He held a gun nonchalantly as if it was something he had done forever, and he clearly hated the military. He sat and watched them out of the window.

The soldiers were mobilized with trucks and armoured vehicles, some of them had megaphones that could be heard in the distance.

'How long ago did it happen?' asked David.

'Three days ago, they forced their way in, I had to defend the hotel but I wasn't fast enough. Khin was out getting food, it was all over by the time she came back' said Senal.

Senal took him to one side as Khin left to go to the bathroom, he said that they had to hide the bodies of the soldiers they were forced to kill. He showed David a different side of him, not on purpose. His eyes were cold, he held the gun and never put it down once, the events he described were as if it were purely factual. The shock had turned his persona robotic, stony and although they had a mutual reason to unite and establish a reasonable friendship at the moment, he saw that he was still nothing to this man and if David were to be killed it wouldn't cause him to stray towards any negative emotion. David placed a hand on his shoulder just emitting the sense of understanding, not necessarily comfort.

Dan called him over to the window to look at something. David took this opportunity to go next door and see Khin, the strong connection didn't seem to take dominance right now but he so wanted to get it back. She could hear him coming and turned to face him as he entered, she didn't shy away now, and she wrapped her arms right around him holding herself close to his torso. Shelling her with his arms he was afraid to ask what had happened, he quizzed himself and went through all the possibilities but was always drawn back to the worst.

After she recovered she relented on how they had been attacked. David became wide eyed when she mentioned that their bodies had been left downstairs, the chill that went through his body made the hairs on his neck raise and his knuckles quiver. He didn't see any sign of a struggle or damage as he passed downstairs and couldn't quite believe what she was saying. She seemed hurt that he found this alarming but clearly had re-ignited her emotive confusion. She took him by the arm and dragged him back downstairs to the room he had stayed in when he was first here. Nearly knocking over one of the chairs by the breakfast table in the hallway she scrambled out of the way hiding from the images as she opened the door for David. He looked in to find a smear of blood across the floor creating a trail leading to their bodies. He inched forward, eyes to the left of the doorway where the bed was and caught sight of the victims' feet, then their legs, and then their bodies in full, fully clothed. He tried to hold his breath unable to tell if it was fear or respect. They had been placed together; it was obvious they didn't die in this room. Their father had been shot twice in the chest, a few cuts were on his arms as if he had been fighting up close and personal with a soldier. On closer inspection without moving closer he found his nose was broken. He couldn't even bring himself to look at the mother who was draped next to him in the bed on the far side. David closed the door behind him as he came back out and held Khin who had her back against the wall.

Senal and Dan came running down with their weapons realizing they were no longer upstairs with them. They started shouting at them to get back up out of sight and that the army were moving again. Khin lost it. She started screaming at both of them, she batted away David's arms and started toward them grabbing chairs from the dining area and launched them their way. As she started kicking walls and doors like crazy David shot back to his instinct and grabbed her, locking her arms to her body to contain what damage she could do. Her brother and Dan were startled and just stood at the base of the stairs, she was never this fiery towards them. The loss of her parents had long set in but her anger for their killers was merely controlled, not dormant.

She simmered as they fell slowly to the ground within David's bear hug. All he could do was whisper *'it's over'* into her ear as the tears streamed down her face and caught breath.

Senal helped get her to her feet and guide her back upstairs to the room to lie down. Dan peered out the window keeping watch behind them, he had a heart set for the visual distance, it gave him an unnerving predatory sense. He reminded David of the animal who attacked him and his friends, laying in wait for the best time to move, glad that this time it was on his side in human form.

'How long do you think this is going to keep up?' he asked him.

'Not to tell' he said shaking his head. It appeared his English was limited rather than taking the remark as secretive.

David started to use more hand and body movements to get his words across to him. He stared at the rifle he was holding.

'How do you know Senal and Khin?' he asked.

He just repeated their names back to him clearly not understanding the question. David re-worded his sentence slower.

'Senal and Khin, friends to you?' he said pointing and expanding his arms.

'Long time,' he replied, 'many years.'

'I see, you keep the guns for emergencies?'

'Gun?' he replied holding it closer to him.

He then started to walk toward the kitchen door further behind David by the back of the building which had been locked. He took the key out of his trouser pocket; David saw every muscle in his skinny forearm ripple as he rooted for it. Opening the door, David was treated with the answer as to where they got the guns, two dead soldiers lay on the floor. They were both face down and still fully clothed, it was obvious they had taken out their wrath on these men trying to avenge their parents. The kitchen was a worse state than the bedroom. David felt the same sick feeling in his throat again but less so than before, inhaling the stench they had started to give off after being in there for three days. Dan remained cold and just raised an eyebrow when David looked back at him.

'Come, we go now,' he said as he lit up a cigarette.

Diary Entry 9

Where the hell do I pick up from? The last two days have been in existence with someone else who inhabits my body and mind. I am calm, but that is probably because I am safe, for now. The road from Kalaw wasn't the easiest ride I've been on. Tanner became close and then distant again within every two hours or so. Meeting Kate was a pleasure, she's from England and should be a step closer than me towards home now, I hope they are both alright. We all owe Shael our lives. He has driven us over endless roads overnight, stopping at Bago for a short time and then unintentionally pitting us against a Burmese Clouded Leopard has turned out to be the most unreal journey so far. I am now back in Yangon, infiltrated through back doors of checkpoints on highways and bridges. Shael is driving them both on to their embassies and I am living back in the hotel with Khin, Dan, her brother Senal and four corpses of varying condition. We are in hell. The uprisings have not stopped for nearly ten days and Yangon is under what we from the western world would know as 'Martial Law'.

We have weapons that I pray we don't have to use, we have food that I pray will last us long enough, we have shelter that I pray we can continue to be safe in. Not ever considering prayer before, I have no idea if I'll be granted these wishes, if not for me though, I hope for the people with me, they have provided beyond their means and I'm going to do everything I can to help them. I guess it's the Buddha I'm praying to, he seems the closest to this part of the planet, but I'm still not sure.

It's too dark now and I haven't raised the discussion with anyone yet, but we do need a plan. They have been camping in the highest room in the building for days, keeping watch on the militant animals that roam the empty streets. Gunshots and engine noises are all that's heard through day and night, no shops are open anymore, no transport outside of your own seems available anymore. It seems like they have barricaded the city all because of a badly planned movement which has upset a weird form of legislation regarding a political prisoner. The perpetrator or freedom fighter that carried out the idea has been deported, now the whole country suffers for their acts. There must be countless others here, hiding behind the walls. I have no one else to blame for me being here, it's out of pure blindness for Khin. I could have gone to the embassy with the others but I have this feeling about her, it's not love, I don't know if I've ever felt that but it's a connection and I feel responsible for her, more than ever now. Both her and her brother are heavily traumatized and are concealing it only too well. Nerves have been touched already and nightmares have been lived, albeit whatever has happened to me has happened in tenfold to them and now they are forced to sleep in the same building as their dead family, how did it ever get this far? Tomorrow, I plan to go out, I don't know where and I can't see any of these guys coming with me too easily, but it's a fact that I can't stay here. I have a mere few days left before my flight out. No footage of distress is reported on TV here and with no outside connections I can't even find out if the airport is still functioning. The other guy here, Dan, reminds me of a killer in an old computer game I played when I was a kid, he is a warm and cold guy. Seems like a good heart holds him, he speaks minimally and smokes a lot but I get the feeling he's the one who would keep it in hand for us if we ran into big trouble. He'll be awake all night if he thinks it's wise, watching and playing cards with himself. I'm going to sleep soon, Khin is next to me asleep and holding onto me *mentally, it's not the way it should be though. Senal seems to have accepted the lesser enemy in me and stepped back from his wariness. They are all exhausted from keeping low. There is something telling me that we aren't meant to stay here, nothing we can do tonight though, I'm going to read up on another option and try and get some sleep. At least my dreams can't get any worse now right?*

Day 12

David awoke to gunshots in the distance again, and faint shouting. Dan and Senal jumped up and took a bracing stance behind each side of the window with their guns. They opened it wide and inconspicuously started peering in all directions for where it was coming from. There were other noises, it was a bit muffled and blotted out by itself. They were all disorientated by it, along with not being fully awake and functional. Khin was still sleeping next to him, she had rolled over, but he felt there was no need to wake her yet.

He forced himself up as a matter of duty and felt his heavy eyes try to focus on the image beyond the bright light of the window. He knelt behind them, all he could see were the tangled wires slung around the street on poles sending electricity and phone cables in all directions. They gathered in silence and waited, the distant noise became less after a few seconds, and then it became clear. *Knocking.* Someone was knocking on the glass sliding doors downstairs. They looked at each other as if confirming the noise and all instantly assumed it were soldiers. David crawled to the edge of the window to look directly below them, they could now hear voices. Dan raised his gun, although there was only one of them knocking, they had no idea how many of them were there. He crept to the edge and looked over the small gaps through the bars and then let out a short, deep breath to find Tanner and Kate at the front door. Kate was knocking, trying to get some attention, whilst Tanner was sitting on the curb just as David had before. He still looked injured in some way as he got up. David shouted for them assuring the others that they were his friends. Before they could ask questions he turned and ran downstairs to let them in. He tripped the latch on the door and slung it open for them, he acted as fast as the others did for him with getting them upstairs. They all adhered to hurry inside.

'What's happened? Why are you guys here?' asked David.

'We missed ya buddy! Thought we'd check in see if you wanted to shoot some pool!' said Tanner sarcastically as he pulled a pistol out from his back pocket and waved it in front of them smiling.

'What the hell? Where did you get that from?' he continued.

'We ran into some trouble, the embassy was unreachable. Shael dropped us off at a derelict house and headed back,' said Kate with a more trusting voice. She looked hot from dragging the bags around for Tanner. It was clearer now that he *was* injured.

'He just left you guys?' said David.

'No, it's not as simple as that, it wasn't anyone's choice. He left for our safety but we're not even sure if he made it back out of the city. He could well be in more danger than us right now,' said Kate.

Kate looked harassed, not as fine cut as she was yesterday but sleeping rough was probably the main factor of it. Her hair was messy even though still tied back, her clothes looked that bit more worn than before. Tanner seemed to not stand out as much.

'So where did you go last night and how did you get here?' David asked.

'We walked, we only ended up about five blocks away and I remembered where this place was. Sule Paya in the distance and all,' said Tanner.

'We slept in the derelict house, it wasn't all that bad. We got hungry though, so we thought we'd sneak out to come find you,' said Kate with a one sided grin.

'Geez, you've had it worse than us then, not half as bad as these guys though,' David said lowering his voice and gesturing back at the others. They were now downstairs urging them to come up with them to the top floor.

Returning from a well earned shower, they were faced with breakfast, brewed up by Khin and Senal who seemed happy to be cooking in the kitchen now. It was similar to Mohinga but with added toast and eggs on the side, everyone was hungry enough by now and ready to form a plan. Tanner had limped upstairs and was tending to his leg which was still causing him pain from the animal attack. he changed the bandage he had on it for a new one. They all introduced each other as they were eating.

'Hey Tanner, did something else happen to your leg? It looks worse now,' David asked.

'Nah, it's just gotten worse, it was the branch more than the animal. Must have got infected or something, feels weak, ya know? I'll manage,' he replied.

The distress was clearer as his tone was shaky and he was much quieter now than he had been generally.

Kate just listened quietly on their conversation, she was also a little surprised at how well Tanner was coping. She changed the subject for them eventually, seeing that it might agitate him. He didn't seem to like being looked after, he was a guy who didn't accept pity or praise very well, especially from women.

'What do you think we should do?' she said looking directly at David.

He was taken back with being plucked out as the one in charge of this question, but he presumed he would only be asking himself the same thing in ten minutes time anyway. He thought for a few seconds and recalled the loose plan he had conjured up the night before whilst reading the guide book; although it had limited information on the dealings of where he selected, he thought the others might be able to fill in some gaps.

'I think we should head this way, if we can reach the border of Myawaddy we can cross into Thailand for a small fee. The fee might be higher now if they've caught on to what is happening,' he explained, holding the book open at a map.

The others listened in whilst finishing their meal, they were attentive and valued his options, even Tanner had been sucked in. It was the kind of thing he liked, the only times he had been emotionally all over the place was when they had no solid plans; this course of action was set up in stone for him.

'Fucking aye!' replied Tanner, 'we got access to any transportation here?' he asked looking around at the locals in the room.

'We have the minivan,' said Senal in approval.

'Well, are we all in for this idea?' Kate asked the group.

Everyone looked at each other except Khin and Senal. Khin felt ashamed of wanting to get away, as far as possible in fact, he knew it too. She also knew that Senal wouldn't want to leave his country, although the danger was clear and despite nothing tying him anymore, his country was everything. It was the Myanmar way, their heritage, their roots. Many of the people thought the same and remained, regardless if they had to keep fighting for it every day of their lives. Moving all he had to Thailand would just be another piece of ground beneath him, with similar but still, very different people that he was living amongst. Dan didn't have much to say on this matter, his parents were lost already. He had started over from scratch and he didn't care about much except quality of life for others these days. For someone so young he was no stranger to the pain that they all felt in their own ways, he would help them leave but not leave himself when it came to it. He nodded and wrinkled his chin in agreement just to please the crowd.

'I will come,' said Khin making David feel comfortable. She didn't look at him, only Senal this time, causing both of them to feel her regret.

'So is it possible to get to Myawaddy before nightfall?' Kate asked Dan, forgetting his language barrier.

He looked lost for a moment trying to form a sentence in reply before Senal took over from him.

'Yes, it is very possible. I can get us to Myawaddy in about five to six hours if we get a straight run. Getting out of Yangon will be difficult though,' he said.

'Do you think they will have sealed off the city on this side?'

'Not just the city, the border as well. The problem that comes before this will be fuel. I don't think we have enough fuel to get to the edge of the city, we will not make it to the border for certain,' he revealed.

The atmosphere sunk within the room, no gas stations would be operational at this point and some gas bottles were sold at the sides of roads unofficially, but not within Yangon. The law stated that this act was actually illegal but it was overlooked by the military due to using the service themselves, they had been known not to pay sometimes when filling up from one of these stations. The stations usually resembled a small, outdoor table sale mixed in with snacks and bananas to buy.

'Do you know where anyone might be selling petrol?' asked Kate.

They all gave each other their blank looks.

'How much gas do you have?' asked Tanner.

'Perhaps enough to get to the airport, about ten or eleven kilometres?' said Senal in estimation.

'Enough to get us to a supermarket?' said Tanner.

'Yes, but a supermarket will not sell petrol,' he stated with an uncertain expression.

'I know that, but I got an idea! '

Shael turned the car around slowly, it was the first time he had ever managed it in one manoeuvre in Yangon due to the usual busy traffic—now they were hollow and empty roads. Tanner and Kate in the back were huddled and losing ideas by the second. They were on trail back toward David, who they dropped off at a hotel, not knowing if he may find the girl he loved. It was a risk he was willing to take, if she was still there, there was no telling as to what he may have done or where he may have gone. They would hope he would come up with the same idea they had.

The engine ticked and whistled, the brake pads let out a dull screech when Shael turned the corners, one corner became too many. Shael had seemed to have lost his sense of direction, he wasn't used to Yangon everyday. The roads were an endless, nameless, grid like maze. There was a military tank in the distance pointing right at them with ten or twelve soldiers standing around by it. Shael kept his tether but stopped, and slowly reversed back around the corner. Tanner and Kate felt their weight shift back towards the cab of the truck and turned their bodies slowly to see what was ahead of them. Shael pulled around the edge of a building blocking the soldiers' view of them around the corner but made sure they could still see the headlights and part of the bonnet. It was an awkward moment but it was the only way he could get away without them firing upon them.

Showing his retreat clearly but at low speed and staying in sight by parking up was a sign of backing down, not running away. He hoped they had not seen the two passengers. He got out of the truck slowly and explained that they would have to get out right now. He helped lift their packs out as he explained, he was brief about it all, but had to be. He looked around and noticed a building about three doors down that was disused.

Its bricks were old and rotten, sweating with grimy colours, the front door was hanging off its hinges but still just about useable. Suggesting that they stay in the building until he came back for them while the soldiers questioned him made them act quickly; they already knew the risk they caused him, they didn't ask a single question and followed his suggestion to the letter.

Shuffling into the building Kate kicked the door open and went into the main room to the left. It was better condition inside than they expected but definitely not habitable. The second room at the back was completely out of sight from the road, she pointed and Tanner followed. They knelt behind the doorway to the larger second room and angled a line of sight that could see the rear end of Shael's truck and watched him. They noticed a soldier had approached him and started questioning him, they could barely hear and were just left to assume that he was being asked why he was out during the curfew and where he was going. They were confident that he would give a quick answer and worm his way out of any trouble.

The quick and necessary actions they took were silent and methodical; it did however mean that they couldn't get to say a proper goodbye. After a mere minute of chatter from the other side of the wall, the soldiers stepped away but escorted Shael visually back into his vehicle, watched him perform a U-turn and drive away slowly. They stayed silent and looked deeply at each other as they heard the sound of the engine fade and then eventually disappear, they were now alone.

'Shael, the man, the legend, good luck man' whispered Tanner quietly.

A startling sound of something being knocked over rang out from behind them causing them to swing their heads around to home in on its source.

Before them lay a young mother cradling a small child wrapped in a blanket on the floor, she was next to a cabinet. She was concerned but not terrified that someone had broken into her house, but the chances were it wasn't hers anyway. Kate dropped her jaw to see the girl in a sorry state; she was obviously a peasant but had stayed there silent, knowing that they were hiding. She could have easily screamed or made any sort of noise knowing they were unaware of her presence, she could have blown their cover completely. She just looked at them wide eyed, dressed in a brown t-shirt and a tattered longyi. The baby she held was small, but not noticeable of gender as she held it close in its dark blue blanket. It looked like it needed a wash, but they seemed to look OK health wise. Kate drew a comforting smile at the girl and her baby as her heart extended a warming generosity toward them, she then looked back at Tanner who met her smile with a blank look.

The young girl spoke no English. Kate looked at her guide book and sat next to her as the night fell, trying to speak her language badly with the handful of phrases inside the back cover. She managed to introduce Tanner and herself and learned that her name was Siboungkshe. When Kate asked about her baby she didn't answer, perhaps it was nameless. They had no idea if either of them had eaten, they didn't seem to be hungry or distressed, and although she could only see the baby's face as the girl tilted it for her, it looked peaceful and made quiet noises. The most unstable emotion at this point was within Kate, not being the type of girl to settle for a baby or even think about children, she surprised herself at how affected by this she was. She could feel tears hiding behind her watering eyes, trying to evacuate en mass, but strived to hold it back. She looked at Tanner again, who was across the room leaning back to the wall with his eyes closed. She was hoping for a thoughtful conversation with him but didn't miss the fact he wasn't awake at the same time. Kate felt that it was OK to unpack her bag. It was obvious they weren't going anywhere tonight so she changed her clothes even with the girl in the room watching, it made them both feel safer and Tanner wasn't going to wake up any time soon, the last time he had slept well was back in Kalaw.

Soon after, the sun concealed itself and with it all sound. Wrapping herself with her spare clothes and even sharing a few with the young girl and her baby was enough to relax her constantly elevated nerves. Tanner had shifted around to lying on his back amongst his clothes too, the hard wooden floors were cushioned enough to be comfortable and strengthen their already well conditioned bones. Kate lay awake for a while thinking of where she was, like so many other travellers, including David, she had waited for the situation they were in to overcome her, she welcomed it with a frown. It never came. The more she stared at the decaying ceiling with no light fittings, the more she realised she was breathing in and out slowly. Her pulse was slow and steady; she could even feel it without touching herself if she really tried. The darkness as a child would have had her terrified, now it was comfort, her eyes became focused and adjusted to seeing better in it by laying still. She could pick out the icons and brand names on Tanner's clothes and boots, she could hear vehicles and the wind from a wealthy distance. She was alive and well and becoming closer to noticing it more everyday she was in this country. She now knew what it was like to live like the indigenous people here, was more confident in herself than she had ever been and now living for a night under an unstable roof with a guy she wouldn't normally get on with. A mother also slept silently was next to her with an unbreakable love, smiling as she held her child in safety. Nothing else mattered.

'OK, this is risky as fuck, but if it works we might actually get ourselves a ticket out of here,' said Tanner getting into the planning trend enthusiastically, 'there's no petrol stations open in Yangon, right?'

'Right' they all agreed.

'This is to keep people within their fucking dirty Omni-coloured clutches of evil, I know, but if we can get hold of a vehicle of theirs, we could drive out of here with what could be a full tank. Their Jeeps and trucks and stuff have got to be loaded with jerry cans right? Otherwise how would they get around on patrol?' he asked the group.

'This is where the flaw of this plan might be,' said Kate looking at David. Her expression was to portray her superiority over the idiot speaking.

'I know what you're thinking,' Tanner replied before anyone could say, he slid across the floor to Dan and wrapped his arm around his shoulders just because he was the nearest. 'Hear me out, if our glorious enlightened friends here would perhaps be willing to, we could perhaps dress them up as soldiers from the guys they wasted downstairs and drive us outta here as undercover prisoners. We could also, maybe, stop for supplies at a liquor store on the way out across the border to Thailand, like David, he who conquered Goliath, suggests.'

'Sounds just like a fucking movie,' Kate spun out with a sigh.

'You say that my dear, but who's to say it would be any more like a movie than what we've already witnessed. Those who don't think it's possible never know if it's possible' he replied in his effortless, sarcastic, slapstick voice.

Senal and Dan didn't say anything, but looked away from him. It was no secret that they loathed the idea, dressing up like a soldier was like admitting defeat, or defecting. They couldn't explain the betrayal they would have felt or possible death sentence if they were found out.

'I suppose you would dress up in a dead guys outfit and feel no remorse huh? Taking a punch for the good of the crew?' said David, raising his voice more than he expected.

' . . . I suppose I would, why not? But it would make no difference, because it would be obvious from the colour of my skin that I am *not* a Burmese soldier,' he fought back, slowly and clearly.

'Well, it's actually a good plan, but we can't expect these people to dress up as something they're not. This isn't a road trip either, we've got wanted posters out on us' said Kate.

Tanner moved over to the window and tried to persuade them by being calm and positive for a change. He then switched the attention straight back to Kate.

'So how do you reckon we get out of here then?'

She thought about it for a second, she didn't like the route she had taken with her thinking. It seemed she had been pushed by Tanner's crazy ideas to think of equally radical directions. Unwillingly she then relented and replied 'I can think of three ideas, all ridiculous, but it's all I can do right now.'

'Number one . . . we steal petrol, from a military jeep. You said they carry jerry cans right?' she confirmed with Tanner.

Tanner was wide eyed with her words and replied 'yeah, yeah they must do'

'OK, number two: we raid a petrol station' she said, pointing out subliminally that that was her preference.

Before she could carry on, Senal and Dan shook their heads and advised against it. They said they would be taken control of by the Junta, raiding it with guns is also useless because they wouldn't be able to fire anything in risk of explosions. The idea was pretty much ruled out instantly, it had to be more covert as priority.

'Number three . . . we raid a local store' she then paused.

They looked at each other not grasping the concept, she knew it too, intending to make a fool of Tanner, it backfired and she was forced to carry on.

'Why?' asked David.

'We steal every drop of alcohol we can and use it to get to the border, most vehicles will run on whiskey if it's filled' she said.

The idea was not what they were expecting but no-one could think of anything better, everything involved stealing or breaking a law of some kind. Senal started translating to Dan the rest of what he didn't pick up, his eyebrows raised and smiled creating a 'no chance' expression in Kate's direction. She was overcome with guilt at the exposure of these ideas and hung her head slightly. It revealed to everyone, including herself, just how bad she wanted to get home now. David saw that the bad ass style she gave as a first impression cloaked a normal, scared young girl clutching at any attempt to get away, but then the reality was that they all thought the same in their heads. He never thought for a second that one of them wasn't entitled to say it, but they were willing, after everything, to give back some damage to the people who took no responsibility for anyone in their country.

The three locals started talking very quickly together, all conversation was soon dominated by them. It escalated to a stronger pace and then evolved into what could be classed as an argument between Khin and the two guys. Dan was the most controlled and ended his abrupt tone without raising his voice. He then put a cigarette back between his lips after making his point. However, Senal carried on and started pacing around, rubbing the back of his head and then leaning against the wall with his forehead.

'Hey, hey, look, we don't want to cause anyone any distress . . .' Kate ensured with her hands out in an attempt to steady the situation but she was interrupted by Khin.

'No, not your fault, we do not fight over what you think. Senal does not want to leave. It is not something we would usually think of in these times. We have no options but are very used to it, we will see things settle again after a few days' she said.

'But you shouldn't have to, this is no graze upon your country or its legislation, but people are much more contained within this country than they are in others and we are not expecting you guys to risk your lives or do anything for us at all. We can get out of here ourselves, everyone has done so much for us already,' she said in reply.

'It does not change our situation. We can help you as much as we can, you are our priority,' Senal said, flicking the gun up in the air gently. He switched places with Dan and went for some air by the window, once again looking pained and leaning on the sill heavily. 'It is my sister I am worried for, she has done everything she could to get away and I don't want her using you as her ticket out of here.'

Tanner looked around in a state of excitement and confusion as to what the new debate had raised. One wanted to leave badly, one wanted to stay badly, the other didn't seem to care as long as everyone was safe. Dan easily had the best call, but a long term plan was out of sight for the westerners.

'Hey, er, maybe we should give the guys some space. We should head into the next room or something to have some cool off time. Kate is right, we don't wanna push you guys around, your freedom of choice is more valid than ours on your own turf,' said Tanner, saying something understanding by surprise.

David agreed first, followed by Kate and they stepped into the next available room on the same floor. Tanner took the pistol he had with him and stuffed it into his belt by his back before flopping onto the bed.

'Fuck man, call me corruption, but I'd down every one of those army fuckers if I had the chance!' he spat out.

Loud voices were heard from next door, they also heard Dan trying to calm them. He soon gave up and walked into the room with the westerners. He spoke slowly as soon as he entered the room with the gun still in hand, wrapped around his rippling, tendon covered shoulder. He glanced around realising the noise from the room he had just left and told them he would help them get home. He added that it didn't matter to him about getting out across the border and shook each of their hands in turn.

'That's one' said Tanner in delight, as if he were tallying up a basketball team.

The argument next door simmered, but still continued on a lower volume. David and Kate just slid down against the walls, blocking it out with trivial conversation, they included Tanner but he didn't really seem interested. He was more complimentary to Kate for coming up with plans that he never would have dreamed of. Stepping out of routine was his forte, he loved the unpredictable. He was proud of his thirst for destruction and believed it was justified for who it was for, the others still found this unnerving. He lay on the tidy bed with white sheets and quilt and took deep breaths.

As the debate continued at a reasonable volume, David remembered his question to Tanner earlier.

'Hey buddy, you never told me, how *did you* get hold of that gun anyway?' he asked.

'I found it outside on the side-walk this morning, by the place we slept in,' he said.

Silence fell and Kate once again obtained the dread she couldn't shake, she didn't trust him. She never knew how he got the gun; she threw up visions of him having it all along, being some kind of megalomaniac who was looking for something to take control of.

'Just lying there?' David questioned further.

'Yep, just lying there.'

'Is it loaded?' he asked, his brow pulling ever closer together.

' . . . Yeah, one magazine . . . four bullets . . . M1911 pistol,' he said slowly, in a state of delirium, staring at the ceiling.

David saw Kate's worry and dropped the conversation for another time, he wasn't an enemy but none of them knew how they would react under pressure. It wasn't the time to be causing any more tension.

' . . . point four five calibre . . . standard issue' he mumbled softly, almost dozing off.

Kate and David just stared at each other, unable to find the need to speak.

The morning hit them hard, Kate was warm and tried not to move, she was aching on one side more than she wanted to know. It wasn't the first time she had found herself sleeping on a slightly cushioned, but still hard floor. Moving slowly, she felt her stomach rumble and contort inside from lack of food. Although breakfast wasn't going to be served or easily obtained, she knew she wouldn't die. It was just a meal missed, just a meal that is easily missed at home on a busy day, just that day at work where you forget your lunch. She would eat again, and with a strong sense of will she thought that it may well be on the plane journey back to England. She missed the cold mornings in bed where she needed to get up but couldn't, tied by the heat of the covers and hearing the rain outside was a perfect lull. Needing to get up here was different, sleeping in was just not beneficial.

Wrenching her creaking body up, she looked around in a fuzzy world of ill surrounds. Tanner wasn't there, the girl with the baby was still sound asleep next to her. She started thinking of the poor child not yet awake, opening its eyes to a hungry and fading life. It almost brought tears to her eyes thinking of how she wasn't even sure if it were a boy or girl, a large feature she felt guilty of overlooking. Without waking them she forced herself to her feet, checking that all her things were still around in the room. She lost her balance not being able to clasp the strength from her leg she had been sleeping on and nearly fell into the wall. She staggered into the front room and clumsily looked out the window to find Tanner. He wasn't there, only an empty street, so hot today that it felt as if it were about to catch fire. Every speck of dust across the street seemed to sparkle. She then lurched around to the alleyway and heard a gunshot in the distance from outside. Stopping and panicking, she suddenly didn't know where to turn, she pushed against the dark walls and was forced backwards by a psychological reaction to find she had walked into a door. It was not well made, the wood was dark and not easily seen from the bright light outside.

Hearing another gunshot she grabbed the handle and pulled, it wedged open but not far enough to open fully. It swung with stiff and ungainly order, only to be wedged against the wall. She entered to find a well made set of wooden stairs; she followed them to reach a door at the top of the building. Opening the door gingerly with a shaking pair of hands, she was blinded by light as it shone across the rooftops like a blade, piercing everything it could. The heat was received across her face as the door moved. She stepped out still fearing for her life but not knowing what from, her heart pounded within her chest.

Tanner was crouched on the roof but suddenly sprang up with the sound of the door. Kate was smothered with a feeling of hopelessness, her forehead pulsed seeing Tanner raise a gun and fire just as she opened her mouth to scream, it was silenced by the sound of the shot. The bullet rang through the air ripping every atom out of its way. She cowered in fear holding her head and falling to her knees crying, it was worse than dying. The bullet missed her and hit the door frame beside her, splintering it and flicking debris out onto the roof. He came running over to her, she was beyond control and too unsure of what he was going to do next. *Had he flipped and started a rampage?* He was the type of guy subject to that kind of event. He crouched in front of her, placed his hands on her shoulders and asked if she was alright. Still holding the gun lazily in one hand, he awaited her recovery.

'Jesus, you scared the shit outta me,' he said.

She launched up and lashed out, punching him straight in the face. The gun went flying down the stairs as he dropped it and Tanner slumped back onto the roof. No holding back, she got up and pushed him back towards the ground before he could get up again, splitting his lip and stunning him.

'Scared the shit outta *you*, you arsehole?! Scared the shit out of you?!' she shouted at him, tailing away to hysteria.

Tanner just lay back accepting the blow. He turned on his side and recovered while nursing his now bleeding lip which was staining his shirt and sleeve.

'Fuck! Come on, how was I supposed to know it was you, huh?' he said, 'there's soldiers crawling around everywhere.'

She got to her feet again after slumping near him, her eyes crazy, her mouth wide and sucking in breath as if she had been starved of it, her fingers rigid and hexed, ready to tear bricks from the wall to throw at him.

'You had a gun and fucking fired it at me! You're a fucking maniac and a liability I didn't ask for!' she shouted back.

Catching their breath they sat for a while to simmer down, gunshots were still heard in the distance, they hoped they had not drawn any attention.

Kate sat, closed her eyes and knelt down. Eventually she crawled over to the edge of the roof near Tanner; he kept watch over the buildings like a bird fantasizing about prey. The girl downstairs must have heard the drama, she must have been terrified but neither of them had the strength in their legs to descend the stairs and check. The cool breeze and sun was easier to deal with up on the roof. They sat saying nothing for some time but Kate eventually spoke up.

'You need to get a grip,' she said, showing no animosity.

He looked around at her for just a second and then away again. His lip was still bleeding. He was pissed off, but knew he was losing his mind and didn't throw any comment back to her.

'If you don't want to travel with me its fine, but you have to know that there's nothing I can do about it. You have to leave to get your own way,' she said quietly.

'What makes you think I don't wanna travel with you?' he replied, 'don't you think I realise that we wouldn't be together given the choice? Where would you go without me anyway?' he asked, feeling slightly insulted.

'Anywhere I want. You know, I had a friend once, we did everything together through high school. We studied together, played out together, we were like sisters and not a single birthday was missed. One day she turned around and said to me straight that she didn't want to be friends any more. When I asked why, she said she had found everything she ever wanted in her new boyfriend and had already made plans to emigrate to Spain working for a hostel with him.'

Tanner listened, even though wasn't truly interested he was urged to ask the question. 'So what's wrong with that?'

'Nothing, she made her choice and I respected that. I was more angry about it than anything at the time but I knew there was nothing I could change. Her mind was already made up. Just after a year later she called me up again,' she explained.

'From Spain?' said Tanner.

'Yes, she made it out there, did everything she said she would, but she was unhappy this time, not so cold, begging for me to come over there and save her. Her boyfriend had drained her accounts and flown to some other country overnight leaving her with only her passport, which I thought was generous,' she continued.

'Did you go get her back?'

'I didn't go to her, but I sent her some money in the post for a flight home, couple of hundred or so. I included a note saying that whether she used the money or not, it came with the deal that she never spoke to me or bothered me again. That way she could never leave me for somebody else' said Kate.

'So you've got trust issues, why are you telling me this?' he said, still dismissive.

'It's just so that you know I won't think anything of ditching you if I have to, so don't feel obliged to stay with me because you think I need it. I can see you're the kind of guy who detests sensitivity,' she said, losing enthusiasm with her own words.

'So if I go out alone from here you think I'll fuck up like your friend did?' he said.

'No, not necessarily, but you're not out to make enemies right?' she said.

He just sighed and shook his head.

'Can we stop talking about you now,' he said, 'I need a god damn cigarette.'

'You selfish son of a bitch,' she said, this time spitting with hatred as she got back up and started for the stairs again to pack her things together.

As she reached the base of the stairs she heard the baby crying. She turned to the wall to see the mother was awake and breast feeding the young one, it wasn't going very well and she was struggling to get it to feed. She just smiled at her, making sure that if she was scared at any point it was defused now. Feeling footsteps behind her and a hand on her shoulder she closed her eyes turning cold again, her body didn't pulse any more, she felt dead to the emotion she felt so strongly last night. She was now steady as a rock and turned around armed with volatile words to find, not Tanner, but a soldier, armed with a rifle and a glare of imposing accusation.

Her natural reaction was to step back, but her instinct fought against it so she didn't attract attention to Tanner. The soldier was broad, his face flatter and fuller than some of the others she had seen. He seemed gentle; his eyes were dark brown and stained in patches around his iris. His uniform was spotless as if new issued; his gun shone and sparkled, giving a smell of fresh polish and metal. The most intimidating feature of him was how calm he was, he seemed to be alone.

He started to speak but Kate couldn't answer as he obviously spoke very little English. He was tall, over six feet with a deep, soft voice. She gathered that his words were in the form of questions. He walked her into the main room with one hand on his rifle and looked around, as if inspecting the property for a safety check, but soon turned his attention towards the girl in the corner as Kate expected. He pointed his gun each time he spoke to her and she answered him in her frail tone, shying away each time. Kate looked up through the ceiling, hoping Tanner had latched on to what was happening, regretting her previous words already. If he had been watching from the roof he surely must have seen him approach?

The soldier frowned at Kate and then turned back to question the girl. She hid in the shadows hoping it would provide shelter from him but the more she spoke the shorter his fuse became. Not knowing what they were saying was hard enough but Kate was forced to intervene. She explained, in English, that they had nothing to do with each other, but it only came to nothing. The soldier took hold of Kate's arm, she pulled away but he persisted as if he were going to arrest her. He reached for his cuffs causing Kate to struggle some more, demanding an explanation of what he was doing. He soon had his hand around her neck. Kate turned red, she considered using her knee and striking him between his legs but then wasn't sure of how bad it would make it for her. Would he take that as an answer or would she literally have to kill him to stop him? if she even could. Luckily, her decision was made for her and severed completely when they heard a gunshot ring out from the roof. His attention turned and was about to run upstairs letting go of Kate. She ran to the girl in the corner to comfort her and her baby, who was now crying louder than ever.

Not quite knowing what to do next and feeling the guilt of standing by, she ran upstairs after the soldier. The rush was loud and clattering as she saw the soldier at the top of the stairs boot open the door and bundle through to the roof. Kate stopped halfway up with the silence and realised she was trapped between a rock and a hard place again, even more scared to turn back, she carried on up. Peeking around the edge of the doorway, she found the soldier with his hands up and deadly still. Tanner had been hiding behind the door as he opened it, letting the soldier bolt right past him not knowing he was there. He felt the familiar, cold metal against his neck held by Tanner's steady hand. Tanner disarmed the soldier by pulling his pistol from his holster. He tossed it straight to Kate and held his current weapon of the same type firmly with both hands, pushing the soldier to move forward.

'I knew there was another one of you, you fuck!' he said with fury, knowing the man wouldn't understand a word.

Kate found herself holding the new weapon but like a small child would, in fear, as if not knowing its power.

'Tanner what are you doing? We can't do this!' she pleaded with him.

'Shut up! Don't say my name, he might pick up on it,' he said, not hiding his anger and malice he felt for the man.

Tanner kicked him in the back of the knee to get him to drop to them. Kate knew that this was where it had all gone too far, no turning back, one way ticket out to prison, possibly death sentence. Whatever the case, this man would not be able to live to tell this tale in order for them to get away. Being quite submissive showed that he may have been trained to deal with capture or hostage situations, staying arms distance from him was the key for them due to not knowing how many times he had experienced them before. Either way, in his eyes he would see his captors were two amateurs and would easily slip up.

'We need to tie him up with something, do you still have any tape in your bag?' he asked.

She just nodded and awaited the next instruction, not feeling completely satisfied that she wasn't about to be held hostage too.

'I need you to watch him for a minute' Tanner said.

'Why?' she threw back.

'Somebody has gotta get his buddy inside before someone finds him.'

Kate walked over to the edge of the roof overlooking the street, her gun now held solidly, fastened on the man. She looked over the edge to find a jeep a few paces down the road and a dead soldier, face down, about half way up to it. The blood from his chest had leaked into a darker shade of crimson on the dusty pavement suggesting Tanner had shot him in the back. She looked away with disgust and took deep breaths.

'OK, I see your point. I'll get him in the building, you stay and watch this guy,' she stated. Tanner was fine with this and awaited her return as she leapt to the inhumane duty.

Being left on the roof with the man, Tanner started to feel his leg curdle with blood. It was strange, it was still strong but only because he had less feeling in it. He felt the wet and sticky texture though, which rolled down his shin and shook it off, using more insults toward the soldier as a remedy.

'How do you live with yourself? Following orders every day, handed out by a maniac . . . how many people have you killed, huh? I bet you wouldn't even admit it if you could understand me would you?' he rambled on. 'You're not getting away this time soldier boy, you're gonna be a martyr for a fallen regime, just like all the others,' he went on, inching closer to his subject who was now sweating in the rising sun.

Plucking off his helmet, he found he had thin and finely woven dark hair and a scar on the back of his neck. Tanner dragged the tip of the gun around his head and back, jabbing him a few times with it.

'I wish you could translate this, bitch, because I my friend am your living version of karma that has been waiting for you. Another family gets to feel the pain of losing someone in a gruesome way, that's out of a citizens control . . . this time it's yours,' he voiced to him, fading out to a mere whisper in his ear.

Kate crept out slowly from the building, passing the post, wrapped in broken wires, to the dead body. She grimaced as she pondered about how to hold him, it seemed to just be a matter of dragging. She quickly concealed her gun in her belt behind her back and grabbed the man, feet first. She dragged him across the dirty pavement, throbbing with heat haze, it left a dirty blood stain as she dragged. Realizing this, she was forced to turn him over and drag his back along the ground. His face was peaceful, his chest was caved in but not quite as bad as she expected it to be and found she could contain the giant blockage in her throat. She tried not to heave at the thought of miniscule parasites, already feeding on the flesh. She glanced around foolishly, worried about being seen. Any slip up from this part of their journey meant game over, but was dragging a dead body down the street worse than holding a soldier hostage on the roof in silence? His boots proved a good handle for her to facilitate her pulling. He was much shorter and smaller than the soldier on the roof and so she eventually dragged him around the corner of the inlet by the doorway and hid him, so that he could not be seen through the large opening at the back. The girl with the baby just watched in terror, it was at this point Kate knew their bond was over. Expressing a face that claimed desperately that it was not her usual business and she was genuinely not a threat to anyone was now hard for the girl to believe. Right now she didn't have time to try and explain through sign language, she ran back out to the pavement where the smothered blood was. She covered it over with a few handfuls of dust she had gathered from the corners of her room and from the joints by the stairway, it wasn't the most effective job, but she tried.

Feeling the strain of hauling the body, she took each step back up to the roof with weak knees, grabbing a blanket of her own on the way. Trembling as she reached the top, she found Tanner stood over the soldier, who had obviously stayed silent the whole time but was now on the floor, flat, face down from being hit with the hilt of the weapon Tanner held.

'Did you bring the rope?' said Tanner, still in an aggressive stance.

'There's no time, we have to go now. We can't leave him here alive, he'll track us down,' she said, slightly out of breath.

Tanner paused and seemed surprised that she had taken control, he felt slightly proud of her, but it made him indecisive in turn. Only the strengthening breeze and the harrowing sound of distant gunshots were heard again. She pulled the gun from the back of her belt and held it in front of the blanket she had picked up. Swinging around, losing patience with Tanner, she pressed the blanket to the man's head and pulled the trigger. It was over. The remorseless actions had frozen her emotions even more so in a deep, deep buried space within her. It was just a soldier, she kept saying in her head. Feeling the body slump behind the blanket, she dropped it upon him, straightened back up and slowly handed Tanner her gun.

'That's one each now, a common enemy' she said.

Tanner stayed for a few seconds longer than she did, holding a pistol in each hand. He looked down at the body, wondering what life he led that they had just ended. Wondering for a split second that they might now be the enemy, feeling like he had gained nothing but knowing that time was now shorter than ever. He used an old trick he had heard of in TV shows back home and placed one of the pistols in the dead man's hand, wiping it with the towel beforehand. He emptied the cartridge of all but one bullet and placed the rest into the gun he kept.

Back downstairs, they threw everything they had back together in their packs and set off, leaving for the hotel David was dropped at. Each bowing their heads and a kiss from Kate, they said goodbye to the young girl they had left terrified, not asking for any of what she had been dragged into. Kate tried to explain to her as clear as she could that she couldn't stay here amongst the dead military. She seemed to catch on, but still didn't fully understand why. Leaving her around sixty dollars worth of her currency, they marched out into the streets, leaving everything emotionally they had valued behind them in a dusty, decaying building.

CHAPTER X

Siphon

'How will I pierce the tank?' asked David.

'Not very easy, maybe you will have to use this to open' said Senal.

He handed David a sturdy knife, it was intended for hunting, but he couldn't think why it would be needed in a hotel environment. He didn't feel asking was relevant so he touched the blade with the underside of his fingers, sensing the sharpest edge he had ever felt and placed it back in its holster.

'So I won't be exploding or catching fire?' he made sure.

'No, we say petrol, but fuel is actually diesel, does not ignite. It has to burn for hours to catch fire by itself. Very safe, very economical, military use for these reasons,' he replied.

Thankful to hear that at least, he didn't have the fear of being scorched away under the vehicle when he found it. He did give a thought to the atmosphere and pollution count, not to mention the risk of getting diesel on his skin. He guessed it was something the government had never really cared about, so never educated anyone else on the harm it could cause.

The plan was ridiculous, Kate started to shake involuntarily. Even feeling much more fresh than she had since entering the country, she could feel a sense of several walls closing in on her. After discussing with the others of what action to take, they agreed on one of the more risky courses. Seeing as the guys were refusing to 'play act' as soldiers with the uniforms of the dead, it was now going to prove difficult to steal petrol from the jeep that Tanner and Kate had abandoned after their entanglement. Not admitting fully what had happened, Kate prayed the bodies hadn't been found. There was no real guarantee the jeep would still be there, any patrolling officer would have cleaned up and maybe even called in troops to scan the area of any suspicious activity. The only thing that stopped her from causing them grief about it was when they agreed that the men would check the streets and perform the tedious operation. Even Senal had agreed to help them, but he wouldn't leave his homeland. Block by block, one would stand in the sight of the other, giving a signal that they were all clear. David was the last in line to actually get under the jeep and siphon the fuel out. It seemed a lot of hassle for such little propulsion by his standards. Raiding the minimart seemed a better idea to him and running the people carrier on alcohol. Still, it was agreed and so they stuck by it, the ever dispersing provisions forced the issue further.

Senal strayed out into the open streets first; it was the furthest he actually wanted to go and gave him a place to mellow after a long, emotional display. He crossed the street, headed a few feet down the road and crouched behind a right angle where a small shop joined an internet cafe. From the shadows, he checked both directions and waved Tanner across. His leg was still slowing him down, he limped along over to him, more enthusiastic than he had ever been about anything else he had seen here. Crouching back to the wall with him, he smiled, and got ready for the next stretch.

'You need to stay where I can see you, on the other side of the street, on the next block. If you see someone coming you need to make sure you can hide somewhere,' said Senal.

Tanner gave him the thumbs up and snapped right to it. Sneaking down to the end corner by the crossroads was the hardest part. The dusty sun in the distance blinded him as he reached the middle, looking around in all angles for movement. With nothing boasting too obvious, he started to shuffle faster and shimmied up against a wall on the opposite side of the street. He felt the gun with his fingers as a matter of security for himself before exhaling and moving each time. Senal squinted to see him as he got as far as he could.

Tanner waved his arm in the distance as if flagging down a taxi, letting him know it was safe to send the next runner. From where he stood he waved up to the hotel balcony where Dan came out, all of his and Senal's weapons were left behind with Khin, who was getting the jerry cans ready for David to take with him. His smaller pack was big enough to hold two of them and he could carry the third in his hand.

Dan ran out, this time with a top on, and shuffled lightly toward Tanner afterwards. He managed to get to the same inlet Tanner had found in a doorway of a launderette, without the cigarette dropping from his mouth. Tanner asked him for one when he got to him, congratulating him on his agility. Dan then crept to the corner of the next junction; he could see movement in the distance to the far right at the turn, but couldn't make out who it might be. He had to assume it was militant patrol and waited until they moved out of sight, like an ant disappearing into a crack in a line of bricks. Listening closely for any engine sounds, he was satisfied with his stealth and leapt across the wide road to the next block. Crossing the road he checked back for Tanner's presence and found a perfect alleyway, barely wide enough to fit his skinny frame. Windows, along with a metal shutter from a market stall that had been abandoned, shaded him from the sun. He followed suit and checked around before proceeding too hastily. He then felt the shudder of a straining engine, a patrol truck trundled by, across the path of where the next runner would be. Fortunately, it was well ahead of them and completely empty, bar the driver. He was on his way somewhere and turned his head to see Tanner, monitoring him from around thirty feet away, waving at him. Dan waved in the same way back to Tanner, who was poised like a hawk. Tanner turned to pass on the signal back to Senal, who looked miserable and barely acknowledged him in return. He knew he could see him, but Senal had lost faith in the whole idea before they had begun. Nonetheless, he witnessed him flag it back to the hotel for David who was up next.

'Eesh, that is one aloof Satsuma' Tanner said to himself, referring to Senal.

The sanity of their improvised street running, as crazy as it was, was actually working at a good pace and David imagined they might be out of the city by early evening. As he gripped the jerry cans and shoved them into his pack, emptying it of all he had so far, it suddenly struck him, as if he were in a dream. It was

the kind of dream where you weren't really sure what you were doing, like holding random objects and communicating with people who seemed to think they were acting out the most important event of their lives. Khin hugged and kissed him as if she were a stricken housewife sending him off to war, knowing he might not return. She handed him a screwdriver, it was quite small, but would be a backup tool to drain the fuel tank if the knife were too thick, or too long. Bagging it quickly, he took several deep breaths and flew out into the silence to join his friends. He had placed a pair on sunglasses across his eyes to reduce the glare of the sun. Although the jerry cans weren't heavy, he felt uncomfortable, the bag was bloated and clumsy noises came from it when he moved. Forced to rearrange when he got to Senal, he placed the knife, which was still sealed in the dark orange holster, in the side netting of his rucksack and a bottle of water Khin had made him up in the other side. He felt his stomach move as each moment passed, especially when he knew he needed to be steady with his nerves and erased all time limits from his head. Somehow, the dark was always the fixed time limit here due to the lack of street-lights and product availability, everyone hid away until dawn.

He re-set his mind on the goal at hand, even if it took him all afternoon to get to the jeep, they would still have the fuel tomorrow.

Khin and Kate gave a 'thumbs up' and an 'OK' sign from the balcony as they watched out for the boys. Their thoughts were a comfort, even though the guys on the ground were in a position now to see more than them. He inched forward and strutted across the first crossroads, calmly looking left to right, and soon met up with Tanner. He then took a breath.

'Good going, one down,' he said to himself.

Tanner grabbed his arm to almost reel him in like some kind of fish as he approached, he crouched with him.

'Here, you might need this bro,' Tanner said, handing him his loaded gun.

David took it reluctantly and shoved it in the back of his belt like Tanner did, making sure his shirt covered it.

'Thanks, hopefully not though, right?' he replied.

'Right.'

Raising his silver aviators, he accepted the burning, bright light for a second along with Dan's wave of safety. He hot-footed it this time, not looking anywhere, in a kind of attitude that said *'if I can't see you then you can't see me'*. He nearly slipped when climbing the curb on the other side of the junction by stepping on the shiny grill of the drains in the side of the road. Luckily, it wasn't enough to take him down and he carried on to find Dan. There wasn't enough room in his alley for them both to fit, so he crouched to rest, just for a second, by the market stall table. He checked his ankles and checked the location of the jeep, it appeared that it was just around the corner of the block opposite. Dan would have to move across the road right to the edge to keep watch over him, it wasn't going to work where they stood presently. Dan pointed out where the jeep would be to the right, but he wasn't completely sure. They spotted a derelict building behind the building opposite, the building happened to be the opposite side of the road to where the jeep was parked. They waved Tanner to head down to where they were, hesitantly he abided, and limped over to all three of them. They explained that only one window could be seen from where they were now. If Dan left for the building and got to the first floor, he could see Tanner from the side window and a few steps away would allow him to see David and the jeep from the front window. Dan went first, the building was easy enough to climb, it was bright and dusty with plant life grasping the walls and dust, enough to fill a small beach to pass off as sand. It made him sneeze, even though the air from the lack of roof spilt in. He checked out the front before giving the all clear for David to head around. David then lightly paced around the sparse corner and saw the jeep. It was parked like any other, but looked very out of place. The dark green paint had faded in the sun. The spare wheel attached to the back didn't look roadworthy and was rusted in the middle, which would make it hard to get off anyway.

Tanner hid in the tight alleyway that Dan had once occupied and tried to look all the way back for Senal, but he was way out of sight. Senal didn't seem to care and had not come closer to check for them, he just lit up a cigarette where he was, hunched in the corner of his doorway. The girls would not have known what was happening from their view. Dan saw David slide under the jeep from his viewpoint. It was just a matter of keeping a look out for him. David felt a head rush as he tilted his body to lie on the ground; he placed his palm to the road finding that it was burning hot. The ring on his left thumb heated up and it felt as if his skin was going to peel away as he removed his hand. Still wearing his shades, he saw the sweat trickle across the surface and drop onto his face; this was no time for thinking of comfort though. Even shaded by the vehicle itself, it seemed hotter than ever underneath as if he was caught in a trail of smoke, not allowing his lungs to expand any further. Knowing the trick was not to panic in severe heat, he used his energy on the task at hand. He could only just see Dan in the window across the street. He arranged his pack as quietly as he could, getting out each jerry can ready and hiding them all under the shade of the Jeep. He shuffled up, located the fuel tank, pulled the knife from the side netting of his pack and held it in his teeth. The tank was near the centre of the chassis in an awkward position. He became paranoid of his legs poking out the front so twisted a little to one side. He could feel the soggy ground being created underneath him by his saturated skin, the more he tried to wipe his brow, the more it made the pores on his forehead secrete. Every breath was a chore, and the technical part was just about to come. He positioned the jerry can next to his head and steadied it with his left arm whilst aiming the hunting knife with his right hand towards the curved corner of the tank. He jabbed it a few times, then a few more, trying not to make a loud prang on the metal. Pausing a few seconds in-between, he checked around at ground level for footsteps. The heat was causing a sound in his head that seemed to block every other sense he could muster.

Dan moved away from the window briefly to check Tanner was still in position. He gave his sign of approval with a 'thumbs up' again and Tanner reciprocated in the same way. Moving back into position, he further monitored David. He was proud of his stealth and could barely be seen underneath the jeep unless you were looking for him. A passer by, if the day warranted one, would not notice, even within a joyless street. The tank was well sealed, built to last, but the top layer was shaved and dented by the knife just enough to weaken it. Thrusting it harder into the tank would just cause it to buckle and leak everywhere, to refine the stream he pulled the screw driver out of his bag and jabbed again in the spot. It slipped away the first time, but realigning, he jabbed it a second time and punctured straight through. It made an awful squawking sound of metal but was quick enough to be concealed. The diesel started pouring out of the tank, the odour was strong enough to burn his eyes as it spilt over his hands but he aligned the jerry can underneath so it started filling slowly.

A few merciless minutes passed and the first can was filled, almost to the brim, he watched the fill line and swapped the cans over so a second one started filling. He carefully screwed the top onto the full one and put it to one side. The switch-over made some of the fluid get on his hands and chin, the smell was engrossing, gassy and made him feel light headed.

Dan, still keeping watch, noticed another vehicle coming from the right. He tried to get David's attention to warn him but he was too busy stocking up and holding position. As the vehicle approached, he was forced to make himself scarce behind the wall. David then heard the other jeep pull up right in front of his one. He stayed perfectly still and plugged the hole in the tank with his hand, stopping the flow for the time being. He wondered for a second if it were mere pedestrians due to the talkative nature of two male voices, but was enlightened when he heard the doors of the jeep slam and caught sight of their black, steel toe capped boots clumping around next to his head. He laid there as if he were dead, keeping his breathing down to the slowest rate he could do. Their chatter hadn't stopped, they were clearly questioning where this jeep had come from and as to where its drivers were now.

They paced slowly around the jeep and got to a stage where they were either side of the vehicle, either side of David. David didn't know which one to follow. The one on the left dropped a cigarette butt and stamped out the smoke on the ground. He was the one on the pavement and soon noticed a stain on it. He walked over and scraped the ground with his boot, kneeling down slowly. David inched away, in hope he didn't notice him. His eye line was on par with the soldiers elbows resting on his knees. The other one walked around to join him and leant against the jeep, David felt it tilt under his weight. Around the corner, Tanner started to get restless. He looked back for Senal, no joy, he looked up at the window where Dan should be, still no joy. He licked his lips, developing a thirst, and wondered if something had happened and he should intervene. If he had something to focus on, his attention would have been occupied, but he wanted in more on the little operation. Being an overseer was OK by him, but he wasn't overseeing at the moment. Being part of the action was his forte, but he wasn't part, right now his position was not vital at all to anyone so he felt. Doing nothing and waiting around he couldn't stand, so came away from the small crevasse of an alley and crept to the other side by the corner to look around at the jeep. Straight away he saw the problem and flung himself back to the wall by his corner. The two soldiers around David just seemed to be loitering, making it more annoying for him to know he was powerless. He pictured Dan by his window, feeling the same useless push against him.

David felt a strain that was more than annoying, these guys must have been on patrol but seemed much younger than the previous soldiers they had seen before and were larking about. He heard laughter as well as serious conversation between them. They were smoking, he tried to depict what they were talking about, maybe the day they had, maybe women, maybe something they saw on TV. The more he thought, the less time it gave him to panic. He positioned his arms straight, down by his sides, realizing he could roll over and use the gun that he had, still tucked into his belt, digging into his back. He envisioned the gun being so saturated by now that it might not even work.

Dan still watched closely, as did Tanner, he wondered if he could create a diversion for David. If Tanner pretended to ask for directions he could coax them away from the jeep, leaving David time to get away. That thought was banished as he knew he shouldn't even be outside, or within the city now.

Dan held one side of his face whilst waiting for the men to move, he couldn't hear them, but he knew they were talking about something irrelevant. They didn't seem to be bothered about the jeep or where it came from now, they were just having a laugh. Being this erratic and irresponsible made him worry about what they might do if they discovered David. He wished he had brought his gun with him; he could fire upon them from where he was, with minimal fuss, leaving nothing to trace. Senal was too far away to inform.

All Tanner could think about was if the men found their dead friends behind the walls of the building next to them. Only he and Kate knew about it, but it annoyed him now that it bothered her so much beforehand, but himself right now.

'She's probably playing cards back there with David's bitch' he whispered to himself.

He hadn't told them any details of what happened as he didn't find it necessary, and flew along with the plan, like embers to wind. Giving David the harsh bet of being caught and then being found near a scene of murder doomed him, willing to let him drop that far after all they had been through.

David still felt them on top of the jeep, one was in the back smoking and one was in the driver seat, leaning around talking to him. He thanked his lucky stars that it had not been petrol fuel, the sticky, scolding feeling of the fuel in the tank was bad enough, but with their littering of cigarettes they would have been set alight by now. He thought that he could maybe get away with this if he could only move onto his front. He could sneak away slowly and let them drive off, leaving the jerry cans behind, one and a half was enough to get them out of the city but he didn't have anything to seal the tank off with. He couldn't rip his shirt this time, like with Tanners wound, some electrical tape would be ideal. He damned his failed sense of preparation. He smiled, seeing the ridiculous situation from the outside, stuck under a jeep, hiding from two scouts, holding a fuel tank together with his hand, watching diesel seep through the gaps of his fingers in a heat only a scarecrow wouldn't mind. He wished Dan could take a photo for him from where he was because it would have made a good postcard back home.

Before he could dream on with the event, he felt one of the drivers get out. He jumped off the jeep, climbed into his own one in front and started the engine. He shouted back saying, what seemed to be, a goodbye. He felt much better already and jumped the gun when he pulled away, feeling the draught from the exhaust on his feet and ankles. The guy in this jeep was still finishing smoking, he sat for another minute or two, which felt like an hour, before jumping off and scouting around a little. He was about to walk over by the alleyway that led to the inlet where Tanner and Kate had stayed.

It was at this moment that Tanner couldn't let him go any further, he was forced to cause a distraction.

'Hey dude!' he shouted from across the street, limping and pretending to be more ragged than he was.

The soldier spun around and headed towards him taking him away from the feared building. This one spoke in English to him, almost perfectly.

'What are you doing here?' he said to Tanner.

'Ah, boy am I glad to see you, there's a war-zone back there I tell you,' he said, avoiding the question slightly.

He placed his hand on the soldiers shoulder and leant upon him, the soldier tried brushing him off a couple of times. Tanner asked him for first aid and showed him his leg.

'You come with me, we have first aid for you,' he said, coaxing him into the jeep.

Tanner kept saying how beautiful the weather was and then sat on the pavement, acting light headed as if he were tired or drunk. The soldier started to lose patience and tried to pull him up by one arm, failing.

'You need to come with me, you break laws right now,' he kept saying, in different manners.

David couldn't see what signals Tanner was sending by this distraction, he inched over to see if he could see Dan in the window across the street. He could see him looking out from one side, he was poker faced and more set on what Tanner was doing. With no choice left and at his absolute wits end, he made a decision. Thinking rationally, he knew the soldier wasn't armed somehow so quietly as possible he let go of the hole in the tank placing the jerry can underneath it again and slipped out of the car, roadside.

'You are in violation of Myanmar law, you must come with me to be detained now. This is your final warning,' he said to Tanner, who was still sitting on the ground.

Tanner raised his head up to him slowly and looked him straight in the eye.

'I'm afraid I can't do that bro, you see you're in violation of human rights just because of what you do, regardless of all that you've done' he replied.

'What did you say?!' he asked, puzzled.

'You're under arrest from the Humane Dragonfly Earth Defence Force for mass murder of mankind,' he said, before gesturing behind him towards David, who was standing there with a gun, drenched in sweat and pissed off enough to pull the trigger.

'Come with us, now,' David stated.

They instantly they led him into the building and out the back where Kate had slept, the place hadn't been touched since they left. It felt dangerous for Tanner to be back here but once again, the situation was forced. Keeping his hands on his head, they frisked him for any other weapons and found the standard issue knife along and a pistol. Tanner took it and used it along side David, whose gun was still pointed at the man, happy to be under tolerable shade.

Dan came running out from the building he was in to join them, seeing everything that just happened.

'Somebody needs to go and get the others and bring bus here,' said Dan.

'Great, I'll go, I need the air. I'll check the last jerry can and bring them in. Tanner, do you have all your stuff?' David asked.

'No, I left it all back at your place,' he replied.

'OK, I'll grab it and throw it all in the bus. Dan, take this while I'm gone,' he said, handing him the gun.

David went back out into the heat and found the second jerry can, over spilling by now. He replaced it with the empty third one and allowed it to fill some more, anticipating that there wasn't much left in the tank anyway. He moved the other two cans back inside and left for the others. The way back he enjoyed more, not exactly like a summer walk, but still clinging to the edges of buildings. It wasn't a short walk back by any means.

Explaining as much as he could in the rush back to Senal and the girls, they grabbed all their things together and readied the bus he had entered the country from originally. He hoped that it would be poetic by leaving safely from it in the same way. They loaded up with everything on minimal fuel to drive five blocks away. Kate moved with highly efficient speed, knowing that this was their lucky break. Khin took one last glance into the room where her parents lay dead, she showed no emotion and said a little prayer to herself. Senal was the one who had to pull her away gently, after saying a prayer himself.

'Come, we must go now, we will see them again one day, but not now,' he comforted.

Starting the bus, they pulled away for the others. Creeping up in front of the building, only David got out, knowing that a bad feeling was about to erupt. He hadn't told them about the soldier, only the fuel and what they wanted to hear. He had no idea what Dan and Tanner had thought about doing with the soldier. He asked the girls to stay in the bus but watching David walking through to the back sent shivers through Kate, she had to look away. David had noticed the other dead soldier this time, slumped in the corner of the front room where Kate had dragged him, it explained the bloodstain on the pavement out the front. He walked through to find the soldier on his knees, hands on his head, almost crying, shaking, with the two pistols still on him.

He was not as confident as the others, he was younger than he looked and well educated in English. Tanner had already given him the shock treatment and waited until consorting with David about what they should do.

'OK buddy, I know you're only doing your duty and this is going to be a life changing event for you either way, but . . . you gotta wake up to things. We've got very little time and an equal amount of patience. Your soldier brothers have already put us through enough huh?' he said.

The soldier just looked at him.

'Your life is over. Your duty is over. You can't win, there is no way out of this, ' he said clearly for him. 'I got an idea . . . let me know what you think, huh?' he said, turning to David.

He turned back to talk to the soldier, 'OK, here's the deal, listen to me very carefully, because I'm only going to explain this once. You can buy your freedom back. You need to help us and do everything we say, otherwise we will shoot you, do you understand?' said Tanner.

The soldier nodded calmly. At that moment, Senal burst in.

'Holy . . . ,' he exclaimed, aloud.

'I told you to stay in the bus, I think we have another passenger,' said David.

'I can't take a solider with us!' he recoiled.

'No, but what about a farmer who knows the way back to his farm, by the border?' said David.

'Precisely,' said Tanner, crouching next to the soldier. He turned back to the man in question and said 'you're going to drive us to Myawaddy border and talk us through every gate, every checkpoint, every hiccup on the way out until we cross the border, at which point we consider your freedom . . . and you consider your future business . . . as a fisherman for example?'

The soldier took a long breath and swallowed, taking in some air ' . . . I have always wanted to be a fisherman,' he said hesitantly, looking Tanner straight in the eye.

Tanner looked at the three guys and smiled, 'Beautiful . . .' he then took out a cigarette from his back pocket, placed it in the mouth of the soldier, and lit it with help from Dan. 'Our loyal guest humbly agrees, we'd best get you out of that multicoloured get-up and into some normal clothes.'

Almost instantly they were away, with a fully fuelled vehicle. The soldier wasn't made to drive straight away as Senal knew enough routes to get out to a safe road, leading them to the edge of the city. Stopping for extra fuel was now made redundant. About six hours driving to the border would get them there around 9pm, it wasn't a good set-up but it was the only choice. Camping out somewhere in the bus would be uncomfortable now in their increased numbers.

'I will drive us to Mokkamaw. We will have no choice but to cross the border there, our friend will have to drive us through and the rest of the way,' said Senal.

David felt relief as if it was all over already, his skin was stinging from sunburn but he felt like he could breathe again through cool air as the sun dipped behind the rugged ground. He sat by the window and looked at the soldier, who sat right between Dan and Tanner. He looked scared. Knowing if it was an act or not was hard, despite his age, he still posed a threat and was not to be trusted; he'd had the same training any other of his peers had.

Kate sat right at the back and twisted to look out the back window, seeing no vehicles trail them, or overtake. Senal seemed to be wired with the radio on low, gliding around any back street to get them to the river he mentioned. Tanner had sorted out civilian clothes for the trooper, but had decided to leave him in his uniform until he was of benefit, by blending in.

'What's your name soldier?' David asked him, just because everyone else had neglected to.

'Htet' he said.

'Pleased to meet you, Min-Gala-Ba. I'm David,' he said, holding his hand out to shake.

Tanner couldn't believe what he saw in David's generosity; he didn't understand why he wanted the soldier to know that there was another side of human nature and not to feel threatened by them, they had nothing personal against each other. He didn't want Htet to feel like he was branded as just a soldier, to let him know that they realised there was more to him, a person, a boy with interests and someone who could help, instead of harm.

If Tanner wanted him to learn a few things and change his direction in life it wasn't going to happen by treating him like a prisoner, it would just breed hatred within him and he would expel it upon someone else in the far future. He checked the mustard seeds in the plastic bag he had kept in his daypack. *'One seed could plant a new direction'* were his thoughts.

Eyes became heavy as they drove on through the city alone. Kate and Khin were asleep before they reached the edge. David put his iPod on and rested against the window. He dozed, but didn't fully fall under the veil of sleep that was willing them all. He thought of Shael and hoped he got away OK, a man of his wit and negotiation would be able to slip away to where he needed to go. Things back home seemed like a distant memory, his parents, his friends, Sarah, he missed them all so much, regretting all what he told them via his e-mail. They were probably worrying much more than he was, but the final steps to the exit were in sight.

The night shone for a while and then David was awoken by the sound of heavy rain. Dry, and lumped in his seat, he sat up quickly and a sharp stabbing pain shot through his neck and ribs. The bus was swaying from side to side, the rain made its transition from light spatter to thunderous blizzard. He got up, seeing that Htet was now driving. Senal was right on his shoulder, kneeling down, directing him, the bus was clearly becoming hard to control in the rain. He thought they must had been near the checkpoint, he checked his map and turned to Kate, who was sitting up wide awake behind him, talking to Khin. Khin smiled at him and touched one side of his face with her hand, pleased to see him arise. He felt odd for a second, feeling nothing for her, his aches became a further barrier. He smiled back and tried to pass off the feeling as a one off from bad sleep.

'Have we reached the border yet?' he asked.

'Border was long ago, you sleep for a long time. We are now in Kayin State, many vigilante here, but no trouble so far,' replied Khin.

Checking his map, Kayin State was the third state away from Yangon, he had obviously felt burnt out and slept for longer than he expected. The window showed dense jungle through the steam on one side while the other side bore a wide open space, chopped down trees but not yet built over, almost wasteland, like something out of a Mad Max movie. Steam rose from the ground and the canopy of the trees. The road was partly gravel and mainly mud. He could feel the wheels spinning, trying to get traction, the cold made the area feel like a punishment. Tanner turned his attention to the front windscreen as the wipers desperately tried to clear the steam.

'How has he been?' asked David.

'Who?' said Khin.

'Htet.'

'He's been fantastic, plain sailing. The last border I was awake for, we got questioned by a couple of inspector guys. I don't know what he said, but he had us through within seconds,' said Kate, with high esteem.

David looked around at them at the front and then out the window, to realise the new obstacle they were facing. The left side of the terrain which started as a steaming wasteland narrowed and drew towards them to meet a high rise. They appeared to be on the edge of a chasm on a road, which luckily, titled away from the edge. The bus jolted and came to a stop in the rain. Senal opened the side door and got out, checking the wheels. Tanner and David followed. As David stepped out into the engulfing darkness, he thought about trying to find a waterproof coat, or what he used for his pack, but quickly saw no point and just stepped out in his shirt. They were soaked in seconds, their clothes felt like they were stretching and disintegrating. Tanner's hair darkened and hung lower, shadowing his face.

'What's the problem?' shouted Tanner, over the heavy dwelling sound of the rain.

'The bus hasn't been designed for these kind of roads, not been out of Yangon for ages,' shouted Senal, in reply.

The bus wasn't exactly on a precarious ledge but was near enough to cause concern. The wheels were now caked in mud, reversing wasn't even an option—on the other side stood a wall of thick jungle, but no longer green from the dust that had been thrown up from the rain. It was a dull mixture of umber and grey, made harder to see from the saturation in the air. They felt their heads freeze just above their eyes and their vision retract to what it does within a dark room of a few feet. The distance over the edge of the cliff faded away, giving them an idea that they were alone in the world.

'Well, how do we move on? I'm not wasting our time on the edge of forever here,' shouted Tanner, his hand on his forehead, shielding his eyes.

'Not much we can do, only push, but we won't get far,' Senal replied, pessimistically.

The three of them got around to the back of the bus to push; their feet began to sink in the mud. Lifting their boots high as if climbing steps, they braced against the back hatch. Khin ordered Htet to accelerate as they heaved against it. Tanner felt his leg straining with his wound and David felt heavier than ever before, even carrying nothing. Fumes leaked out of the exhaust and were quickly fused with the rising steam from the surface. It was useless, every push was useless, not one movement from the bus. Giving up and taking a breath, they couldn't see a choice left for them. If it was daylight, they might have retained some traction and had confidence on where they were pushing it, the rain made things further impossible. Regrouping back inside the bus they had noticed a leak near the back, causing a damp smell. David checked his watch, 9pm. He noticed a dirty mark smeared across his wrist from where he hadn't taken it off for so long.

A few snacks were handed around by the two girls who didn't seem scared at all. They were nowhere near the border but the boys were forced to accept the 'picnic' items they had been handed. Tanner kept his hand on his pistol whilst Htet was called down to join them from the front. Khin and Dan seemed to show the least fear for him, so he sat with them opposite Tanner and Senal while they ate a few prawn and chicken flavoured crisps.

'So Htet, how long have you been in service?' asked David.

'About eight months' he replied.

'Ah, a newbie, do you enjoy it?' he asked very patiently, expressing that there might be a wrong answer.

'It has good and bad sides' he replied, after thinking about it.

Tanner cut in, in his usual, sly way of trying to destroy someone from the inside.

'Does the killing represent the good or the bad side? ' he said.

'Shut the fuck up Tanner,' David said, in a dark tone, sick of his bullshit, show-off attitude.

'I have never killed anyone' he replied.

'That's a bold statement' replied David.

He pressed to change the subject now, as his true intention was to not escalate the instability of mood. This man could have been truly innocent enough to have not killed anybody yet, though trust was still an issue. David pictured for a second the barracks at where the soldiers trained, even though never being there in real life. He envisioned soldiers feeding through doors to practice each drill of conduct, firing ranges, hand to hand combat, jungle survival, equipment checks and the last room being soul trade, where their souls were removed along with their remorse, forcing them to kill innocent people who didn't matter. Pure fiction nearly triggered a warm wave of anger within his chest, so he quickly erased his imagination and moved on. He felt sorry for the guy. He hadn't changed out of his army attire yet, if he had, he would look like any other member of society, but still people couldn't forget. It was an occupation that instantly outlined them. He wouldn't disclose any details about his family or where he came from, probably in fear of them being found and some sort of revenge taken upon them, not that it would certainly happen. The conversation drifted into card games. One thing they all had in common was card games.

The hard rain still made the bus rock gently. The storm started for the night and lit up the sky, with forked lightning this time. David took a pack of cards he had had with him for a long time, they were given to him by someone on a plane who was heading out on holiday and found that card games were illegal where he was going. David wasn't sure that they weren't illegal where he was now. It wasn't going to plan but until midnight, they sat and taught each other card games of varying styles. Now the thought of union between them became clearer, a Burmese soldier, three Burmese citizens, two English and an American, sitting stranded in a bus on a high peak, in a rainstorm, playing cards together. Seeing Htet smile was also a strange comfort, he looked genuinely happy, for brief moments, everyone did at some stage. They rested as the night thickened and the storm faded.

Diary Entry 10

It's around 1am on the 14th and we've passed by the day that's an unlucky number for some, it's proving very lucky for me though. It's been such a drag. I slept well last night but most of the others didn't. Tanner and Kate returned to us, not being able to get near the embassies, instead they slept rough in a burnt out building and hiked over to us early this morning. Since then, I have been losing weight in sweat underneath a military jeep, trying to steal the fuel out of it. After a long, painful and scorching process, it was successful. It hasn't done anything for my courage here; I feel dead and am absolutely sick of keeping out of sight. Freedom of movement and freedom of existence are up on our wanted posters now, on top of speech. It gets worse . . . we have captured in all of this process a soldier, yes, captured. He is a young and fragile guy from what I can gather though. We have used him to get through a checkpoint or two and will need him to finally get us out across the Myawaddy border into Thailand, where we hope we can find some rest. It's not proving so easy, as for the last few hours we have been ceased into a cliff-side of thick mud, too dangerous to continue. The guy seems quiet and not really a soldier inside, if you know what I mean. I know how lucky we have been, we are all still alive, we have all eaten well and even had a laugh at such a late stage of our travels together. The fact all of these nations have worked together for this short space of time in these stressful positions must show hope to the rest of the world that it can be done. Senal, Khin and Dan are risking their lives for us all, just as Shael and Cheylam did. This is something that is going to stay with us forever. I am starting to feel less for Khin, the cold of tonight has got to me. It's not that I don't care about her, it's just I'm starting to doubt whether it's worth her while coming with us. We didn't put her in danger, she's coming of her own will to try and set up a new life somewhere else. With me, maybe? We haven't really discussed it. I'm scaring myself at how easily I have been drawn into her before, right now I think dropping her off in Thailand and never seeing her again wouldn't bother me so much. I'm not ready for this. The storm outside is nearly over, the sky has been black and electric blue all night. We can't sleep very well and my little lapse earlier has caused me to be well out of sync now. The storm inside me is just about to get worse. I think I've made a big mistake by finding Khin, but then I wouldn't be alive without these people.

Day 13

The timing was at its worst, but around two in the morning the rain stopped and the storm quenched completely. The ground was still slushy, but the bus was strong enough to pull away from it. About an hour passed while they all rested. Dan was the first to rest this time, it seemed only fair. David stayed awake, feeling it was his duty, the card games had ended and someone had to watch Htet. He was quiet but very durable due to his training and could stay awake for insane periods of time. David wanted him to keep his friendly side up and further pursue the friendly side of Htet. Someone had to be watching him as all the guns, except one, were stored under a blanket at the back of the bus, a further one was constantly with Tanner. Tanner sat slumped with a raised eyebrow, keeping Htet in vision all the time, waiting for him to go AWOL on them.

'Htet, I need to ask you something,' said David.

'Yes?' he replied.

'I was handed this piece of writing by a monk, can you tell me what it says?' said David as he held the scrap up to him.

The yellow writing had stayed vibrant on it. Htet took it and read it over, very carefully, his eyebrows then rose and he glanced toward him.

'This seems to be a very personal message, you say a monk gave to you?'

David confirmed and awaited his next words.

'It says: Breathe deep. Tread carefully. Your kindness will return in Karma and in the end, you will return home.'

David was taken back; indeed, nothing prepared him for a note that personal.

'Do you believe in Karma?' asked Htet.

'. . . I guess so, yes, it's been around too long for me to deny it . . .'

David paused to think. 'Do you think karma affects us all, even if not told so by a priest?'

'Yes, but our thoughts and minds can change any result,' he replied, tapping his temple lightly and handing him back the material with both hands.

'So it will always come back to you?'

'Even if you don't follow, it will follow you. If you get home, you know it will be true.'

CHAPTER XI

The Friendship Bridge

The storm faded and only blue and black streaks lined the skies. Several of them tried hard to force themselves out of the early morning daze. No-one had passed them all night and they were less than an hour away from the Myawaddy border, known as the friendship bridge. The moths dominated the trees next to them and every now and again, released themselves into the black. Senal, Dan and David stepped out into the drying mud to help push the bus out, the rear wheels were worse for being buried compared to the front—almost half way up the wheel on each side was invisible, luckily, some of the moist ground gave way and they released it from the rut as Htet powered the gas again. Tanner was still cocking the gun through the back of his seat, part of him hated the way he wasn't even trembling as he questioned why his manhood had to come to this. He pictured pulling the trigger; he pictured the exit wound in the man's chest as he lay dead.

The girls got out, reducing the weight of the bus for the men to push it free, it worked. Their effort was marked well due to the lack of strength between them. Tanner was still limping and it was getting slowly worse, his wound was now sticky and saturated every time he revealed it. Out of sight, out of mind was his only choice at the moment. He would try to find a decent port of first aid somewhere in Mae Sot, now matter how far off that felt right now. Kate was so tired, the ordeal had changed her, no longer the outgoing, quick answering self she had fallen back on the rest of the trip. She felt out of control and as if she had just jumped on with them from lack of choice, if it weren't for David she would have no faith in their actions. Khin looked relaxed, getting what she wanted was distant like it always had been in her life. The look on her face as she stared at David saw a loving for, not just a desire, but also for a figure to look up to. As soon as the bus hit more solid ground with the peaked road, they took some deep breaths. Dan, Senal and Khin got back on the bus and a much needed boost of morale greeted them as Htet flicked on the headlights again. David rested against the side of the bus and looked out into the beautiful, low lit distance across the rise.

'Are you OK David?' asked Kate.

'I'll be OK, I just need a minute to breathe,' he said, resting on his knees and trying to not get emotional from a reason he couldn't find. His hands were hot, his head felt laboured along with his body. He thought of Buddha and almost prayed for a happy ending.

'Well, if you're sure, I'll tell them to wait a second for you,' said Kate.

Before she could, he walked up to her and hugged her.

'I'm glad you're here, you don't know how much it means, you probably have no idea but I've been trying my best to hold everything together and I've only managed so far because you're here too you know . . . I don't mean to . . . you know . . .' he said, losing his trail.

She stopped him in his tracks and said it was OK, she didn't admit it, but she was relieved and a little choked up that he felt a similar way. It had been a longer journey than it had meant to be but the next part was the most unknown area. He let go of her and cleaned up his pitiful appearance as best he could with his shirt, neither of them could contain every part of their smile but they were happy to have the bond of understanding now. Kate always thought she would be the one to be running to him for council.

'Thanks for everything David, but it's not over yet,' she perked up.

'I know, I gotta buy you a Singha beer in Bangkok remember,' he replied.

'I'll give you a minute,' she said, getting back on the bus.

As she stepped on, he headed around the back of the vehicle, his vision was now worse than ever but he had to get a mental burden away from him. Down on his knees, he took the mustard seeds from his pocket again, ripped the plastic bag apart and buried the seeds by the growth of the tree line. The soil was a little dryer, he had no idea if it would work but it was as good a time as any, he wasn't banking on ever finding out. He closed his eyes over the small mound he had made, pushed it together and smoothed it over. Taking several more deep breaths, he rose and wasted not a second more.

Currently, no foreigners were allowed to travel into Myanmar after crossing from Mai Sot in Thailand, they weren't even allowed to stay over night. Vehicles were also prohibited and that was even for natives. Japan had interest along with the Thais about trading and creating a serious link through the rest of Asia with this bridge. Myanmar politicians were having none of it, for several reasons. One being that the vigilante situation in Kayin state had not been under complete control since day one and to agree with the full opening and free travel would provide a two way road straight through their country, all the way from Mae sot to Bangladesh. As it stood, apart from a visa run, the border was next to useless. Under extreme circumstances or normal, the border was going to be so difficult to cross, they would usually be forbidden from travelling the ground they were on right now. Htet still held the key to their success and regardless of his co-operation, he was still the enemy. Htet was in the driver seat again, silent and steady, with no expression. They all ducked down under blankets and covers they had brought to get the final rest they all seemed to guess they would be able to get before getting to Thailand. David thought about talking to Htet about a strategy.

His army uniform had been more than helpful to them. He asked about what he intended to say at the border. Htet replied in such a way, describing the border as non-negotiable, although it was known as a bridge, it was a well built road, suspended over the river. A toll booth was on each side to deal with the relevant stamping of passports, barriers were also there along with the expected armed guards. He went into detail of what he might come up with at the barriers by perhaps saying to them that he had been given express orders by his superiors to get these people across, hoping that no questions were asked, hoping that they had no phone line to check with his party. If they got away with it, Htet would have to come back, he didn't see a way out into Thailand, he felt the same way Senal and Dan did. A truce would have to be called and he would have to walk off, keeping Dan and Senal well out of danger. As they approached during the small hours, they were the two men who seemed to be losing interest, they seemed to already be whispering about how they were going to get back. David gained everyone's attention for a second, speaking louder, keeping people on their toes and also providing hard proof of the soldier's words. Htet promised to give it his best shot to get them through, after they parted they would have no attachment to each other, no-one would be anyone else's responsibility. A joint agreement rallied around and a few shakes of hands, even a few hugs were passed. David placed a hand on Htet's shoulder.

'Even though we are supposed to, we won't forget you for this if this works,' he said.

Htet just smiled and nodded, trying not to show too much emotion. David turned around and sat down next to Khin who had been looking too relaxed for too long. He took her hand and tried to fight his yawns, with his second hand he pulled his inhaler out again. He took it in two gulps and let his breath out slowly, feeling the sticky, swelling feeling slowly die inside his lungs. It made his voice hoarse when he was able to speak.

'This is it Khin, but you know I can't promise you everything now?' he said, black and white.

'I know, if we both get across OK, it is meant to be, if we don't, then we must use Buddha wisely to get to where we need to be,' she replied.

She was happy with her words, he was happy that she was too but the feeling wasn't promising even as much as they were to each other. She was terrified of asking what she wanted, about whether to stay with him until the end, or how far they were willing to take it. She had seen the way David and Kate acted, although there was no attraction, she saw the easiness of their flow together being of the same, western eyes. She noticed the continuity they had together, and it was something she just couldn't compete with. She knew there would be hundreds of others like her back in England. Her mind was set as far as Thailand now, which was further than she had ever been yet. David gave her some Thai Baht from his wallet that he had been carrying for quite some time, he had transited there before, but not exchanged his money back into what he required.

'Here, take this, it's Thai Baht. If we get separated at any time, I'll meet you in Mae Sot. If we get delayed further, head to Bangkok, I'll meet you there in three days, OK?' he assured her, handing her just a little over two thousand Baht.

'But how will I get there, it is very far?' she asked.

'Mae Sot is easy, even a Tuk-Tuk will take you, but for Bangkok you will need a bus and then a train, this should cover you for then, you can even stay in a hotel with this money,' he said.

He dug around for some more Baht. At first thinking he might need some himself, he was replenished by the thought of a cash machine being accessible somewhere. By approximation, he was positive that he would have around a thousand pounds left to bail himself out.

'Screw it, take this,' he said, handing her another six hundred Baht.

She tried not to accept it but he dismissed the money anyway, saying he really could do without it.

A while later people emerged from outside the bus. Noise from human kind was heard in the distance, the road formed and came together, indicating that nature had met society until eventually they were stopped by an obstruction, a long line of vehicles. The rain started again but not as heavy as earlier, it made the lights and fire flicker in the distance where they could see the bridge. It took them a few moments to realise that the cars were abandoned, no engines were switched on. The line, about thirty or so vehicles long, consisted of cars, trucks, tuk-tuks, small mopeds and a few minibuses like their own. The border was obviously rejecting them, the only chance to find out if it regarded people in the same way was to get out and walk. People, beggars mainly, slept by the side of the road, as soon as they geared up and stepped out of the bus they swarmed in. Grabbing their clothes in desperation for money or food, these were the hands of the rejected. Tourists and backpackers on treks from Thailand were usually permitted entry for a day under instruction to return by nightfall. They were the main targets and possibly income of these people.

No children seemed to be around but the adults adopted desperation, like children hunting for a lost parent. Khin and Senal had to tell them to leave them alone at times as they moved through them. Tanner concealed the gun under his shirt at the back of his belt again and followed Htet.

David was the only one who remembered that there were guns at the rear of the bus.

'Hey! Guys, come back here a second!' he shouted.

Most just turned and waited but Senal, Tanner and Htet came closer as he willed them. He flapped the blankets back and handed Htet the rifle.

'Are you fucking kidding me man?!' said Tanner.

'If he's going to try and do this for us, we have to trust him and make him look like a soldier, if he looks like a prisoner it's gonna give it all away, huh?' he replied.

David stared at Htet, giving him a nod of understanding that he was giving him full control again. He was confident that Htet was willing to stand by his newly returned beliefs of peace.

'OK Mr. Hero, I ache too much to argue now but can we please make the fail-safe aware that if he tries anything I am still armed, so is Dan. I'll trust him merely because of you but I will gun him down if he puts a foot wrong,' Tanner threatened.

Htet got the drift of things very quickly. He looped the rifle strap around his neck and shoulders and led up front as they walked up to the barriers. The buildings in the distance weren't tall but stood high above the trees, which diminished as they moved. The black of night turned into a dark blue and drizzled with an annoying level of rain. Fires were lit like lanterns at each side of the wide bridge as they approached, the closer they got, the more people they saw. Some were crying, panicking about being stranded, some were even building their own camp-site by the side of the road. Others sat in their vehicles smoking, waiting, wondering when things were going to shift. Right where the steep banks met the bridge, there were some travellers who had the same idea as them. David and Kate spoke up to them as if in a conference call about what had been happening here. They replied with bleak news, saying things like the border had been closed for days, from both ways. The soldiers weren't moving and not yet providing an alternative. A pair of young looking travellers sat on the edge of the bridge on the left side quite precariously, they looked no older than eighteen, packs on their backs. The one with curly brown hair was waving a musical instrument around, a strange wooden piece on a string that he whirled through the air in circles, causing an ambient and harmonic sound.

As they neared the left hand building, they had to push through people, seeing Htet in uniform and holding a weapon didn't make them part any quicker for them. Suddenly they could see nothing but the mass of bodies around them, lit up by dull fires and dim floodlights. Htet helped wade through them, all the way up to the toll booth. About twenty soldiers and a few jeeps were blocking the bridge as well as the two heavy duty barriers. The Thai side had people in the distance, too far to make out but they seemed to be waiting for something, the chances are they had been told to stay clear of the entire fiasco.

Although nobody was being threatened, a height of emotion was present and nerves were disturbed. Htet ducked straight under the horizontal, rigid barriers with an extra suspended weight hanging from it and spoke to the guards. They looked back at the situation together and all the desperate people. No matter how much pleading they were doing, none of the soldiers would take the slightest notice. Senal and Dan hung back, behind the others. Senal spoke with Khin, their conversation was muffled by the undulation of sound and speech around them, the rain caused a further distance between everybody, no matter how close they were.

Tanner stayed at the barrier, poker faced. He watched every curve and crease that came from Htet's mouth, even though he didn't understand what he was saying. He handed him his thoughts that he blended in with the other soldiers all too well, like they wanted. David and Kate moved nearer the others and checked over the edge of the bridge, the stony surface was flat and cold, about twenty inches thick but not very high from the floor. The sight over the edge was the low river, it didn't look unfriendly though. The rocks scattered the flow of the water near the bottom, the moon was trying to light up parts of the water but was dipping behind the trees. Nothing was said until they went to find Khin and Senal again. They were saying their goodbyes, hugging, as if it were all they ever had and they were about to lose it. Senal held back his tears but Khin wasn't so well balanced, Senal had to push her away into David as they parted.

'You look after her my friend, make sure she is OK, whatever happens to you both' he stated to him.

'I will, I promise, and look after yourself my friend,' replied David, and shook his hand with a strong grip.

Senal stepped back a few feet and watched from a distance with Dan. David took Khin to the edge of the bridge through the people. He stood her up straight and placed his hands on the side of her arms.

'This is it; if this works then it's OK. I'm just going to check with Htet what the deal is. OK?' he said.

She nodded, too choked up to say anything yet.

'Stay here for a minute, I'll be right back' he said, and took his hoodie off, putting it on Khin as a replacement promise to her.

He went back to the front but Htet was nowhere in sight, he became hesitant and felt a wave of heat across his forehead. The white noise and push of everything caused him to breathe through his mouth and show how tired he felt to anybody with eyes. Before the motion of sickness could take hold, he was clasped on his shoulder by Tanner from behind him.

'Hey dude, we gotta go now,' he shouted from behind, still almost drowned out by a sea of people.

'Go?! Did it work? Where's Htet?' he asked, not knowing which question he would prefer answering first.

Tanner pulled him around to face him, ignoring the crush of people, he greeted him with a positive smile as if they had passed an exam together back in college.

'Yeah! It worked, he took a while and when he went in the building with them, I thought he fucked us, but no. He said all we need is our passports and we can get through. Get the others!' said Tanner, through his frazzled hair and strained grin.

David reached back through the crowd. His larger pack was knocking some people around as he turned, but he didn't care any more, he just wanted to move whilst they were given the green flag. His sorrow for anyone else here vanished within seconds when he let Kate in on the news, but then he remembered Khin wasn't so blessed as to possess a passport. Tanner hadn't clarified if she was in on the deal.

Dan moved forward to them, keeping watch and attempting to wave goodbye as they pushed back towards the barrier to find out what would become of them. Neither of them had heard about their chance through the confusion. All he caught sight of was David whispering, at a higher volume than usual, into Khin's ear the whole way.

As they approached, they all stood as near to the barrier as they could but the forces of people seemed to be building up. David found Tanner floundering, as if in a torrent filled stream, so grabbed hold of his pack and pulled him back towards him, to the dismay of the impatient people around them.

'Where do we go now? Where is Htet?' he shouted in his left ear.

'I don't know, I got pushed back and I lost him!' he exclaimed.

David stood high on his toes to try and look over the increasingly swaying crowd. He was landed back on the flats of his soles when a man at the front, with no top on, released his anger. His protest for not getting through had been taken to a new height by standing in the under-hanging, smaller bar of the barrier and shouting abuse at the soldiers. A gunshot was fired into the air by a nearby soldier to regain authority. Chaos ensued. People fell back, including David, who then pulled Tanner by reflex, still holding his bag and attempting to not get separated. A violent scramble was caused by some who climbed over everyone else to get out of the way, but the majority remained courageously and stood closer to the barrier. Htet was still nowhere to be seen. Getting back to their feet, their eyes scattered and found a handful of soldiers that only resembled Htet a little through the lit fires. Kate started to look panicked and worn out, it was like being in the mosh pit of a heavy metal festival, a battle to stand up amongst uncontrollable people; except this time the crowd control had guns and the crowd weren't fans. She pulled Khin and David away from where they were to the edge where the building was.

'Excuse me!' she shouted trying to get a guards attention, 'excuse me!'

She even tried waving her passport around to make a statement of her rights.

'This isn't working, he must have fucked us. We've got to find another way. Come on!' urged Tanner.

Tanner started pushing through to where they had came from, they didn't get far before another shot was fired. The crowd screamed and hit the floor as much as they did the first time, then another shot went off, then another. Down on their knees, they started crawling away. Another shot went off, making people scramble and run more than ever. A man and woman at the front barrier had been shot, one badly wounded, the other one, most likely already dead from his lack of order. The soldiers started to advance over the barrier and walk amongst the people. David checked back to find one pushing a woman out of the way onto her knees. People flocked back out to the road and the opening of the bridge; some got in their vehicles and started up their engines. A shot raced past David as they shuffled away. David dropped his day pack but Khin picked it up for him and hung it over her shoulders. The shot had blasted through the windscreen of a minivan that they were passing, causing the windscreen to crack like a spider web. As he raised himself up, his knees still bent from fear of another shot, he saw a creation of crimson spill, obscured through the windscreen. A man lay dead behind the splintered glass, the keys were still in his hand, no way of telling if he was picked out and aimed for as he was higher than the rest of the crowd but boxed in to a standstill from the cars behind him. Something in David turned as he watched the blood run down the native man's throat. His hands shook from adrenaline, his head rocked erratically from side to side. David felt the boost of adrenaline himself, he was scared beyond his wits but his head seemed to fire up like a steam train that had just been shovelled a pallet full of coal. His acts soon became quicker than his thoughts; he spun around and shouted at Khin, Kate and Tanner.

'Go! Do what I said to do!' he said, mainly directing it at Khin.

He reached over the dead man, whose blood had now reached the seat he was slumped in, and grabbed the key from him. He started the minivan, not occupied by anyone else, and flicked on the headlights to full beam.

It was the first high vehicle pointed in the direction of the soldiers and blinded what vision they had beyond the light. He shook off his larger pack and instructed Kate to do so as well, who followed his lead without question. He ran to the edge and launched them over the side of the bridge. They were nearly at the mouth but the bags still fell a good twenty feet with no regard for anyone in their path if they were.

Tanner was taken back with his actions, secretly loving the quick thinking, like some sort of extreme sports junkie. He kept one hand on his pistol, still concealed in his belt. Jumping over the last part of the lip of the bridge, he helped Khin and Kate over. Tanner stumbled with his leg suffering but didn't complain. They landed on soft ground, with the rain making it softer as they moved.

Moving on through some trees, the light faded behind them and eventually, they turned back on themselves. David ran like a robot, as if programmed with a mission to find water. He grew impatient as no-one could keep up but turned, against his head, realising how selfish it was in hindsight for the others. The light split through the trees behind them as they entered deeper into the jungle brush. They felt their ankles get caught on vines and they soon became shadow puppets in the trees, even to each other; featureless figures. They felt the downward slant as they heard the trickle of the water from the river, their ankles now strained at the front from the descent. David was the first to hit the bottom, actually falling into the river from moving too fast out from the tree line. He fell, hands first and saw figures in front of him standing, wading around in the river, knee deep. He couldn't make out a single friend or foe. Khin and Kate helped him up and he noticed his hand was now bleeding from his palm from falling on something sharp in the river. Endless and unreasonable shouting came from all sides. All he wished was for it to cease, clearly a few people had the same idea he had by crossing the river by foot, but the frustration of trying to do it discreetly obviously couldn't be induced by anyone else.

As the water hit their feet, it was ice cold, within seconds their feet were embedded and felt as if they weren't there any more. They waded into the water and got as deep as the others. They found their packs bobbing in the water, hooked together against some small rocks. They grabbed them and pushed them across as they waded. None of them seemed to struggle too much with the weight of their bags, or the water shifting around their feet. They lifted their knees as high as they could before they were forced to go waist deep. David was forced to open his mouth to breathe as the feeling of the water rose, like a set of cold snakes, wrapping around him under his shorts and shirt. Three beams of light appeared from over the edge of the bridge above and hunted out the people in front of them. More shots were fired and the water splashed up, like timed drum beats in front of David who shook his bag loose from his arms and took cover at the water line. Khin screamed behind him and clasped onto his waist that she had already been using to steady herself. As Tanner edged into the water he felt a stinging pain from his leg as it covered it, but his pack was much lighter in general. He pulled Kate more to one side, to get under the bridge. As they looked to the right under the vast concrete, a human body had been thrown off of the other side of the bridge from the top and splashed down into the water, like a dead weight. Kate grabbed Khin and pulled her and David in under the cover of the bridge with her, leaving the main bags to float off downstream.

'They don't matter now, let 'em go!' she voiced.

Keeping the relevant pace, they edge closer to the other side of the bank. The shots from the soldiers fired out still, all around them, it sounded like a small explosion had happened above them on the road. It was nowhere near enough to rock the strong foundations of the bridge but it had clearly done some damage in some way. They were now deep enough to be partly floating in the water, they looked up, sheltered from the rain but seeing another victim fall from the edge nearest them, this time alive. The man who fell landed with a hard smack, mere feet from them, but to their surprise he then sprang up and started swimming strong towards the opposite side, as if he had intended the whole stunt. Smoke started to reign above them, flowing out like gas. It soon engulfed everything in the slight breeze, causing an even more clouded vision and the rain didn't seem to disperse it much. Blindly pulling each other along, Tanner was heard now, desperately trying to conceal the pain of his leg, breaking through each barrier of it by pushing himself further. It was the best use of his stubborn nature so far. He took the lead and started swimming creating a guideline for the others. David forced Khin and Kate in front getting the girls up the other side of the bank first as they approached it. They led themselves through the mist with no vision of what was up ahead; their prayers were confirmed as they hit the bank before they could see it. They could see on both sides and even under the Thai side of the bridge that people were waiting. They started helping them up the bank, which was not as steep, but much longer than the other side to reach the join of the bridge, and dry land. Tanner stopped at a small breach in-between the trees on the higher land to help the girls step up. Their legs were shaking trying to hold their new increased weight as they got out of the water. In the trees behind them David could see a figure jogging around the trunks to join them and help them up; as he got closer they found it was Htet.

Htet stepped down to the edge of the bank and held out his hand for them, he let the girls go up the hill between the thicker brush to find the road. Tanner could barely move as he exited the water, he started crawling, trying not to get dirt in the wound on his leg. The first aid patch he wore had come away and had bunched together in a soggy patch of material. David, still wading, really felt the help from Htet as he pulled Tanner up. His heart pounding, his veins now close to the surface of his skin, David saw the dream turn into a nightmare that was forming in front of him. As Htet helped Tanner up, he waited until he was at his feet fully before slamming the rifle butt into the side of his head. Tanner went flying off to the left and fell into the water again, with a rag-doll effect. The thrusting blow left him unconscious. David stood there, watching the now dangerous man in front of him with the higher ground in the misty moonlight. He was silent, the girls, still in shock behind him, let out a cry. Khin tried to shout a muffled warning, but her distance was too great.

David was forced to stand still in the water. He glanced at Tanner who was floating face up in the water, he knew he had the gun; he was their only chance of attacking the rogue soldier. Htet stepped in the water towards David, pointing his rifle at him.

'Welcome to Thailand David,' he said, with menacing tone.

David took a worried second to think of something that might stall him.

'What the fuck are you doing?' he asked him straight.

'My duty to my country,' he replied.

The feeling of everything being washed down the drain became apparent to David, living proof that people could only change themselves, but surely Htet was not born this way. David lowered his hands and punched the water around him, mentally spitting at the loss of a life before it knew it.

Htet raised the rifle higher, still pointing it at David. A lapse in time occurred in his head now as he closed his eyes, waiting for him to pull the trigger. Before the next second could pass, he plucked words from the air that came to him as if he were meant to say them, in release that the end was already over. He spoke with the boldest confidence.

'Tell me again before you pull that trigger soldier.'

Htet cocked his head to one side speaking up in reply.

'What now?'

'Do you still believe in Karma? Or was *everything* you said to us a lie?' he asked.

Kate and Khin had been received in the sight of aid workers and natives of Thailand who were trying to pull them to safety, but they misunderstood their struggle to get away, they wanted to help. From David's viewpoint he couldn't tell if they had been abducted by other members of the military. It injected him with a loss of hope. Yet still he wanted Htet's response to his question.

'I believe for sure, but I don't think Karma believes in you any more,' he finally said in return.

Aiming down the sight and raising the gun to pinpoint David, Htet pulled a face that stated the people around him shouldn't be here, he said in his head that they shouldn't be anywhere, because of violation of rights on their side. As he pulled the trigger he felt the usual tilt of the gun, but it was only imaginary. After the initial half inch, the release of the bullet from the trigger felt too easy, it clicked and slipped back. He tried it again, and again the same 'click'. He folded the gun down to check the magazine chamber, it was empty. His face became angry, he checked his body to find nothing of the usual ammunition to load it with. The travellers had even stripped him of his knife when they first interrogated him.

'Do you still believe it will always come back to you?' said David, in the mist.

He held the bullets from the clip in his hand up to show him, before throwing them downstream. Htet looked up at David and saw him running towards him in a rage. He raised his gun to use as a beating weapon again. David thrust himself into the body of the soldier and took him down with the style of a rugby tackle that he had not tried since his school days, but managed to floor him with great technique. A heavy handed fight between them broke out. He started out on top, Htet took some heavy blows to the face but he was soon overpowering David again. They grappled in the now disturbed, swamp like surroundings, to end up against the foundation wall of the bridge. Htet gained the more powerful side and held his arm up against David's neck. David found his strength failing him this time but his voice was still clear enough to understand over the soldiers arm.

'You didn't think I'd give an animal like you a loaded gun, did you?' said David, now bleeding from the mouth, pinned against the wall.

Htet was in a much worse state physically, but again, his durability served him well.

'You have no rights here, you have done just as much wrong as I have, you won't live to be arrested,' he shot back, in a formal way.

Pushing his arm into his neck harder and holding one leg against his groin he spoke again in an intimidating manner.

'As I said, we can always change life into how we want to be.'

'You don't want it to be anything but fucking miserable,' spouted David, 'why don't you spend some time making something worthwhile for somebody instead of shitting on your own beliefs, do you think this is poetic? Do you think killing *me* is going to change your miserable future soldier!?'

'Are you saying you think *you* are my Karma?'

Well and truly overpowered and helpless against the wall, David noticed a figure step up behind the soldier from the corner of his eye.

'No, but maybe *she* is mine.'

The last look on Htet's face was a confused one as the figure behind him raised a knife and thrust into his neck. It tore through him from one side at a steep angle, causing him to choke and fall in a jittering way. Blood spewed everywhere as David fell to his knees and saw Khin through crimson vision in front of him. She dropped the knife and took hold of his face gently, she seemed to ask if he was OK, he didn't answer, he couldn't answer, a short paralysis set in where he lost control of his basic functions. It all went black.

Chapter XII

New Destination

Bright lights above him burnt his eyes, he could feel their heat through his eyelids. Opening slowly, creaking them apart, he saw it, the gridded ceiling. He shut them again, knowing the dream that was about to heat him up inside. He was definitely lying down, he felt like being sick but his mouth was too dry to care. The edges of the oxygen mask pressed around his face and nose, he could feel the enhanced breath retained in his chest at least.

Remembering things wasn't important right now, his worst fear was here and the standard motor skills had to be performed like he always dreamt he might have to do one day. Toes first, he curled the left ones, then the right. It seemed all were present and all seemed in place. Fingers were next, again he wiggled left to right, the left were fine but the right were very tight—the tendons felt burnt out, but that was a good sign, maybe? At least they weren't broken. Next stage was the neck, although he could feel an achy body attached, if he couldn't move his neck, he wouldn't feel convenience any more. With an exhale and a painful slow wrench, he rolled to the right and found an empty chair staring at him. *Figures*, he thought, before he could no longer prevent another blackout.

3 Days Later

'How does your arm feel?' asked Kate, sitting down on the other chair at his table.

'Still rusty, but I think it will do now.'

'Can't wait to get home now you're all fixed up? '

'You bet . . . is it weird of me to say I'm going to miss this place though?' he said.

'What Thailand? You've only been here a few days.'

'No, Myanmar, the people, the food . . . you know,' he said, picking up his sunglasses.

'Not the war-zone though, huh? Here, I bought you a coke,' she said, placing a bottle for each of them on the café table.

He took a deep breath and felt good to be in freshly washed clothes. His bones ached, but it was the kind of ache that represented a clear sign of healing rather than constant half-way pain. His eye was bruised and his lip was swollen, his right hand that he had fallen on felt like it was lined with metal that just wouldn't let him flex, his back and legs just ached like any Sunday morning spent in bed too long.

'I can't thank you enough for everything Kate,' he said.

She smiled and didn't take it as emotionally as before but mocked him for saying it again.

'It's been a pleasure, who wouldn't have stuck by you in this? I wouldn't be here if it weren't for you . . . fancy a beer later in Bangkok?' she replied.

He put on the sunglasses he had and looked across the street at an old man selling fruit to passers by in a large, woven basket. He kept batting away flies that were around him, but other than that he didn't seem to be bothered by much; he smiled when he caught sight of him. A dragonfly circled above his head in a robotic, plotted pattern. It eventually came over towards David, hovered above him and perched on the edge of the tin roof. He looked up, seeing one set of its wings spread out and pierced by the sunlight, the vein stems and each segment that made up the wing were clearly visible for a few seconds. The colours on the tips when it flew away shone green and a deep blue. Thoughts of his grandmother were brought back to him with what the fortune teller back in Kalaw had said; *'Someone close is watching you, through the eyes of the dragonfly'.*

'Yeah . . . yeah that sounds good.'

Final Diary entry

Air never felt so good, we take so much for granted. I just bought a fruit seller a bottle of coke, which never happened to him before. I just had one myself, with a good friend of mine, Kate; she has been looking after me since we got here. Here, is a café down the road from Mae Sot general hospital, Thailand, where they let me go yesterday. Luckily I didn't have to explain a screw driver that was left in my bag and they even got me a new inhaler. We got admitted emergency status visas and have fifteen days free entry. I have been in and out of waking life but feel OK now. I had been starved of oxygen to the brain slightly, from a fight that occurred with a guy who thought he knew his way forward in life was clear. He became very afraid when he found out it wasn't, tried to change but couldn't, at least that's what I think. I, on the other hand, have changed completely, me and my new friends have been through it a bit the last seventeen days, but we are all OK. Tanner high-tailed it while I was out, he got patched up along with me but then took the antibiotics and ran to find his brother on Kho Pagn Ngan. Khin . . . she went too, we said our goodbyes yesterday, and it wasn't as hard as I thought it would be, our attachment was genuine but in another land, another world. We still feel something for each other, maybe we always will, but we both knew it wasn't going to be possible to go anywhere else. She's starting a new life here and seeing where it takes her. I might see her again one day I hope. Kate has been here like I said, proving a great companion so far. We are waiting for the bus to Bangkok and we are going to get each other home. I've sent a message to my family and Sarah, saying we got through it all, they should be waiting for me at the airport when I get home in a few days. I don't think I feel the same for Sarah any more either, I've heard that things like this can change relationships, so I guess I'm lucky to not be in one at the moment. I'm going to ride the waves like Khin and Tanner for a while, see what happens. I hope Myanmar recovers one day, I proved myself right and wrong with my first aspirations on arrival. There is an undiscovered civilization and culture there, not the same place that everybody hears about; it lives within the people you speak to and in the short distance between you and their kindness.

I just saw the most amazing dragonfly land above me . . . home is going to be great but I'm patient enough to get back slowly now, take in the view . . . tell a few stories. I've still got my iPod that miraculously didn't get wet, my passport and money, oh and a little poem called 'Karma' that was given to me as a souvenir by a monk. I wish Maung Win Zaw was here . . . I think I might be able to tell him now that I've found what I was looking for.

Lightning Source UK Ltd.
Milton Keynes UK
UKOW051127150612

194458UK00001B/55/P